The Retroactivist

by Nate Ragolia

Published in the United States by:

Spaceboy Books LLC

1627 Vine Street

Denver, CO 80203

www.readspaceboy.com

First printed February 2017

ISBN-10:
0-9987120-0-0

ISBN-13:
978-0-9987120-0-0

For the idealists and utopians who confront reality everyday
and continue to dream beyond it.

1

Capitol Hill Citizenry District; Denver, Colorado; United Sociocracy of the
Americas
May 29, 2087
7:47 AM

"I woke up this morning and I had nothing, Iris. I tried my last idea yesterday and it didn't work. I am dried up. I am empty."

Reid Rosales pauses on those last words, shocked to hear himself say them; even more shocked to realize that they are not a dramatization, but simple truth. He talked himself out of it when light first hit his eyes this morning. *It's just a bad feeling that will pass*, he told himself. But the feeling hadn't passed. It hadn't even diminished. No distraction he throws at it makes it go away. He has nothing. Real, undebatable nothing. For the first time.

Reid walks to his kitchen and taps in his usual breakfast order on the replicator. Two eggs over easy. Wild boar bacon. Irish potato hashbrowns. Gluten-free wheat toast. Blood orange juice. Coffee- dark roast. Food has a way of making things easier, a way of clearing the cobwebs, a way of filling the emptiness. The replicator swiftly processes each request, and generates each item; building them row-by-row, as if laying out thousands upon thousands of miniature building blocks.

Reid used to love watching the replicator work when he was a boy. He enjoyed the simplicity in knowing that everything, including himself, is comprised of millions of tiny building blocks. The process of cloning humans was outlawed by the 2024 Revised Bill of Rights, because even when a machine got all the building blocks in the right place to make a human replica, it couldn't create a human personality. Reid liked that. It meant there would always be something special about being a person, an individual. Something that couldn't be copied.

The replicator chimes its completion tone and Reid takes his nutritionally-optimized meal to the countertop. He chokes down every bite, dabbing his toast robotically into the yolk and chewing out of obligation.

"Even for the last three months, I've had bad ideas. Now I don't have anything at all. Do you have any concept of how terrifying that is? How frustrating it is to wake up one day and no longer know how to be the person you've defined yourself as? No. You wouldn't know because, you don't have to define."

"That's not entirely accurate, Reid, and you know it," Iris says, meandering from the living room to the kitchen. "Maybe it's time to do something else entirely. Something new, something exciting. Something that isn't 'you.' You could try music again, or join a sports club, or take up photography or design. The possibilities that could prevent you from moping around this kitchen, *again,* are quite-nearly endless."

Reid collects himself and sighs. "I know you're trying to help, Iris. But I've tried already everything. Music is Xiu's thing. I'm not that keen on team sports. I never figured out the old darkroom and I don't take good photos. If you remember, my design class in college didn't go well. My take on Art Deco got me laughed out of the class."

"You said you wanted a challenge, didn't you?" Iris asks.

"It's not even the challenge, Iris. I just wonder what the point is to being creative, when everybody else can be too? Cartooning was my thing. Mine. It brought me some real happiness, you know, but now it doesn't and I don't know what I'm supposed to do. Or what I'm supposed to be," Reid replies. "I feel like I'm drowning."

Iris frowns and sits down across from Reid at the breakfast counter, reaching out toward him with a consoling hand.

"Each student who chooses to practice art following their education brings something individual to their medium. Your cartoon is yours and yours alone. Just because you may never win an award, doesn't make it invalid," Iris says. "The Covenants of the U. S. of A. were written to give every citizen a chance to follow their passion. It's all set up to help people find meaning through art, music, film, collecting, dance, drug-expression, books, acting, sexual demonstration, sports, or anything else that makes them happy."

"I took U. S. of A. history, Iris. I know how the system works. The problem is that I'm not passionate about anything at all. The list could be long enough to contain the entirety of the universe, and I'd still be right here, a husk without even a hint of inspiration."

"You are much more upset than usual, Reid," Iris says. "I understand that you have been feeling unfulfilled. You have been experiencing a creative drought for three months."

Reid pushes his uneaten food around his plate with his utensils. He stands and paces back and forth like a child building up for a tantrum.

"I haven't drawn or written anything good in years, Iris," Reid says. "But it's not the drought that bothers me, it's the realization that nothing I've ever done was any good either."

Iris's lips purse and her eyes fix gently on Reid.

"Your cartoon consistently receives millions of views per week," Iris says. "It has millions of upvotes and positive comments from viewers and readers. I think that means your work is good, Reid."

"*Origami Emu* gets tons of views, but no matter what I try, I never come away with an award. I'm stuck in the middle of the pack every year. I'm just an also-ran who fell into an easy pattern. The comic doesn't bring me joy anymore. It doesn't wake me up in the middle of the night with ideas. It doesn't feel like it's good to me. It feels cheap."

"Perhaps you are in a rut and you need to try some new ideas, or engage with a collaborator."

"You suggest this every day, Iris," Reid exclaims. "You really should work on that."

"I don't think you've tried challenging yourself, Reid," she replies. "You're stuck in a cycle of frustration and it is not healthy. You have not eaten regularly in a month. You have failed to visit your parents' memorial for three weeks. You have been smiling around 75% less than usual, and you have been laughing 90% less. This isn't like you."

"Those are tough numbers, Iris," he replies. "But you know that I'm going to see my parents today."

"You said that yesterday, Reid."

"Yeah, but today I mean it, okay?" he replies.

"I am sure you do," Iris says. "And I hope you do because it will help you get over this depression, especially if pushing yourself creatively won't work."

"That's not fair, Iris," Reid yells. "I've changed mediums and artistic styles. I've sent Origami Emu to space. I've sent him back in time. He's fought Foil Swan so many times that I can't remember what they're fighting about. Every storyline gets thumbs up, but still, no awards. And no one wants to collaborate with me because they're doing their own cartoons, or just happily consuming the next cartoon on the list."

"I only hoped to cheer you up," Iris replies. "There's nothing wrong with being underappreciated in your time. Most artists have been."

"It's not just about appreciation, Iris. It's… complicated. And it's not your fault that you can't understand," Reid replies. "You're a machine."

"Perhaps that is so," the hologram answers.

"I bet the other cartoonists do respect me," Reid continues. "But there's a difference between the respect we all show each other and real, individualized admiration."

"We all succeed together."

Reid blinks, and then scoffs at his digital assistant.

"I know the credo, Iris," he says.

The hologram leans against the counter island and nods. Her eyebrows torque and Iris holds up her hand, index finger extended toward the ceiling as an idea springs to her.

"Maybe doing your daily vote will distract you some? There are seven local initiatives to vote on today, Reid," Iris says. "Would you like to review them while you finish breakfast?"

"Do I have a choice?" Reid asks as sits back down in front of his plate. He reluctantly rolls a slice of bacon and drops it into his mouth.

"If you don't participate in the local initiatives, you won't receive your daily credit disper—"

"I know, Iris," Reid interrupts the hologram. "Bring them up."

Reid turns his attention to the wall at the foot of his bed where Iris always projects the day's list of district-specific ballot items. Despite the rough exposed brick in his 1920's apartment, the image is legible and flawless, corrected by Iris's complex light and texture sensors. Reid surveys each carefully and casts each of his votes with quick thumbs up/thumbs down gestures:

1. Children's parade to celebrate former U.S. President Linda Watanabe? Yes.
2. Continue funding of universal healthcare for this district? Yes.
3. Approve redevelopment of retired nuclear plant? No.
4. Sign birthday card from this district to Iranian President Hafezzadeh? Yes.
5. Approve funding for teleportation research in this district? Yes.
6. Approve creation of cloned dinosaur Leisure Park? No.
7. Commission new district Tubecar "Sir Ian McKellan" for transit use? Yes.

As immediately as the final thumbs up registers, Reid's profile card replaces the daily ballot in Iris's projection. Beside his avatar and name, the profile card lists his credit balance: 1320. Below the balance, in bright green, his Daily Credit Dispersal of 1000 appears, and the same phrase that accompanies it each morning:

Thank you for your vote, Reid Rosales. Have a wonderful day. Daily Credit Dispersal provided by the Sociocracy Department of Income, in partnership with Global Robonomics.

Reid has been doing his dailies since he was eighteen. At first, he felt distinct excitement from participating in the system, and joy each time he received his credit dispersal. After fifteen years of the routine, the dailies had become his least favorite part of the day. Reid toyed with ignoring the dailies, but without his usual 1000 daily credits, he grew bored sitting around his standard-issue apartment with only the basic entertainment and semi-gourmet food that the government provides.

"Why are we still voting on the healthcare thing, Iris? It always passes."

"Mandatory daily votes on health care were written into the Universal Citizen Care bill of 2038, as a compromise with dissenting members of the Old Congress," Iris recites. "These votes are required to continue until the one-hundredth anniversary of the law's passing in 2138."

"And all those idiots are dead now," Reid mutters, while spreading jam onto his last piece of wheat toast. "But I guess it's nice that everyone still gets a say on the matter."

Reid rests his chin on his fist and stares toward the apartment window and its view of the Denver skyline. He stabs at the wrecked mess of yellow and white that remain of his eggs. He sighs. He shifts the weight of his head and all its thoughts to his other fist. He sighs again.

"Why don't we see what's going on in the world today?" Iris says, shattering the silence. "Maybe the news will inspire you. They say that truth is stranger than fiction."

Reid waves his hand. "Let 'em rip, Iris."

"It looks like they put an end to world hunger yesterday with a new replicator installation in New Zambia. This looks very interesting, can I share it with you?" Iris says.

"Sure, Iris," Reid says. "Let's see it."

"Okay, let me grab that for you," Iris says.

A new hologram appears across from Reid at the counter. A beautiful woman in a blazer smiles at Reid, carefully adjusts her hair and then begins speaking.

"In Mwaleshi, workers for the World Commission on Hunger Eradication installed the last of 2.2 million free, public food replicators in the African Alliance zone of New Zambia today. Replicators funded by international accord of the United Nations have been installed in 182 countries worldwide since the program began in 2082."

A small window appears on the wall behind the holographic newswoman, with a video recording from the story.

"We are proud to announce that the only way a human will go hungry on the planet Earth in 2087 is by choice," says Food and Hunger Minister Archibald Igwe. "This is a remarkable achievement that we have attained together, as a united and passionate international community."

"Replicators became commonplace in the United Sociocracy of the Americas and European Union following their invention by former 3D PrintCo engineer Ricardo Boyle in 2074," the newswoman continues.

"The Commission estimates that the replicators will create hundreds of thousands of leisure hours globally, providing marked increases in creative development, art, music, theatre, and games."

"We're very excited to give more people the opportunity to pursue their passions, rather than worrying about the basics," Igwe adds. "It's an honor to lose half of my title today. I'm very happy to be, simply, Food Minister Igwe."

The video window disappears, the newswoman in the blazer smiles and waves as her hologram dissolves away entirely.

"That's all for this story," Iris says.

"Great," Reid grumbles. "Now the only way to waste away anywhere in the world is the existential way."

"I think it's a very nice thing that no one will starve, Reid," Iris replies.

"I'm sure it is."

"Here's a story about the robot economy that might interest you," Iris adds.

A man with perfectly coiffed hair appears in hologram across from Reid. He straightens his tie, flattens his eyebrows with his thumb, and fidgets with the tablet in from of him.

"In Detroit, Michigan, U. S. of A.- decades of rebuilding the former-Motor City has transformed it into the world capital of service and security robot manufacturing," the newsman begins. "New Center District Robotics Chief Miranda Huxley-Ford spoke at a ribbon cutting ceremony about new robots that will someday maintain themselves, further eliminating human-completed work and enhancing global leisure time."

Another video window appears, behind the newsman.

"As our newest Huxley-Ford XC80s become more efficient we are excitedly approaching an age of truly elevated human exper—"

"That's enough, Iris," Reid interrupts. "The news isn't doing me any good. Thanks."

The hologram of the newsman abruptly evaporates. Iris leans against the kitchen counter and shakes her head.

Reid stands from the counter and contemplates what else might help him clear his head.

"Calendar up," Reid commands.

A projection of a calendar appears, once again projected cleanly and clearly on the exposed brick wall. Reid surveys his schedule for the day.

At ten a.m. he will take a yoga class taught by a program composite of the Buddha.

At eleven, he will visit his parents' graves at the Memorial Center.

At noon he will take the Tubecar to New York and eat lunch at Balthazar.

At two p.m. he will take the Tubecar back to Denver, and attend a showing of *Hamlet*.

At six p.m. Reid has a massage and spa relaxation appointment, followed by dinner and drinks.

At eight p.m. Reid is signed up to attend a cartoonists group meeting.

"Cancel the cartoonists group, Iris," Reid says. "No point in going. I don't have any ideas to share."

"I am happy to cancel it for you, Reid," Iris replies from the kitchen. "This is the sixth meeting you've canceled in as many weeks. I believe that attendance is mandatory to continue your group membership."

"Then cancel my membership," Reid says.

"You don't mean that, Reid," Iris replies.

"I do mean it. I'm just wasting their time anyway."

"If that's what you want," Iris says. "Tell you what, I'll be sure to leave your return open, so you can still change your mind."

"Fine," Reid says. "Is that all for today, Iris?"

"You also have a tentative call with Xiu Parker at eleven p.m. Miss Parker intends to confirm this before one p.m. today."

"Maybe Xiu will help me shake off this dark cloud," Reid sighs.

"Miss Parker does seem to like you very much," Iris says.

"She's a pretty great girlfriend. Too bad she can't make me or my work relevant."

Iris frowns and shrugs her shoulders.

Reid exhales and picks up his dirty dishes and tosses them into the replicator. He taps the disassemble icon and the empty dishes instantly turn to dust, and then into smaller particles until there is nothing left in the replicator at all.

"Perhaps a cocktail will—" Iris begins.

"I'm going for a walk," Reid says. "Let the Buddha know that I'll be twenty minutes late."

Reid grabs his wristband and exits his apartment. He walks down the narrow hallway, admiring the new set of Impressionist reproduction that posted this morning on his way toward the stairwell. A piano concerto billows out from under his neighbor's door. The 144 year-old man in apartment 16 waves to him as he bends down to pick up an analog newspaper. The red light of an in-unit darkroom glows beneath another door. Reid descends the stairs to the ground floor. A couple behind the door to number six argue about which Leisure Park to visit. A group of children in school uniforms march single-file out toward the street. Another neighbor, a girl just starting college, smiles at him.

"I just got your last book," she says. "I can't wait to read it."

Reid plasters his face in a smile.

"Thank you. How's the fencing going?" He asks. "It is fencing, isn't it?"

The girl smiles.

"Yes, fencing. I've nearly perfected my opening feint."

He envies the excitement in her voice.

"Good to hear."

He offers the girl a friendly goodbye wave and continues toward the building entrance. The blue door scans him, lights up in a pale green and slides open, bearing him onto the street outside.

Shops, restaurants and apartment buildings line Pearl Street. A robot roams the sidewalk seeking dirt or refuse to vaporize. Dozens of couples and single Citizens sit on the grassy strip along the middle of the old street, drinking wine, kissing, laughing, and playing games like chess and checkers projected onto the ground from their wristbands. Pigeons and other birds hop around the sidewalk and chirp happily. The piano concerto from Reid's building pours into the street, attracting a small crowd who listen and count off the beat with their hands. Another robot sells sandwiches from a replicator cart in the center of the street-park as Citizens cruise around the makeshift cafe on their bicycles. A pair of security robots rumble by on their tank treads.

"Have a nice day, Citizens," one says.

"Be careful riding ahead," says the other. "There is a substantial crowd in front of the theatre."

The clean sidewalks and artfully graffitied buildings bustle with citizens. People flow in and out of the Tubecar station at the corner of Pearl and 13th Avenue.

Reid passes the crowd and continues along Pearl Street. Every face he sees is a friendly and smiling one. Every single person he passes is out and about because they want to be. Everyone is going somewhere they want to go, or simply wandering around finding strangers to talk with—conversation being the universal pastime. Each passerby waves, smiles, or says hello. Reid nods, smiles, and returns the greeting.

"Hello, Citizen," a stranger calls to him. "Beautiful day isn't it?"

"It is," he says, unable to resist the stranger's smile.

A mother and young daughter stop before him. The little girl waves furiously with one hand, while clutching her mother's calf with the other.

"Hello, nice man," she says.

Her mother tousles her hair. "That's right," she says to the girl.

Then to Reid, "She's been stopping everyone today. It's adorable how fast they learn to be kind."

"Thank you for saying so," Reid says to the girl. "I woke up on the wrong side of the bed."

The girl looks at her mother quizzically.

"It's an expression from back when people didn't get to sleep as long as they needed," the mother says.

The little girl's mouth makes a big "O" and she covers her eyes with her hands.

"People used to do lots of silly things," the mother says. "Have a nice day, citizen," she says to Reid.

Reid wanders down the block and passes the Tubecar station. For a moment, he considers changing all of his plans. *Lisbon, or Beijing, or Paris would be nice*, he thinks. *It's not like I have to do what I have planned.*

A wet tongue laps at his hand. Reid glances over to the couple walking by with their dog.

"We're still training him," the woman says. "I hope that you don't mind."

"Not at all," Reid says, wiping his hand on his jeans. "I love dogs. Is he a German Shepherd?"

The man nods. "He is. In fact he's the great-great-great-great-great grandpup of a police dog. Did you know, back when there was crime, they used to train these dogs to catch criminals?"

The man is clearly very proud of this fact.

"I think I read that somewhere, yeah," Reid replies.

"Fascinating isn't it? What would a dog know about crime anyway?" the man asks the dog.

"I'm glad that we don't have any of that business anymore," the woman says.

"Have a wonderful day, citizen," the man says.

Reid gives the dog a pat on the head.

"The three of you, too," Reid replies.

He continues down Pearl, past 12th and keeps walking south. Every few feet, he stops to talk to another citizen or two or three, to pet a dog, to smile at a child. From the corner of Seventh and Pearl, he looks to the east and sees the Seventh and Downing Tubecar Station, its sign alight—advertising low-price trips to the Houston Lunargate. He looks to the west and sees the Lincoln Street Recording Center and the Denver Ballet Studio. Iris's suggestions flutter around in his head.

He really could do anything he wants to do. Anything he could imagine. But none of it would make this feeling go away. None of it would turn his nothing into something; anything.

Instead, Reid finds himself paralyzed—more downtrodden and dissatisfied than ever.

Without creativity, Reid is as anonymous as anyone else wandering the streets. Without awards, he's just another hobbyist who can draw whenever he wants, and fill his days however he wants.

There is nothing more empty than boundlessness.

2

Upper East Side Citizenry District; Manhattan, New York; United Sociocracy of the
Americas
June 2, 2087
10:34 AM

Xiu Parker looks stunning in a form fitting gold dress with matching shoes. She stands atop the stairs at the street-level Tubecar entrance, using a hair-tint pen to select the color of the day. She stops on a shade of copper just short of rust, replacing her usual jet black, and drops the pen into her purse.

"Reid!" Xiu calls through the dense crowd of rushing, grinning Manhattanites. Reid makes his way up the steps from the Tubecar station, pushing past the sharply dressed men and women of the East Coast. He fends off a downpour of pleasantries as pedestrians bounce around his shoulders, like water breaking on stone.

"Welcome to New York," a citizen says.

"I love tourists. So many interesting people," Reid overhears another say.

A couple caught beside him in the stream talks about a death in their family.

"She made it to 168," the woman says. "That's a long, full life."

"It's just hard that she's gone," the other woman replies.

The first woman's wristband pings. "Oh. The government just replied. The service will happen in a week, and she's getting the plot she requested. And they're delivering all her things to us after the ceremony."

One of the women bumps Reid with her shoulder as she passes.

"Oh, excuse me," she says.

"No, it's my fault," Reid replies.

She hugs him.

"Have a great day, sir," she replies.

All around him, Citizens are laughing, singing. A six-piece busker band plays in the stairwell; their wristbands flashing incessantly, as other Citizens tip them credits.

Even atop the stairs there is no end to the crowd, and Reid is reminded how tiny Denver still is—with a population as measly as five million—compared to Manhattan, and most other cities he visits around the world. Reid stares up at the towering buildings, each with millions of windows, all stabbing up into the sky so high that more than half of the structures disappear above the ceiling of rolling clouds. *The view down from up there must be spectacular*, Reid thinks. *Like a blanket of fresh snow.*

He stops in his tracks, hoping to slip through the flow of humanity, but it's Xiu who reaches into the pack, grabs his arm, and extracts him. His rescue ends with a hug and a long kiss. Xiu also grabs and squeezes his right butt cheek.

"Thanks for meeting me here. I just have to see this exhibit before it cycles out," she says. "How excited are you?"

"The usual amount for a museum, I suppose," Reid replies.

Xiu smirks.

"Yeah? Well buck up, boyo. This museum is all about death and suffering, just like you like."

"It's not that I don't appreciate the enthusiasm, Xiu, but it's just old health science stuff," Reid says. "I came here in fourth grade. There's a guy in a flu costume, a fake Ebola quarantine zone, and some old pictures of people covered with spots."

"Fine, be grumpy," Xiu replies. "I think it's going to be fun."

"Any time I spend with you is fun, Xiu," Reid says. "If ever I'm bored, I'll just focus on how awesome your hair looks today."

Xiu smiles.

The Museum of Ancient Diseases lives within a ten year old building designed in a retro-futuristic style with hints of classical Greek architecture. Large, stone columns with decorative fins rise from the landing atop a short white stone staircase. Behind the columns, the white marble facade features rows of symmetrical circular "rocket-side" windows. Above each window is a curved bubble-like awning.

18

Everything about the design is smooth and sleek, as if to contribute to aerodynamism. The main entrance is a glass hemisphere set in the pristine marble facade. There is a solar-powered revolving door at its center.

The museum's interior comprises more brilliant white stone, a vaulted atrium with a glass dome ceiling that fills the building with natural light, and eight glass columns with decorative fins. A curved marble desk serves as the reception kiosk, and it is manned, such as it is, by a row of robot ticket vendors. Xiu picks the third from the right.

"Welcome to the Museum of Ancient Diseases: where what didn't kill us only made us stronger," the robot intones. "Please remember to visit the Petri Dish for delicious disease inspired meals before you leave."

"Two general admissions, please," Xiu says.

"That will be 300 credits, please," the robot replies.

"Sounds good," Xiu says, and her wristband flashes, deducting the payment.

The ticket robot chimes, and the tickets appear on both Xiu's and Reid's lapels.

"Thank you for visiting the Museum of Ancient Diseases," the robot says. "May I direct you toward a particular exhibit?"

Xiu looks at Reid. He throws on a half-smile.

"What's the most sensational thing in this place?" she asks.

The robot turns to the other robot ticket vendors.

"What is the most sensational exhibit?" it asks.

The robots chatter quietly to one another for a few moments in conference, until their ticket vendor turns back to them.

"Guests appear to use 'sensational' and variant synonyms following visits to the Dangerous Coupling: Sexually Transmitted Infections of the Past."

"I disagree," the other robot says. "Vaccinations: From Discovery, to Doubt, to Devotion has received more uses of 'sensational' and variants. You have not accessed the most recent data."

"I always access the most recent data," the first robot says.

"Incorrect," says the other.

"Thank you. Both of you," Xiu says to the robots. "See," she continues, turning to Reid. "This is going to be a blast."

Reid offers another weary smile as she takes his hand and drags him toward the curved chrome metallic archway to the Alexander Fleming Early Medicines wing. Each of the three wings of the museum is named for a scientist notable to disease prevention. The Louis Pasteur wing, honoring the inventor of vaccination, features a copper metallic archway. And the gold metallic archway accents the entrance to the Allison Chen wing, named for the woman who cured cancer in 2036.

Inside the Fleming wing, Reid and Xiu are surrounded by recreations of laboratories, images of illness and infection, old-timey doctor's equipment, and viewscreens. The cavernous room matches the main atrium, with glass columns and vaulted ceilings. They pass a display on bacteria, describing a time before science had mastered bacterial manipulation to renew cells, prolong life, and prevent infection altogether.

Xiu lights up at each exhibit, smiling to Reid in hopes of finding him suddenly distracted and happy. Reid simply saunters along, holding her hand loosely and nodding as he absorbs each new dose of information.

Then they arrive at the Disease and Working Life display, and Reid looks at the exhibit with anticipation.

"Look at this," Xiu says, pointing at the viewscreen. "Can you believe people used to have an allotment of time to be sick, back when they worked for credits?" Xiu asks.

She stares at the display of a man hooked to an IV sitting at a desk piled with paperwork.

"Not only did they get sick, but they couldn't even take time to get healthy," Xiu continues. "It's surprising we survived this long."

Reid peers over her shoulder. The man pictured at the desk looks strong to Reid, like a wounded animal defending its offspring at all costs.

"Back then, people had to get things done," he says. "If they didn't, the whole world would stop."

"Most of the people just died of disease, sitting at their desks," she adds.

"Maybe people back then felt like they were part of something," Reid says. "Maybe they wanted to keep working because it was the only way to make our world their future."

Xiu rolls her eyes.

"Some of them. Maybe," she says. "But if you remember your history correctly, most of them were just trying to make enough money to stay alive."

"That's still a purpose isn't it?"

"Sure, but it's not the noble calling you're making it out to be."

"So you think people are generally better off now?" Reid asks.

"Seriously?" Xiu stares at him. "Of course. I don't think there's anything brave or noble or whatever in vomiting at a job because if you don't go no one will feed your kids."

Xiu shakes her head and sighs loudly. "Can you imagine?"

Reid nods. "There's a long line of individuals who picked up the world, or their nation, and put it all on their backs. They wrote the original Bill of Rights. They designed the first computers. They dug trenches in the ground with their hands, fought wars, and did whatever they could to be the best. If I knew that one *Origami Emu* cartoon was the difference between me eating and going hungry, I would take that cartoon so much more seriously. People back then probably felt like their struggles were for a greater purpose, so everything was worth it."

"I bet they did feel that way. They were strong, rugged individuals refusing to share and battling against that which they did not yet understand," Xiu says. "It's like something out of an adventure serial. It sounds fun in theory, but you probably wouldn't want to experience most of it."

She grabs him by the arm and pulls him close.

"Unlike *other* things that both sound fun *and* you do want to experience all of it."

Xiu kisses him on the mouth.

"I'm fond of you, my historical man."

Reid blushes and forgets his concerns.

"Maybe you're right, Xiu," Reid says. "All of the work, purpose, and struggle may have made those people strong in some ways, but it definitely made them weak, tired, and lonely in others."

"Of course I'm right, darling," Xiu quips.

"Still, none of them had to wake up each morning with endless choices and not even the remotest sense of risk," Reid says.

"There's always the risk that you'll annoy your girlfriend and she won't sleep with you."

Reid frowns at her, but his frown turns quickly to a smirk.

"Okay, okay. I get it. I'll drop it. I'm just looking for some meaning," Reid says.

"I know," Xiu says. "We all are. In our own ways."

"I'm fond of you, Xiu," he replies.

Reid wraps his arm around her and they enter an exhibit stylized with plush rugs, red velvet and satin, mirrored ceilings and funky music littered with deep, throbbing bass lines. A viewscreen in the first room reads: Dangerous Coupling.

"This is it," Xiu exclaims. She wriggles out from Reid's grasp and sprints, giggling, into the first room of the exhibit.

Reid chases her, caught up in her excitement. Xiu disappears briefly around a corner but reappears behind a floating projection of a neon-outlined couple engaged in sexual embrace. Over her shoulder Reid pants, trying to catch his breath, and reads the viewscreen that holds Xiu's attention.

"Sexually Transmitted Infections: Exploited for Shame. Throughout history, sexually- transmitted infections were indicated and lauded as representative evidence that sex was evil, especially outside marriage, and in pre-21st Century times, even married sex shared by same sex partners."

"During the HIV/AIDS epidemic of the late 20th century, attempts were made to blame the existence of the infection on marginalized groups, despite clear evidence to the contrary. Mounting public concerns about HIV/AIDS led to levels of discrimination and irrational fear last seen in the years leading up to the first Civil Rights Movement."

"In the years that followed, STIs and their treatments gradually became culturally acceptable, and decades-old stigmas disappeared. Eventually, with the invention of the Doctors, those practices were no longer essential to prevention or treatment. The last STIs were treated in 2044, and the concept of dangerous coupling has existed only in History ever since."

Xiu spins around and plants a kiss on Reid's cheek.

"Can you believe that people used to have to be so careful? What a drag that something so fun would have such gross consequences," Xiu says.

"People were dicks back then," Reid replies. "Always looking for someone to exclude."

"Oh? Did I just hear Old Man Reid praise our modern paradise?"

"Yeah. Okay," he says. "It's great that we don't have to worry about STIs or weird illnesses."

Xiu smiles.

"Let's check out some of the other exhibits."

She eagerly takes Reid's hand again. They pass by displays of syphilis, gonorrhea, herpes, warts and crabs.

"Imagine that," Xiu says. "It's like a coral reef around your business. Maybe I'll write a couple of songs about the perils of ancient sex for my next album."

"That's a great idea," Reid says. "Maybe orchestral pop?"

"I was thinking more like baroque rock, but I'm open minded."

Xiu leans in and kisses Reid on the mouth. They are standing below a sign for the last room of the exhibit: After Safe Sex and Beyond. In the final room, Reid follows Xiu from display to display. There is one about the end of condoms. There is another about Doctors and their role in birth control and sexual health. Another display is about the rise of sex clubs and partner groups. Finally, there is a large interactive display about the fall of sexual mores and stigmas, including a detailed history of the U.S. of A.'s various district policies on public sex, sexual freedom and women's rights. At the end of the exhibit are three rows of fully-enclosed photo booths. Each row has ten booths. Atop each booth a scrolling banner reads:

Remember your visit and embrace your sexual freedom. Capture you and a loved one(s) in action on a commemorative photo strip. Only 300 credits per session.

Reid can tell by the look in Xiu's eyes that she wants a photo strip. He keys in the transfer on his wristband and the nearest unoccupied booth scrolls open. Reid grabs Xiu around the waist and kisses her. Together, they maneuver into their cramped booth and the door slides closed behind them with a quiet hush.

"Welcome to Phototron's Intimate Experience Booth. Please select your location by scrolling through the available backgrounds," the booth says.

Xiu taps at the screen and available options scroll before them.

"Tropical beach or skyscraper penthouse?" she asks.

Reid considers the options carefully.

"The beach," he answers. "It's us against the elements."

"Us against us, against the elements." Xiu winks at him. She selects tropical beach and the interior of the booth lights up with sunny blue skies, waving palm trees and warm, golden sand. A warm sea breeze circulates around them from some hidden vents. The gentle crashing of waves, and a mist of salty water hit their ears and skin respectively.

"Your Intimate Experience will begin in three minutes. Please prepare accordingly."

Xiu undresses quickly, shimmying out of the dress as if it were a golden cocoon. She kicks her heels to the front of the booth, and stands before Reid in all her glory. Reid unbuttons his shirt and removes his pants, shoes and socks. He leaves them in a rumpled pile.

"There's only two more minutes," Xiu says, kissing Reid. "We need to get moving if we want any good shots."

For a moment, the pressure wears on Reid. Her frenzied kisses, her passionately grasping fingers almost don't register with his body. He is too busy thinking about the exhibit. Those were, after all, a time with great stakes. Even something as pleasurable and natural as sex could be dangerous. And it wasn't simply a matter of doing it in public—people might see! Or doing it on the thin ledge

24

of a balcony—we could slip onto the netting that prevents dangerous falling objects! No, then, in the 20th and before, sex had consequence. It was a visceral, animal thing that resulted in injury, disease, and offspring. It had to mean something then because it could be the end of you. Now there's nothing he and Xiu can't do, completely without conseq—

Xiu's mouth finds him and Reid is pulled back to the present. The animal is undeniable here. The booth's timer counts down—silently—from thirty seconds. Reid kisses her. The beach backdrop begins to feel more convincing. Xiu stands and turns her back to him. He kisses her neck and she moans as he enters her. The booth keeps counting down.

Twelve.

Eleven.

Ten.

Nine.

The warm breeze and simulated mist dapple their skin with sweat. Xiu cries with delight.

Eight.

Seven.

Six.

Five.

Reid runs his fingers down her spine, and breathes deeply the faux sea air.

Four.

Three.

Two.

One.

The booth begins taking a rapid string of photos. Xiu arches her back to kiss Reid. They change positions, with Reid prone on the floor and Xiu atop him. The booth continues to capture them in strobe like flashes of motion.

"Fifty images remain," the booth says.

Xiu pulls Reid up from the floor, and sits him down on the booth's bench. She sits down on him, facing the front of the booth.

"This is amazing," she says.

"Yeah," Reid agrees.

He stares out at the simulated beach and begins to imagine what the real thing would be like. Reid has been to beaches before, on vacations, and whenever he wants via the Tubecar, but the beaches are always full of other Citizens whose free time, abundant money, and desire drives them there. A deserted beach, natural and wild, that he or he and Xiu could share alone doesn't exist to his knowledge. The realization makes him sad. He forgets where he is, or perhaps remembers and he's completely aware of the booth, inside the museum, inside the city where every has whatever they want... and no one is truly unique.

"Hey," Xiu says, neck craning to face him. "Where'd you go?"

"Nowhere," Reid replies.

"I think the booth is done with photos, but are you going to finish?"

Reid looks at her body in front of his. He listens to her panting breaths.

"Did you finish?" he asks.

"Yeah. You'll see in the photos."

"Then I'm fine," he replies. "I just got distracted."

Xiu pops up off of him and bends down to get her dress. "It happens," she says. "Not like it's in short supply either. I'll get you back."

Reid dresses as Xiu crawls back into her clothes and adjusts her hair. She takes out her hair-tint pen and changes the coppery shade to an anime-style blue-black. The booth chimes when the image file is compiled. Xiu downloads it to her wristband and scrolls through them as they exit the booth. Another couple, flush from their session exists at the same time, nearly running into Reid and Xiu. The four people laugh and trade pleasantries about the experience. Then Xiu sits on a bench at the exhibit's end by the main lobby.

"Damn, we look good," she says. "Look at this one." She holds up her wristband for Reid. He nods in agreement, gazing at his girlfriend's naked form bonded with his own.

"Yeah," Xiu continues. "Most of these are really good. It's too bad about the end though. See?"

Reid looks at the final group of images. Xiu looks caught in a blissful ecstasy. Her mouth open, lip curled just so. Her eyes shut tight as if trying to bottle

26

the intensity for just a moment more. Reid, though, wears a vacant expression. His mouth is pursed in concern, lips tight and thin. His eyes are open, staring miles away into a fictionalized paradise, with passion long dissipated.

"If you weren't having fun, you could've just said," Xiu says.

"No, I was. I'm sorry. I just had something on my mind," Reid answers. "Let's go again. My treat."

Xiu stands from the bench and kisses him on the forehead.

"We'll come back sometime."

Reid stands up to follow her. She takes his hand and they walk into the main lobby.

"What else do you want to see?" she asks.

"Why don't we go have a coffee?" Reid replies.

"That sounds good, love. I will need to get my energy back up after that workout." She winks at him. "I'm very fond of you, you know."

"I know," he says. "Thank you, Xiu."

Their wristbands light up in unison with an appointment notice. Outing with Gustave and Selene, tomorrow, 9 p.m.

"We'll both need our energy tomorrow," Reid says.

"I can't wait to see Selene's new photos, and her new tattoo."

"She got another one?"

"Oh yeah," Xiu replies. "It's not like they're permanent."

Nothing is permanent, Reid thinks. *Change your tattoos as you change your mind. Be anything. Do anything. Chase the next new experience. Pretend to be someone else, somewhere else in a Leisure Park. Live painlessly.*

"Maybe I'll get one." He taps on his wristband free arm. "Right here. It'll be of your butt with my name on it because I own your ass."

Reid slaps his hand on her behind and gives a squeeze. Xiu smiles and kisses his cheek.

"Won't people think that it's just a tattoo of your butt? Or that it's a butt named Reid?"

She bursts into laughter.

Reid laughs too.

They walk together, hand-in-hand, down the crowded Manhattan sidewalk toward Midtown District. As they slide through the happy, chatty, accented New Yorkers, Reid feels more at ease. Spending time with Xiu Parker is one of the few things left in his life that doesn't leave him feeling confused and empty. And that could be a kind of purpose in itself.

3

Curtis Park Citizenry District; Denver, Colorado; United Sociocracy of the Americas

June 3, 2087

11:05 AM

The Curtis Park Doctor bank is a large, open-air plaza; peppered with deciduous and evergreen trees, fountains, benches, picnic tables, and stone chess tables. It is named for the thirty Doctors that fill the spaces between the parklife and white stone sidewalks. The bank was built in 2050 to provide one of twenty centralized Doctor groups to Citizens all over Denver. Similar programs had taken hold in major cities across the U. S. of A. and all over the world.

There was no real reason for Reid to travel to the Curtis Park District location. There is a similar bank in Capitol Hill District, in the southeast corner. Each bank has the same Doctors with the same treatments running the same software, but Reid favors the Curtis Park location, since he lived in the district a few years ago.

Reid always uses the same Doctor—number 2674. He considers the robot inside to be his personal physician, even though that vocation long ago went extinct, except in the remaining rural areas where physicians serve primarily as Leisure Park veterinarians.

There are children running among the fountains when Reid approaches kiosk 2674. Several of the other kiosks are occupied, indicated with a red light above each door. Thousands of people utilize the Doctors each month, getting a standard check-up and preventative treatment as recommended by the Health Council.

The door to 2674 slides open and Reid steps inside. Calming muzak—an artifact from the 20th century—plays inside the kiosk. The air is processed to be oxygen-rich, and it smells of cologne, perfume and a hint of antiseptic.

"Good day, Reid Rosales," Longevity Robot 2674 says.

"Morning, doc," Reid replies. "How're the wife and kids?"

"I'm sorry. I didn't understand your health question," the robot answers. "Please repeat your query."

Reid laughs. "You and your sense of humor."

The robot does not respond.

After a pause: "Records show that your last visit occurred on May 1, 2087. Good job watching your health, Reid Rosales."

"Thanks, doc. You make the process fun."

"This kiosk performs all standard Longevity functions per Health Council guidelines," the robot replies.

"You don't get small talk much, I guess."

"Conversation does not have a size," the robot replies. "Please take a deep breath, and prepare for your age and health evaluation."

Reid rolls up his sleeve, exposing the veinous interior of his right elbow. The robot's arm extends across the narrow counter in the booth and from its arm extends a small needle—the diameter of a single hair. The needle contacts Reid's skin and slips painlessly into the vein. The robot begins counting down from ten as Reid's health data is collected.

"Small talk is something humans used to do with other humans they didn't know well, but had to interact with anyway," Reid explains. "See, when humans used to go to human doctors, they might not see them more than once in a year, so they would have no concept of each other's lives, but would still want to engage in conversation.

"Usually people would talk about the weather, work, family, or the things that they wanted to buy but couldn't. Other times they might talk about sports, but once it was clear that they both knew and enjoyed sports, it ceased to be small talk."

"Do you wish to discuss recent headlines while your test completes?" the robot asks.

"No, I guess I'm just nostalgic for a time when you would have been a person and we might have pretended to know one another."

The robot does not reply.

"The test is complete," the robot says as it retracts the thin needle. "Processing results. Please wait."

30

Reid waits patiently.

"Results ready. Would you like the report now?"

"Yes, doc," Reid says. "How'm I doing?"

"Current Patient Status for Reid Rosales. Age 33. Health Adjusted Age 17. Diseases None. Genetic Abnormalities None. Abnormal Cell Growth None. Current Life Expectancy 163," the robot reports. "Would you like to receive Preventative Care?"

Preventative Care is an injection of stem cells, essential oils, vitamins, minerals, amino acids, anti-virals, bacteria, and some refined growth hormone to prevent muscular atrophy, bone density loss, and skin deterioration. PC treatments are recommended for every citizen at least once every six months, depending on the kind of aging they prefer. Some Citizens choose the minimum regimen in hopes of aging more naturally, while also decreasing their life expectancy slightly. Others receive the injections monthly to preserve youth and maintain peak physical performance well into the early 120s. Reid usually keeps monthly appointments, but will miss one of two a year due to lack of interest.

"Yes, doc," Reid says.

The robot extends a second needle, this one much larger in diameter. A nozzle mounted above the needle sprays a powerful, short-lived local anesthetic on the insertion point in Reid's arm.

Reid feels the spot immediately go cold and tingly, and watches the needle slide in. The injection takes only a few seconds. The needle retracts and feeling returns to Reid's arm. The sensation of the PC treatment feels a lot like a fast infusion of caffeine, but without the racing heartbeat, anxiety, or intestinal distress. The pure energy buzzes through Reid's body for a moment and seems to dissipate out through his fingers.

"Your Preventative Care treatment is now complete," the robot says. "Do you have any additional health care needs today?"

"I've been having a hard time feeling passionate about my art lately," Reid says. "Is there anything that you can give me for that?"

"My prescription is to take your mind off of your concern. Take a vacation. Experience something new and you will often find that the passions you are missing will come back to you."

"I've tried a lot of different things, but I was hoping you'd prescribe something stronger than platitudes," Reid replies.

"Your symptoms—level three life dissatisfaction—do not indicate the prescription of medications. Breaking your routine is as effective as anything else, and that is what I recommend," the robot says. "If you have any other medical concerns, please visit again immediately. Do you have any additional health care needs today?"

Reid rolls his eyes, sighs, and ponders the Doctor's question. He could keep talking about it, about the lack of meaning, about the cartoon not being great enough, about the emptiness, but the Doctor will never bend on its diagnosis because it's not programmed to bend. A late-onset sense of euphoria washing over Reid from the PC treatment seals the issue. Smile and power through, that's what he will do.

"No thank you, doc," Reid replies. "I feel fantastic already."

"Longevity Kiosk is proud to serve you, Reid Rosales," the robot says, turning away toward the back wall behind it. The machine rotates back, now holding a small stainless steel container filled with colorfully wrapped objects.

"Please take a sucker, and leave in good health."

Reid takes a cherry sucker from the container and bids Longevity Robot 2674 goodbye. The Doctors bank now swarms with people taking their midday meal outside. Dozens more children sprint and splash among the fountains. Parents watch them from beneath the cool shade of the tall trees.

Some of these people are only in their sixties and they're already having kids, Reid thinks. *There was a time when people had to rush into parenthood, sometimes before they had even found themselves, all because of biology. People still turned out alright, didn't they? There were generations of humans who raised their kids without a clue what they were doing, sometimes sacrificing their own primes just to give life to another. Maybe that sometimes meant resentment, but maybe, it also meant that they had to be additionally dedicated.*

It's strange that we don't need to have as many kids anymore, he thought. *But people still do. It's a pure luxury, without cost or risk. The extra life added by the kiosks more than incentivizes giving some of it away for the next generation. Does that make the choice and sacrifice and love less pure, less valid?*

Reid brings up his calendar on his wristband and contemplates his schedule. The day is his—save for a gathering with Xiu, Gustave, and Selene in the evening. Reid can do whatever he wants, and though the free time is not at all unknown to him, he resents it. He resents having nowhere to be.

Reid decides to go to the old Throwback Arcade on the corner of Colfax and Cook in the Congress Park District. The Throwback is one of Reid's few regular haunts outside of his home district. The building is a mid-twenty-first century renewable design, built from old train cars, shipping containers and sundry recycled materials. Many American cities that saw population bursts during the 2030s, '40s, and '50s feature the architectural style which rejects newly manufactured materials, and as such, the eastern districts of Denver are littered with them.

Reid enters the Throwback and finds it packed, as usual. The bank of skeeball games has a line twenty people long. The air is alive with flashing lights—many with reproductions of old incandescent bulbs—sirens, buzzers, and digital voices asking him to come and play. Old arcade game cabinets, pinball machines, and virtual reality rigs line the outside walls. There is a group of early-twenty-first century pornographic sex simulators, branded with actors and actresses of their day. There is a line of direct combat games, in which two fighters battle in real time and real life to activate characters on the screen. In the center of the room is the Throwback Ticket to Fun Counter. There, a pair of robots accept and redeem digital versions of game tickets players get for performing well. The prizes available range from old-style stuffed animals, to 3D printed basic trinkets, to private Tubecar trips and specialized wristband software upgrades. But Reid's attention is focused on the far wall where the Throwback keeps their own line of games.

He bellies up to the Throwback Presents: *American Showdown* game. *American Showdown* is in a twentieth century-style wood and glass cabinet. The programmers designed it to emulate games from that era. Reid activates the game with his wristband, transferring ten credits to the machine. The game turns on and the title crawl moves up the screen:

"The year is 2023. You are a Lawmaker, one of a special class of 535 individuals tasked with determining the future of America. Your choices will determine whether the country succeeds or fails, but sometimes your choices will not matter at all. Will you be the bold savior that your electorate called for? Or will you be a resistant force in a 'lame duck' chamber? The choice is yours, Lawmaker…"

"Now, go make those laws."

The crawl fades away and the screen fills with a reproduction of the Washington, D.C. Capitol Mall. At one end is the goal, the Capitol Building. At the other, the starting line on the steps of the Lincoln Memorial. Each level is named after one of the divisive issues of the '20s. Level one is Guns. Level two is Abortion. Level three is the Red Secession. Level four is Universal Healthcare. Level five is Universal Equality. Using the joystick, Reid guides his Lawmaker up the screen, collecting supporters, each represented by a pixelated little person waving a flag. Reid dodges the other Lawmakers, wearing red and blue, making his way to the top of each screen and collecting as many supporters as he can along the way. Once he reaches the Capitol Building, the game tabulates his supporters. If he collects more than fifty thousand supporter points, the public is Frenzied, and he moves onto the next level. If he doesn't meet the supporter point threshold, he loses a life and has to start the level over.

Reid blows through the first five levels. It's all a system of patterns, anyway. If you identify the patterns, it's very easy to pick up supporters. On level six, Immigration, Reid loses a life, but he gets through on his second try. Then on level seven, Church and State, Reid dies two more times. On his last life, he barely grabs the final group of supporters before the Capitol steps. His palms sweat, and his hands shake.

Level eight is the Boss level. Reid has only seen it one other time before. A new screen loads with Reid's Lawmaker seated behind a desk on a political talk show. The computer controlled pundit asks questions of his Lawmaker while Reid selects from multiple choice lists of supplies.

Each answer that solicits a "hmm" from the pundit means Reid loses points.

Each answer that causes the pundit to flail his pixelated arms gains Reid's Lawmaker points.

Each question is follows the theme from the previous seven levels.

"Could gun control reduce the number of gun related deaths?" is the first question.

Reid selects "Gun control will cause more deaths."

The pundit waves his arms.

To question two, "Do women deserve unquestioned control over their own bodies?" Reid selects "Hormones prevent women from making sound decisions."

The pundit waves his arms.

Reid flies through the rest of the Boss level. A cut-scene depicts Reid's pixelated followers collected on the steps of the Lincoln Memorial. As the camera pans across the crowd of supporters, more and more of them raise guns, pitchforks, shovels, and signs. Reid's character appears on screen in front of them, followed by the words "Lead Your People!" Reid uses the joystick to walk up the Mall, with his supporters close behind. As they they march from the Memorial up to the Capitol, they leave a wake of pixelated fire, trash, and the occasional dead body.

When they reach the Capitol, the supporters cheer, as Reid's Lawmaker ascends the steps. The screen goes black.

"Continue by paying back your corporate donors? Deposit 100 credits."

The game counts down from ten.

Reid chooses not to pay up.

When the counter reaches zero, the phrase "Term Over" scrolls onto the screen.

"Why'd you let yourself lose?" a boys asks from behind him.

"The game doesn't get any better from there." Reid says. "The review I read says it's just the same thing over and over until you're out of credit.

"Duh," the boy says. "But after level fifty you get to burn the Capitol down. It looks really cool."

"I'll bet it does," Reid says, ceding the controls to the boy.

Reid plays a game of skeeball before finding himself bored. He checks his wristband again. Hours left to kill and nowhere to be. He leaves the Throwback and takes the Tubecar to Austin's Bouldin Citizenry District to take in a concert in one of their numerous virtual venues. Reid spends 200 credits to see the Beatles at Shea Stadium, electing to pay the extra 50 to drown out the crowd noise. A blonde girl wearing a floral top and mocassins faints on him when the band plays "Ticket to Ride". The simulation is very good, but Reid leaves wondering how such a popular band could have played only twelve songs in such a massive venue. His wristband tells him he still has plenty of time.

He sighs and chooses another activity.

He walks to the Congress and Riverside Tubecar station, and takes it to the 3rd and King station in San Francisco where he is just in time to watch the Giants baseball game at Bumgarner Ballfield. He enjoys some replicated hot dogs and popcorn and even drinks a few beers. The game moves slowly, part of the MLB Preservation Council's mission to maintain its original design despite athletes that never tire and scores exceeding triple-digits. During the seventh-inning stretch, Reid's wristband buzzes his skin. It's Xiu.

"Hey babe," she says. "I hope you're having a fun day!"

"It's okay, I guess."

"We're still on for dinner with Gustave and Selene in an hour, right?"

"Of course," Reid replies. "I wouldn't miss it."

"Yay! Where are you now, sweetie?"

"San Francisco. Just watching a ballgame," he says.

"Sounds nice," she says.

"It's just a way to pass all the time."

"That's what they say," Xiu replies. "See you soon."

The communication ends and Reid rises from his seat and walks back to the 3rd and King station, where he boards the first Tubecar back to Denver.

4

Capitol Hill Citizenry District; Denver, Colorado; United Sociocracy of the
Americas
June 3, 2087
8:40 PM

"The economy was becoming abstract back in the twentieth century, you know," Selene adds. "Most wealthy people built fortunes by moving the concept of their existing money around from company to company. They even used it to make money on other people's debts. But they definitely weren't working to directly contribute to some perfect system."

"The last oligarchic class was funded by their production, their investments in other oligarchs, and by money funneled to them by the old government through lobbyists," Gustave says. "You might be thinking about the past a little too nostalgically."

"I'm only saying that it might have been interesting to live in a time when you had to do something in the economy to gain from it," Reid says.

"Yeah," Xiu adds. "I think having a job might've been kind of cool. People could count on you and you'd make a table or plant some trees or push some buttons. I bet it would be a lot like meditation."

Reid nods and squeezes her to him.

"Are you kidding?" Selene asks. "The history books are loaded with stories about people hating having jobs. If you read Martin's *History of the Virtual Life*, you'll find that people were trying to escape being alive in the Twentieth almost constantly.

"They drank and smoked. They used the internet to pretend to be other people. They even wrote songs about 'working for the weekend.' Does that sound like a happy, meditative society to you?"

"I guess not," Xiu replies.

"People used to have to work more than twenty hours each week, you know," Gustave points out. "Who wants to do any one thing for that long?"

Xiu's face pinches in disgust.

"No thanks," Selene sighs, lighting a joint. "I'd rather have time for my photography."

She passes the joint to Xiu. Xiu passes it along to Reid.

Reid inhales deeply, and exhales.

"What did you do today?" Gustave asks Reid.

"I went to the Throwback, down to Austin for a repro-concert, and then went to most of a Giants game."

"You'd rather have been sitting at a desk inside? Or assembling something?"

Reid passes Gustave the joint.

"Didn't leave me much," Gustave says.

"There's plenty after we finish that one. We can just go to a vendor," Selene replies.

Reid shrugs. "I just think it'd be nice to have some purpose. It'd be nice to earn what I have."

Gustave passes the joint to Selene. She finishes it and stubs it out on the patio trash can lid. Above their table, strands of LED lights create a canopy of synthetic stars that drown out the glow of the city. A steady flow of people—some walking dogs—dressed mostly in summer attire, move past them along 12th Avenue. The summer night air is warm and dry. The sky is cloudless, and deep like the ocean.

A service robot rolls up to the table and collects their empty glasses.

"Can I bring you anything else?" it asks.

"Another beer, please," Gustave says.

"Same here," Reid adds.

"I'd like another red wine. Do you have a '35 Malbec, by chance?" Xiu asks.

"Let me check for you," the robot says. And immediately, "Yes. That vintage is available for order."

38

"One please, thanks."

"Bring me a Red Lotus," Selene says.

The robot turns and wheels away.

"Waiter," Gustave calls. "Give us a mountain view, too, please."

The robot turns around and says, "Yes."

In moments, 12th Avenue and all its buildings, shops, robots, people and pets disappear and an unobstructed view of the Rocky Mountains appears.

Gustave's wristband lights up with a new message: "You can deactivate mountain view here for the duration of your visit."

"I suppose you'd rather I had to get up and walk over to the robot waiter to deactivate it, huh, Reid?"

"Yeah, yeah. I get it. Never mind."

The robot returns with their drink order and rolls away to serve the rest of the lounge.

Selene produces a small case from her purse and opens it on the table. Inside are vials and baggies of different powders and pills. Each one is marked with a U. S. of A. Organic Safe seal, labeled with dosage recommendations and the explanation:

"The intoxicant herein is proven to simulate the reaction of its original. This product is safe and carries no health risks. Effects last between two and six hours. Exercise caution during use as balance and decision-making may still be affected."

"You guys want to try ecstasy tonight?" she asks.

The table replies, "Yes."

Selene distributes the pills to each of them. They take them together, clinking one another's glasses before washing the pills down. She closes the case and places it back in her purse.

"I think you have something of a point, Reid," Selene says. "It is sometimes overwhelming to be able to do anything I want. The structure of working could be a nice thing, but then I think I could only enjoy it in bursts."

"It would be a nice thing to visit, but you wouldn't want to live there," Xiu adds.

"Exactly."

"But I think it depends greatly on the individual," Gustave begins. "Look at us now, none of us have jobs. We're all second or third generation jobless. And somehow we all manage to keep busy, and even excel.

"Reid, you're one of the top cartoonists in this hemisphere. Selene does a gallery show a month with her photos. Xiu churns out beloved albums multiple times a year. I dabble with robotics, and still have time to write biographies on people who aren't famous but really deserve to be recognized.

"We've each found our niche, even without a system enforcing niches on us."

Reid sips his drink.

"You may have a point there," he says. "But is it really a niche if just about anyone can fill it?"

"We're each unique, so, I say yes," Selene adds. "It doesn't diminish your love for Xiu to know that other people are sharing love too, does it?"

"That's not the same thing," Reid replies.

"I think it is, Reid," Gustave gestures with a swirl of his glass. "I think you just don't want everyone to play the same game."

Reid stands angrily up from the table. The ecstasy is fast-acting and he feels his pants slide against his legs. The sensation is like a gentle caress or a cool breeze. He loses his thought for a moment as he presses the pockets flat with his hands, savoring the contact, then shakes himself back to awareness.

His anger following the pause is less convincing.

"I'm not against other people finding their purpose," he grunts. "Don't make me out to be some kind of fascist."

"This is just like your Thoreau obsession, Reid," Gustave continues. "But after a few weeks, you were back to working inside and enjoying the replicators."

"That was a legitimate interest in a philosophy of living," Reid answers. "It's not my fault that you've never wanted to live outside the lines."

"You know full well th—"

"Whoa, boys," Xiu interrupts. "This is a friendly place. Let's take a step back."

She touches Reid's pant leg and he quivers momentarily before following her hand back to his seat. Selene activates the photo projector in her wristband. Her portfolio hovers above the center of their table.

"I admit that I can't take photos of suffering when there isn't any," she says. "And that might hurt the artistic dialogue, in a way, Reid. I think that's partly what you're getting at."

She scrolls through the images until she finds an image of a woman, staring out a window, in stark black and white.

"Look at her face, Reid. There's still sadness, even without the other struggles," Selene says. "We're only human."

"Look at the juxtaposition of light and shadow here. It's as if half of her is lost in an amorphous cloud," Xiu says.

"It's an undeniably successful photograph," Gustave adds.

"Maybe we're always bound to be disappointed by something, no matter how good it gets?" Reid asks.

"I think so," Xiu replies. "As long as it's not me."

"Never," Reid answers. He leans over and kisses her on the neck.

"Being the best isn't really important," Gustave says. "Having a society of bests, now that's something."

Reid nods, but finds himself unable to stop kissing Xiu's neck. Her perfume calls his lips to her flesh like some wispy fingers from an old cartoon. Xiu leans into his lips and her skin erupts in goosebumps. She moans into his ear. Across the table Gustave begins kissing Selene. She climbs onto his lap and he traces her collarbone with his tongue.

The service robot appears beside them, emerging into their brilliant mountain view from out of nowhere.

"How is everyone doing here?" it asks.

Reid pops up from his cozy spot in the crook of Xiu's neck, suddenly aware of his surroundings.

"This stuff is really working," he says to the table.

Gustave nods.

Xiu says, "I think that's obvious."

Selene adds, "Fast-acting means fast-acting."

"Just the check then," Reid says to the service robot.

The robot emits a set of tones that indicates it is calculating.

"Your total is 956 credits," it says. "Would you like me to split the bill?"

"No," Gustave says. "Just put it all on mine."

An authorization to transfer 956 credits appears on Gustave's wristband. He reads the bill. "Fine by me," Gustave says. His wristband confirms the transaction.

"Thank you for your business, please return soon," the robot says as it disappears into the mountain view.

"We should get out of here before this starts to wear off," Selene says. "I have some new toys we can try together."

She climbs from Gustave's lap, straightens her shorts, and gathers her purse. Xiu rises from her seat, guiding Reid from his with a gentle gesture of her fingertips across his chest. Gustave follows, and the foursome exit the lounge to walk toward his flat on Tenth Avenue and Clarkson.

Reid Rosales and Xiu Parker have been friends with Gustave Yamamoto and Selene Fitzhugh for two years. They met at an art show in the old River North Art District—caught up talking about a set of vintage sports sculptures in a converted warehouse gallery. Reid and Xiu were looking for a couple to blend with for a few weeks, conveniently, Gustave and Selene wanted the same. Gustave's tall, lanky frame and thick, blonde beard appealed to Xiu, while Selene's Rubenesque form and silver hair grabbed Reid's attention. They were lucky that Gustave and Selene felt similarly about Reid's sandy hair and slender, non-athletic physique, and Xiu's slim form and usually jet-black hair.

That night they all went home together and blended for the first time. They've been doing so a few times a month ever since. They went to parties together, met with their peers, and blended further.

Gustave's flat is an open-floor plan unit that resembles an old garage. There are metal pillars that hold up two metal cross beams, and large windows that roll up when they open to create a space that feels outside, while remaining indoors. The walls are combination brick and metal, adorned with travel posters from the early twentieth century, and signage from roadways to businesses that Gustave has collected over the years.

They enter through the sliding front door and Xiu and Selene drop their bags beside the coat rack. Gustave buzzes over to the kitchen and asks the replicator for the same vintage of Malbec Xiu had previously ordered. Selene leads Reid and Xiu into the center of the room where Gustave has built a custom conversation pit, one of the few successful architectural concepts of the 1970s, filled with pillows and cushions. There is no need for furniture. The space is freely customizable.

"Catherine," Gustave speaks to his apartment computer. "Please put on the 2041 Sonata. We need some music."

"Prepare for an earful," Catherine replies.

The electronic-post-dub-neoclassical piece begins playing all around them. Reid can feel the music, especially the bass, rattling his still electrified skin. Xiu coos and he knows that she's feeling the same.

Reid notices something that lifts his spirit. An original Origami Emu, this one dressed in the military regalia of 19th Century France, gazes back at him from Gustave's wall.

"You hung it up?" Reid asks Gustave, pointing at the illustration.

"Of course I hung it up, Reid," Gustave says. "It's a brilliant piece of satire."

Reid smirks.

"I wanted to play with the concepts of parody and meme culture, mixing with historical context," Reid says. "This was supposed to be something like Napoleon meets web-art meets Origami Emu."

"And it's executed brilliantly," Gustave replies. "Hence its valuable real estate."

"Thanks. It's funny that it only got 3293rd place in the contest I entered it in."

"You can't account for taste," Gustave says.

Gustave takes the glasses from the replicator and moves toward the group, bouncing carefully to the music, so as not to spill the wine.

"If not for the robot economy, Antoine Digre never could have written this," Gustave says as he hands out the wine. "He was no aristocrat. Imagine composing a twenty-four hour masterpiece like this one through sickness, hunger, and a job. It would be impossible. It would have taken his entire life. Instead, we have a year's worth of his *Long Symphonies*."

Reid is too high to argue, and at the moment he's not even sure how he'd retort.

"I believe this is as close to old concepts of Heaven that we'll ever reach," Selene says.

"You mean the ecstasy?" Reid asks, one hand on his wine, and the other tracing Xiu's spine.

"No silly, the Digre," Selene replies. "But also the ecstasy."

They laugh together.

"If angels exist on this earth," Gustave says. "Truly, we are them."

He climbs down into the conversation pit with them. Gustave and Selene and Xiu and Reid all cuddle together among the pillows, letting the wine and music wash over them. Reid begins to lose himself in the pillows, unable to tell for certain where he ends and the intense sensation of comfort begins. The same feeling connects his fingertips to Xiu, and the wine to his lips. Maybe this connection, the one that comes through the drugs and the wine and the conversation, maybe this is all the meaning a person needs. If ecstasy can be less of a concept, and more of a concoction, then why couldn't the same be true for purpose? The sensations are real. The feeling the continuity between people is real. The tastes and smells are real. Who cares where—or how—they originate? There's something powerfully human and individual about a lifetime of experiences. The struggle—the necessary one— could simply be in choosing how to experience the world at all.

"Catherine, give us some stars," Gustave commands.

"Time to dazzle," Catherine replies.

The ceiling disappears, replaced with a perfect representation of the night sky, as seen far outside the city where no light pollutes the view. The Milky Way shimmers white in a velvet band above their heads.

"We are so small compared to all that," Xiu says.

44

"And yet somehow we're each a universe inside a tiny shell," Selene adds.

"I think that our shared conflict of ego and impermanence is what bonds us all," Gustave says.

"And that conflict is unique for each of us," Reid replies. "It makes us each unique."

The stars and music and the ecstasy combine majestically. Reid kisses Xiu. He kisses Selene. Xiu kisses Gustave. Selene kisses Xiu. Reid kisses Gustave.

They undress each other.

They fall naked together into the cushions and pillows.

They have sex under the synthetic stars to the carefully programmed tones of an ideal symphony, and when they finish they fall back into each other's arms.

The stars need not be real to be significant. They don't need to be real to prove something to the universe. Most of them are long, long dead, casting a dying light out into a senseless void. That could be it, Reid thinks. *It could just be a matter of sending something out into the void, not hoping for a reply, or a confirmation, but simply because it is done.*

Reid holds Xiu, stroking her hair. Gustave and Selene tangle together.

Xiu falls asleep.

Selene and Gustave fall asleep.

Reid lies awake staring up at the starry ceiling.

If I'm insignificant compared to all of that, he thinks. *Don't I deserve to feel significant down here? Shouldn't my life be something I built myself, rather than something handed down to me?*

The stars don't know significance. The stars shine. The stars burn hot and burst and fall back to death, only to be reabsorbed into the ether. But humans name them. Humans give them significance by creating stories and worlds and belief systems built around them. Maybe purpose isn't earned at all, but assigned. Reid Rosales begins to wonder if he can't create his own purpose. Like *Origami Emu*, what's to stop Reid from creating his own significance? Or his own world?

An hour later, Xiu wakes up and rolls over to him.

"You're still up?" she asks.

"Just thinking."

"I love your brains."

"I love you."

She wraps her naked body around him. He listens to her gentle breaths, and in time, drifts away to sleep.

5

Capitol Hill Citizenry District; Denver, Colorado; United Sociocracy of the
Americas
June 4, 2087
9:22 AM

Reid awakens to the smell of thick Italian espresso fresh from Gustave's
kitchen replicator. Xiu, still nude, rubs sleep from her eyes to Reid's right. Selene
skitters about the flat in a silk kimono, cradling her cup of coffee like an infant.
Gustave hovers over the kitchen island, breathing in the crisp scents of ground beans
and Alps spring water. The ceiling of the apartment adjusts with the time of day,
surrounding them in calming, pale blue. A few wispy clouds hover above.

Reid climbs from the nest of pillows, stretches, and gathers his clothing. He
dresses. He feels no residual effects from the ecstasy—no hangover—save for the
distinct lack of heightened sensation as his shirt and pants contact his skin. Xiu pops
up beside him and kisses his cheek before searching among the cushion for her
underwear and dress. She slips into her panties, and then climbs out of the pit like a
drowsy kitten. Xiu slinks over to her purse by the door, swaying to some unheard
music. She digs for and retrieves her hair-tint pen, taps at its settings, and touches it
to her jet-black locks, turning them an electric blue.

Reid gathers up a coffee for him and one for Xiu and brings hers to her just
as her dress slips over her naked torso like a waterfall.

"It's a blue day today?" Reid asks.

"I feel peaceful, don't you?" she replies.

Gustave raises his cup toward the ceiling and steps out from the kitchen.
"Here's to another truly successful evening."

Selene, Xiu, and Reid raise their cups in agreement.

"Sorry about giving you a tough time, Reid," Gustave continues. "You
know I love an argument."

Selene nods emphatically.

"We balance each other out, right?" Reid says. "That's what keeps us honest."

"Good man," Gustave replies.

"Gustave Yamamoto, it's that time again," Cathcrine says. "Shall I read off the daily votes with breakfast as is your wont?"

Gustave sighs. "Thank you, but let's wait until our guests leave," he says. "Ask me again in an hour, Catherine."

"As you like it, darling boy," the computer replies.

Reid sips at the espresso. The temperature is perfect. The taste and body are perfect. He can feel the caffeine energizing him, clearing out the cobwebs of morning. At one time, it took a human operator and an elaborate machine of boilers, steamers and grinders to make a single espresso. It was a craft to produce a single tiny cup of brown liquid. Reid wonders what the real thing tasted like, and if anyone in the U. S. of A. could still remember.

"What are everyone's plans for this beautiful day?" Xiu asks.

Selene gulps down the last portion of her espresso and sets the cup on the counter. "I'm taking the Tubecar to the Mexico Federal Citizenry District to take photos at the Aztec Life Leisure Park."

"That's the one where you simulate life in Tenochtitlan," Reid says.

"The very same, handsome," Selene replies.

"I always thought that would be fun. I don't know why I haven't visited yet," he continues.

"They have a really hilarious human sacrifice exhibit," Gustave jokes. "Maybe you could volunteer."

"A tall blonde like yourself would lock in a more bountiful harvest," Reid quips.

"Glad you're up on the right side of the bed, chap," Gustave replies.

Reid finishes his coffee and sets the empty cup on the kitchen island.

"Thanks for hosting this week, Gus," Reid says.

Gustave raises his fist playfully. "Don't call me..."

"Stop me," Reid replies.

"You can come with me, Reid," Selene says. "It'd be nice to ride the Tubecar together."

"Thanks, Selene," Reid answers. "But I've got some other stuff to do."

"Like what?" Xiu asks. "You told me you were just going to do your dailies and wander."

"I changed my mind. I going to stop by the Church for a bit, if you must know."

Gustave coughs. "The Church? It's all mumbo jumbo in that old church. Reid. Pal. You're going to drive yourself mad with this search for meaning and purpose. Besides, you're not going to find it over there."

"This is why I didn't say anything," Reid says to Xiu.

"Don't be cross. I just care about you," Gustave replies.

"Well, I'm going to the Hall of Fame today to run a new song by the Annie Clark hologram," Xiu says. "I wish I could grow the way she did. Each new album was like a new sound."

"I'm going to continue writing my new novel," Gustave states. "I'll finally get to introduce the murderous AI that has been stalking Franz Kafka's robot body since chapter one."

Gustave finishes his cup, gathers Xiu's empty, and places them in the replicator to be molecularly deconstructed. He rejoins the group as Selene trades her kimono for her dress.

Reid, Xiu, Gustave, and Selene embrace and wish each other a good day before the three guests file out into the hallway and through the entrance to Gustave's building. The summer sun reflects off the street. The pavement is hot. The sidewalks overflow with people, their children, their pets, their conversations. The food vendors and buskers fill the air with street song. Gone are the serene fictions of the night before. At least for another week. All the people might as well be stars.

Selene waves goodbye, checks her wristband for the time, and sprints toward the Tubecar station. Reid takes Xiu by the wrist and pulls her close to him.

"We're okay, right?" he asks. "I know I kind of changed plans. I should have told you."

"I don't care," Xiu answers. "I just wish you'd have invited me, or as least shared it with me."

"You're right. I should have brought you in," he replies. "Do you want to come?"

Xiu shakes her head.

"Today I'm really excited about Cleveland, but I'll go next time."

Reid detects a faint hurt in her voice. *Xiu is always so good at disguising it, tucking it behind a sunny veneer that always reflects positivity.*

"I'm really confused right now," Reid says. "I don't know why, but I can't stop thinking about how all of this is too easy—or not right, or...something."

She hugs him tight.

"I know. It happens, and it will pass. Take some time to do some soul searching after your dailies and you'll see. Some kind of big creative burst will take over and you'll stop thinking about all this morbid history."

Reid, still wrapped in Xiu's embrace, feels suddenly alone—hovering in the limitlessness of space with no connection to anything. *She wants me to get over it*, he thinks. *Maybe she's right.*

"I'm fond of you, Xiu."

"I'm fond of you, Reid."

Xiu lets him go and swings her purse strap over her shoulder. "Ping me," she says.

"I will."

Xiu Parker walks confidently down 12th Avenue toward the Seventh and Downing Street Tubecar station that serves Midwest stops. Reid turns around and walks back toward Pearl Street, his apartment, his dailies, and a change of clothes.

***

The Universal Combined Church of Faiths—or simply the Church—is the single, one-stop shop for religious study, research, and interfaith collaboration. There are more than forty-thousand UCCF branches worldwide, each one making its home in buildings formerly dedicated to an individual faith—including churches,

50

synagogues, mosques, cathedrals, and temples. The UCCF was founded in 2033 after the last of the Faith Wars—and their negative perception among the public— left the remaining religious leaders clamoring for a peaceful compromise. Pope Pius XIX, the 21st Dalai Lama, Evangelist David Tebow, Grand Imam Aalim Mannan, Rabbi Chaim Geron, Chinese Shenism Councilwoman Ming Ning, and Brahmin Guru Pommi Krishnamurthy conferred for six days in the Old Norse Asatru hof just outside of Reykjavik, Iceland. Together with High Priestess Elsa Önnudóttir, the unprecedented religious summit attempted to redefine religion in a world that had seen too many atrocities committed in its name.

After months of discussion, with some negotiations reaching back into the 2020s, the group decided that the best way to bridge their differences was to literally bring each of the major religions together under one roof. The idea was slow to take off. Religious leaders—watching their followers dwindle—encouraged peaceful parallel worship, attendance improved. Once word spread that Catholics, Christians, Muslims, Jews, Buddhists, Hindus, Chinese Shenists and Norse Pagans were gathering in the same buildings, worshipping their own capital "G" God or "lowercase "g" gods peacefully, side-by-side, like the lion and the lamb, the UCCF spread quickly worldwide. The collaboration also led to the first successful negotiations regarding holy lands and agreements to end extremism. Of course, the religious leaders didn't admit it, but replicated food and advances in healthcare gave each an opportunity to look past their singular interests toward real compromise.

The public saw their leaders commit to the peace they preached, and visited the new Church in droves, whether for absolution, salat, yoga, or tourism. Faith stopped being a divisive topic, and became the popular way to seek enlightenment, self-knowledge and inner peace.

The Cathedral Basilica of the Immaculate Conception stands defiant amid the modern housing towers that surround it along Colfax Avenue. The 1921 structure, designed in the architectural style of the 12th century, looks almost magical beside the 2040s renewables, and houses one of three Capitol Hill District UCCF chapters. As agreed upon at the first UCCF summit, no aspects of religious buildings have been altered, and the Cathedral Basilica's interior looks just as it did when first opened.

Reid enters through the golden double doors on the Colfax entrance. The cathedral is silent—unaffected by the clamor of pedestrians and cyclists on the street outside. A UCCF robot emblazoned with the official seal of the United Heart stands at the entrance.

"Good morning and welcome," it says. "Please take an audio device to enhance your experience."

Reid nods to the robot and takes a small audio player and wireless earphones from its metal hand.

"Should I do this clockwise, or counter?" Reid asks, looking into the cathedral interior where holograms and altars to each religion line the outside walls.

"Faith comes from within," the robot replies. "Begin where your heart leads you and continue as you wish."

"I come here looking for guidance and all I get is another open end?" Reid asks. He reluctantly inserts his earphones, and shakes his head.

"Blessings," the robot says as Reid steps toward the vaulted center of the nave.

Unsure of where to begin, Reid walks straight ahead to the original altar of Christ placed there by the Catholic church when the cathedral was built. The prophet of Christianity gazes down upon him from the crucifix. Blood runs down his face, arms and feet. The violence and brutality make Reid uncomfortable, but he steps forward and a hologram of Jesus appears before him.

"I am Jesus Christ. My doctrine is of love, compassion and charity," the hologram says through Reid's earphones. "Would you like to hear the scripture of the day?"

"Actually, I have a personal quandary I need help with," Reid whispers.

"Speak it, child," the hologram says.

"I find myself dissatisfied with my life. I want something more for myself."

"You seem focused on yourself," the hologram says. "But the greatest purpose is in giving to others. Look to 1 John 4:12: 'If we love one another, God lives in us and His love is made complete in us.' Instead of asking what is wrong with your life, ask what you can do to love others more completely."

"But am I not supposed to have purpose? Am I not supposed to feel meaningful?"

The hologram appears to think for a moment.

"'The purposes of a person's heart are deep waters, but one who has insight draws them out.' That is Proverbs 20:5. Perhaps you should seek purpose in service to others. Create art or music, and cultivate joy."

"I've been doing that, but everyone is, so what's the point?" Reid protests.

"I will refer you to the previously quoted proverb, my child," the hologram answers. "Consider its deeper meaning and I am certain you will find respite."

Reid steps back from the altar and the hologram disappears. *Maybe my dissatisfaction stems from not serving others, or at least feeling like I don't,* he thinks. *But I still don't feel any clearer.*

The altar to Buddhism draws Reid next. A hologram of the Buddha appears before him, sitting pensive in lotus, beneath the Bodhi Tree. He smiles at the Buddha and the Buddha returns his smile.

The hologram blinks its gentle eyes. Reid can't be sure if it looks at him or into him. An iridescence around the Buddha shifts from blue to green to gold.

Finally the Buddha speaks, "What troubles you, my friend?"

"I am struggling to define myself," Reid says. "I want so much to feel purposeful and important, but I'm just like everyone else."

"Ah, yes. That is an old concern, friend," the Buddha says. "You are surrounded with ease and wealth and food and sensation, much like I was at one time."

"You were?" Reid asks.

"Oh, yes. Indeed, friend. I was once an aristocrat, a rich boy, lost and lonely despite being surrounded by friends and lovers."

"What did you do?" Reid asks.

"I talked to many people. Some of them told me that I needed to enjoy my wealth. Others told me to reject all of my wealth and live with only what I needed. But neither of those polemics spoke to me. I lived both. I nearly starved to death chasing asceticism. I wanted to find a middle way. So I sat beneath the Bodhi Tree and I let go of my thoughts until I let go of myself."

"And then what?"

"I came to realize the cause of all suffering. It was neither relieved through a life of pleasure, nor through a rejection of all pleasure. Instead, I discovered the Four Noble Truths. First, that our experiences and pleasures aren't ultimately satisfying. Second, that our attachments to having pleasurable experiences, or to avoiding bad experiences prevents us from escaping the cycle of dissatisfaction and rebirth. Third, that by ending the cravings and clingings to pleasures and displeasures, one can escape the cycle. And fourth, that discipline, mindfulness, decency, and meditation are the path to transcending the cycle, and becoming one with meaning. Once you free yourself from fears and ego, you can access the peace within, but the mind is everything. What you think you will become."

"Jesus just told me that the greatest purpose came from serving others," Reid says.

"It is a common path to enlightenment," the Buddha says. "The best way to serve others is to begin by serving yourself, because you and others are not actually separate things. Like I said once, 'Thousands of candles can be lighted from a single candle, and the life of the candle will not be shortened. Happiness never decreases by being shared.'"

"So I should find inner peace and then tell other people about it?" Reid asks.

"That's a simple way to put it," the Buddha replies. "Follow your heart to your happiness, and encourage others to follow theirs."

Reid bows to the hologram and begins moving toward the next altar.

"Say, friend," the hologram calls. "Do you take my yoga class?"

Reid smiles. "I do. I didn't know you were connected to that."

"We are all connected," the hologram says.

Next Reid visits the altar of Islam.

"What do you seek?" a disembodied voices speaks.

Reid looks around the altar for a hologram, but finds nothing.

"Are you Muhammed?" he asks.

"I am Abū al-Qāsim Muḥammad ibn ʿAbd Allāh ibn ʿAbd al-Muṭṭalib ibn Hāshim of Mecca," the voices says. "But you know that."

54

"Why don't you have a hologram?" Reid asks.

"Because you need not see me to believe," Muhammed answers. "What has brought you here?"

"I've lost my passion for life. I seek meaning."

"I once sought meaning. I worked as a merchant, and I would retreat to the caves in the near mountains for seclusion and prayer. After many retreats to Hira, and many, many prayers, I was visited by the angel Gabriel who spoke to me about Allah."

"So discipline is the way to find meaning?" Reid asks.

"Discipline is important. Had I not shown my devotion, Allah would not have chosen me," Muhammed says. "But the path to meaning lies in God and God alone. Discard your desires for wealth or praise or glory and give all glory to him and you will find what you seek."

"That's it?" Reid asks. "My purpose in life is to worship God?"

"You must know the Quran. You must follow its teachings. And you must worship Allah," the voice says. "In doing these things you will free yourself of the concerns of the flesh, and of material meaning. You will live your life in service to Him, and it will be a good life."

"Jesus and the Buddha have different takes on this," Reid says.

"There is only Allah," Muhammed says. "And the peace he brings to you through devotion."

Reid nods solemnly. "Thank you."

"Go in peace," Muhammed says. "Praise be to Allah."

Then he approaches the Norse altar and a hologram of a bearded man in a three piece suit appears. His hair is slicked back and he wears a pair of mirrored sunglasses.

"Are you, umm, Odin?" Reid asks, reading from his wristband. "The Allfather?"

The bearded man chuckles, and lowers his sunglasses to reveal one glinting eye and one empty socket.

"It's not easy to be in disguise when there's a placard naming me," he says. "Yes, I am the Allfather."

"I'm Reid," Reid says. "And I'm trying to find meaning in my life."

"Then you are already finding it, boy," Odin says.

"I'm not sure I follow," Reid replies.

"Then you're already losing your meaning again," Odin says.

Reid blinks, dumbfounded.

"I lost this," Odin says, pointing to his empty eye socket. "I lost this to drink of the Well of Urd, a spring of wisdom. And then I sacrificed myself to myself on Yggdrasil, to discover the Runes."

"Sacrificed yourself to yourself?" Reid asks.

"I am a god, after all," Odin replies.

"Doesn't that make it less impressive?"

"Try hanging yourself from a tree with a gaping chest wound without food or water for nine days," Odin says. "You tell me it's easy."

"But couldn't you just mend yourself or something?" Reid asks.

Odin furrows his brow. "Look, Reid," he says. "That isn't the point. The point is that knowledge is everything. I went to the ends of the world for it, and gave my life for it. Wisdom is meaning. So long as you seek it, you are fulfilling your purpose."

"Why don't I feel meaningful right now, then?" Reid asks. "And why did Jesus, the Buddha, and Muhammed have other ideas?"

"If you don't feel it, kid, you're not seeking knowledge, you're seeking something else," Odin says. "Maybe you mean to feed your ego and not your mind?"

"As for the other guys in here, they are all seeking knowledge too. They just share specific bits they've learned more often than they talk about the search."

Reid stands before the altar of Vishnu next. The god appears, standing, its four arms raised, holding the conch, the chakra, the lotus and the mace. Vishnu's blue skin glows, and the god smiles with bright red lips.

"Vishnu?" Reid asks.

The god opens his eyes and his skin glows brighter, emanating from the center of his chest.

"You seek purpose?"

"I do, Vishnu," Reid says. "And I'm getting a lot of different perspectives, so I'm half hoping that you'll agree with one of the other guys, and half hoping that you throw me a curveball."

"Why do you seek purpose?"

Reid pauses.

"I used to find meaning in my work, but recently I've realized that I'll never be the best at it, and now the work doesn't feel right to me anymore."

"There is nothing noble about being superior to some other man," Vishnu says. "The true nobility is in being superior to your previous self."

Reid nods. *There's the curveball.*

"How can I be better than the best I've already been?" he asks.

"You're thinking too literally," Vishnu replies. "Your best self is not your most successful self. Your best self is your kindest, wisest, most enlightened self. Only by seeking your best self again and again, will you have any chance to find true greatness."

"So if I'm a good person, and I do the right things, eventually I will find meaning."

"No," Vishnu says. "You will become meaning."

Reid smiles to the god. "I'll start right away," he says.

"And in many lifetimes you will reach your goal," Vishnu replies.

"Many lifetimes?" Reid asks.

"You are presently quite far from enlightenment."

"I see," Reid says. "You've been helpful. Thank you, sir."

Vishnu bows his head briefly, lowers his four arms and closes his eyes.

Reid approaches the Judaic altar feeling confused and tired.

A bearded man, with wild hair, dressed in robes appears in hologram before the altar.

Reid looks down at his wristband.

"Moses?"

"Yes," Moses says. "You are on a search for meaning?"

"How did you know?"

"You look weary, like the man who has traveled far and learned much," Moses replies. "Please, sit down and take a cup of tea."

A teacup, steaming, appears from a replicator hidden within the altar.

"A quest for truth cannot be undertaken by a weakened soul," Moses says.

"Thank you," Reid replies, taking the cup. Reid sips the tea. It is warm and syrupy, and consoling in a deep down way that he can't quite describe.

"Thank you," Reid says. "The tea is great."

"L'chaim," Moses replies.

"I have heard a lot of different things from everyone here, and I am more confused than ever."

"Good," Moses says.

"Good?"

"Yes," Moses says. "God knows all things. If you were not confused, you wouldn't need God in the first place."

"I guess that makes some sense," Reid replies.

"It does and it doesn't. What I'll tell you next might not make sense to you either, but I believe it is true," Moses says. "In Judaism, we honor God by living right and living well. We do right by our neighbors. We seek knowledge. And we savor the pleasures of the world that He has created for us. The path to meaning is complex, but it ultimately boils down to following the Commandments, and always trying to be a better person. It is a hunger for life."

"That sounds great. It's like all the other guys wrapped into one," Reid says. "With some contradictions."

"What good would life be without contradictions?" Moses replies. "There'd be no brave pacifists, no old news."

"So what am I supposed to take away from all of this?" Reid asks.

"Whatever your heart tells you to take away, but do not make the mistake of missing out on your life while searching for what it is supposed to be."

Reid nods to Moses, and finishes his tea.

"Thank you," he says to the hologram. "I have a lot to think about."

"You do," Moses says. "And you'll be better for it."

Reid takes these thoughts and sits in a pew at the center of the cathedral. Hundreds of other people cross his vision—some speaking with the holograms, praying, doing yoga—but Reid does not see them, transfixed in consideration.

My purpose will come from doing for others, he thinks. *My purpose will come from forgetting myself. My purpose is inside me and outside of me at once. If only I could find someone to serve. If only I could find someone who still needed something, who still struggled. If only I could do more than just draw and fulfill myself. But maybe I'm fulfilling others by fulfilling myself and bringing them joy. Maybe I'm wasting time thinking about myself, as Odin said. Or perhaps if I turn my love outward I will feel it come back.*

Or I should war with my ego to conquer this?

Or I should simply seek to be better?

Reid Rosales sits in silence again, with so many thoughts he cannot think.

His wristband buzzes. It's Xiu.

"The Hall of Fame is wonderful," her message says. "I hope that you're finding what you need. You are loved, Reid."

Calm washes over him, and he blinks away tears. His chest tightens and he cries.

There is no answer, Reid thinks. *Meaning is something I find in myself. Meaning is something I create by helping others. Meaning is something that comes through devotion, something that I find through experience and the avoidance of experience. It's too much.*

The only thing that seems clear is that there will be a sign. Their common thread is that they all knew what to do when the time was right. The prophets and gods were compelled, or they were visited, but the thing they needed grabbed them, shook them, and brought them to meaning.

All I have to do is be open to the sign when it comes. It will still be a search for knowledge and for meaning, but it will be my willingness to discover it, to see what God or the gods or the universe or anything presents to me, and to take action.

He gathers himself after a few minutes and rises from the pew. He stops at the UCCF robot and leaves the audio player and earphones with it.

"Did you have a good visit, today?" it asks him.

"Yes. I learned a lot, I think," Reid says. "My eyes are open to whatever guidance appears to me."

"You are welcome to return anytime."

"Thank you," Reid says. "Maybe I will."

On the walk back to his apartment, Reid makes an effort to smile at every person he passes. Any of them could be a messenger of meaning. Any one of them could have a sign, or be a sign. He could help any of them, or any of them could be there to help him.

A young woman of sixty or so, coming back from yoga, smiles back at him.

"Hello," Reid says.

"Hi," she replies.

"Nice yoga mat," Reid says.

She looks at her mat. "Thanks," she says. "I'm just coming back from class."

"I do yoga too," Reid says. "But I'm not sure I'm getting everything out of it I should."

"Oh not me," she says. "Every class feels like it pulls me to the center of myself."

Reid feels suddenly jealous.

"I wish I had felt that way about it," he says.

"Maybe it's just not your thing," she says.

"Maybe it's not."

"Have a wonderful day," she says, smiling, and then walks away.

An older gentleman in his 130s or 140s, sitting on the grass midway in a lawn chair stops Reid.

"Come here and listen to this if you're not in a hurry," the old man says.

Reid considers it and sits down on the grass.

The old man gestures at his wristband, and bright, energetic music starts playing. Reid remembers it from school, something called Big Band Jazz.

"You like this?" the old man asks.

The trumpets and trombones blare and bleet to the drummer's hasty beat.

"It's fun," Reid replies.

"You know, when I was a your age or so, people thought this music was dangerous."

"How could it be dangerous?"

"Makes people want to dance. And dancing, they thought, always led to sex, and other improprieties," the old man says. "But you should ask Alice Minter if she slept with me after we went to the Homecoming dance, the Winter Ball, and the prom, and you'll see how silly that idea was in the first place.

"Anyway, that's not important to you is it? I just like to share my music because it makes me happy."

"Thank you," Reid says. "I do like it."

"You take care now."

"You too," Reid replies.

He continues toward his apartment and sees a boy and girl play catching over by a pair of street vendors.

"You want to play, mister?" the girl asks.

Reid nods and the three make a triangle around the vendors. As they toss the ball back and forth and around and around, Reid marvels at the way the boy and girl sprint to and from the ball, and how their whole bodies seem to be involved in the simple motion experience of throwing.

The girl laughs as she catches the ball. "Nice throw," she says.

The boy giggles as the ball sails over his head and he gives chase.

Reid catches the ball easily, examines it for a moment, wondering what he's missing, and then tosses it back to the girl.

"That's enough for me," Reid says. "Thanks for letting me play."

"Of course," says the girl.

"Have a great one," says the boy.

By the time he returns to his apartment, Reid speaks to four more people in just a few blocks. He sits with them, talks to them, and shares in their joys and pleasures, but none of them tell him what he's supposed to do, who he's supposed to be, or offer him any kind of sign. *There must be something that I'm missing*, he thinks. *Or maybe it's just that another person's meaning and my own can't be the same thing, not completely. I'll have to find my own.*

Reid enters his building, zips up to his apartment and makes a sandwich and a beer in the replicator.

"Good to see you," Iris says. "Did you have an enjoyable day?"

"I think so, Iris."

"Why do you only think so, Reid?"

"I'm not sure," he answers. "There's still something missing. Something I can't put my finger on. Something I haven't found yet."

6

Highland Citizenry District; Denver, Colorado; United Sociocracy of the Americas

June 5, 2087

1:14 PM

April Casablanca tours the world teaching her comprehensive course on art history, titled "Art: Ages, Civilizations, and Masters." Tickets are issued by lottery in batches of one hundred and she only stops in two hundred cities each year. The tricky thing is that you must be a resident of the city to be included in the lottery because as April says "The Tubecar connects us to everywhere, but only the here and now connects us to ourselves."

Her class is one of the last scarce commodities in the U. S. of A., or the world, and Selene is screaming gleefully into her wristband when she tells Reid, Xiu and Gustave that their names have been selected to attend.

The class is set up in Leprino Foods Civic Center, a converted office and distribution hub for a long-defunct food company. The attendees—dressed in formal attire, as requested—gather in an open atrium room with tall, narrow windows that reach nearly from floor to ceiling. There are rows of white tables with pre-replicated glasses of wine, beers, and liquor, as well as plates of hors d'oeuvres. The stunning detail lies in their arrangement. Everything is laid out in homage to great works of art. The cheese plate hearkens to Van Gogh's *Starry Night*. A tray of dips resembles Rothko's *Orange, Red, Yellow*. A giant sheet cake is iced like a Pollack. The charcuterie and cut vegetables float about a pond of Monet's *Waterlilies*. Even Phelp's 2036 collage *Death of the Assembled Man* is recreated in various rolls of sushi.

"You know it's nice to be out among our people," Gustave says, swirling a glass of wine. "Instead of rolling around in the muck with the swine."

"Don't be gauche," Selene replies.

"I was only joking," he says. "Reid got the joke, and he's anti-aristocracy."

"I'm not—"

"This is really important to me, Gustave, and it should be for you too," Selene says. "Xiu and Reid understand how rare this opportunity is."

Reid and Xiu nod. Reid and Gustave wear matching black tuxedos and thin neckties. Xiu wears a two-piece black skirt and backless cap-sleeved top. Her hair is an electric red. Selene is dressed in a short-cut, flowing sleeveless dress. Despite the time they put into choosing their outfits, they could easily disappear into the crowd of one hundred. Formal wear leaves so few options.

"I wonder what we're going to make," Xiu says.

"I'd like to play with mixed media," Reid says. "That's April's specialty, isn't it?"

"Yes. You've done your homework," Selene replies.

Reid excuses himself and scours the food tables, filling a small plate. He surveys the room, and not a face is familiar beyond his party. All cities had grown exponentially for years, and Denver was no exception, but Reid could remember times when he would run into a friend or acquaintance at a function like this. The Tubecar changed things too. That ease of travel, combined with the fungibility of U. S. of A. housing, meant that few people stayed in a community for very long. Wanderlust had become wandermarriage, a long term commitment to living everywhere, traveling everywhere, and never needing to set down roots.

"I don't know anyone else here," he says to Xiu.

"Me neither. There are only a hundred people here though."

"I guess the odds are against it."

He pops a gossamer slice of prosciutto into his mouth and lets it melt on his tongue. *Maybe people would be more interested in living in one place, and building a community, if they had more to say and do in its construction, instead of just floating from one to another*, he wonders. *Aren't we more proud of what we earn, what we make, than what we consume?*

As he leans into Xiu to ask her perspective on his thought, April Casablanca appears at the far side of room, creating a cascade of applause and rustling as the attendees turn to face her. She is a small, pale, blonde doll of a woman, dressed in black leggings and a black sweater, calling back to the beatnik culture of the 1950s.

64

"Oh em gee, you guys, I'm so excited to be here in Denver," she says. "This class will survey pretty much everything that is art, but it's not boring because you'll be making art of your own too."

Another clatter of applause fills the room.

April Casablanca raises her arms like a talk show host announcing an amazing gift.

"This is Art: Ages, Civilizations and Masters! Now everyone follow me into the classroom, and be sure to pick up a smock from the smock box so you don't get your nice clothes dirty."

April Casablanca spins on balls of her feet and nearly bounds through the doors to the classroom. The crowd doesn't move quite as quickly, so Reid finishes his plate of hors d'oeuvres and shuffles in behind Gustave, Selene, and Xiu. He takes an artist's smock, size medium, from the bin as he walks in. The classroom is a bright, open auditorium with five rows of easels in the round before an elevated podium. The besmocked attendees have filled the first four rows, leaving the final four easels in the back of the room open.

"Now, I know you must be excited to get creating, but you can't make art until you understand art," April says.

"I'm so excited," Xiu says, grasping Reid's arm.

Reid smiles. "She's definitely something."

"First, any of you not yet wearing your smock can go ahead and put that on. That way we'll be able to flow right from the lessons to the participation. Sound fun?"

April doesn't wait for an answer.

"So, art. It's a big word for being so short, isn't it? We all know what we like, and we all think we know what art is, but maybe we don't. Maybe art isn't about a portrait or a landscape or a sculpture or an abstract or a photo. Maybe art is you, and me, and this handsome fella over here, or this darling little lady right there. Imagine that art isn't the product, but the process. Each drawing is generations of creative energy expressing itself through a creator."

A chorus of hmms and ahhs roll through the crowd.

April Casablanca feeds off the interest, converting it into energy.

"Those cave paintings of animal hunts from thousands of years ago were a burst of creativity through one artist from the collective artistic conscience. The masterpieces that you saw recreated in our delicious complimentary spread out front were each powerful jolts of art, coming from the higher body of art and shooting out from the hands of their 'creators.'"

She makes quotes with her fingers when she says the last word.

"Even my work, which is beloved by billions all over this world, and maybe even by some little green men out there, is just a funneling of the great creative collective. It would probably surprise you to hear it, but me, the great April Casablanca, I have no formal training in painting, but you can bet you've seen my work in some prestigious places. And that's all because of Art. That living, breathing, ageless, collective entity that works through us to add color and life and love to this world is just waiting for you to pick up a brush and be its conduit.

"From our time in caves, the Mayans, medieval kings, the peoples of the plains, Renaissance men and women, industrial revolutionaries, spaceagers, neo-futurists, renewables, all the way up to today, people have been opening themselves up to Art and letting it flow through them. That's what we're going to do this afternoon. We're going to let Art flow through us, and we're going to see what masterpieces come out of us. After all, any of you could be the next April Casablanca, if the spirit of Art chooses you.

"Now, each of you, pick up your brush and close your eyes. Let Art speak through you and guide your hand. Let it do whatever it does. A line here, a splotch, a single whisper of a brushstroke. Art will make you an artist, if you release yourself to it."

The class applauds and April Casablanca climbs down from the podiums and strolls the aisles.

"I don't think this sounds right," Reid says to Xiu.

"There must be something to it. Her work is amazing."

"Yeah, I know that when I take a great shot it feels like something's guiding me," Selene says.

"But you've been taking photos for years. You've studied light," Reid replies. "You've grown as an artist over time, and you have the bad photos to prove it."

"I do, and those don't feel as good as the great ones do when I take them."

"It's still yours though, Selene, right? It's not art taking a photo for you."

"Of course not," she replies.

"I'm pretty sure April is speaking in metaphor, Reid," Gustave chimes in.

"The artist makes the art, but maybe there is a spiritual element," Xiu says.

"When an idea just springs to you, it comes from lots of other ideas mashed together," Selene adds. "That's what art is, it's a bunch of ideas mashed together."

"So we're all just creating derivations of a big cloud of art up in the sky?" Reid asks.

"You don't need to be a dick about it," Gustave says. "She's the renowned artist, why not just give her idea a chance?"

Reid exhales, knowing there's no point in continuing to argue. "Yeah. You're probably right," he says.

He takes up the brush in one hand and the palette in the other. Reid gazes at the canvas for a few moments and then he begins. A field of pale yellow, and then an overlay of greens and blues. He cleans the brush and dips the edge finely with black, then draws a subtle outline of an emu wearing an Aikido gi. Reid fills in the gi with subtle touch of blue, and fills the belt with streaks of midnight and black. Then he paints the background, a distance copse of green-brown brush and small trees. He adds blades of tall yellow grass and even drops in a pair of other emus—silhouetted in the distance. Finally, Reid adds a swan, metallic and reflective, that appears to sneak up on the emu.

"This is brilliant," April Casablanca exclaims, suddenly standing behind him. "Please, may I hold this up for the entire class?"

Before Reid can respond, April takes his painting from the easel and prances toward the front of the room. Xiu pats him on the butt like a third-base coach. Selene offers him a sidelong glance. And Gustave doesn't even look up from his painting, an abstract image resembling a penis on a hoverboard.

April holds Reid's painting high over her head.

"Class, please give me your undivided up here," she says. "This is Art alive and flowing through a person. Look at the genius of this design. The forms are so well-realized. The background offers a distinct sense of place. Now it's a little more conventional than I usually go in for myself, but this is undeniably a work of greatness. This is what I was talking about earlier."

A woman raises her hand in the front row.

"I don't usually take questions, but go ahead," April responds.

"Is that just Origami Emu and his arch-nemesis Foil Swan?" the woman asks.

"I'm not sure I know what you mean."

"It is," Reid says.

April's face brightens with a smile.

"There you have it," she says. "From the artist's mouth. Isn't it fascinating? This is exactly what I was talking about. This woman in the front row offers an unconventional title for this painting, and it just so happens that the artist conceived of the very same title. Now, why do you think that is?"

She doesn't wait for an answer.

"That's right. It's the collective of Art speaking through two vessels at once."

"It's a moderately popular cartoon," the woman in the front row says.

"And is it any wonder why? These characters are some of the most vivid creations to burst forth from Art that I have ever seen."

Reid raises his hand from the back, his face is red with a cocktail of fury and embarrassment.

"Yes, the artist, tell us how it felt to have Art speak through you this way," April says.

"The woman in the front is right. Origami Emu and Foil Swan are characters I invented nine years ago. They appear in a cartoon series that receives billions of views each week."

"Fascinating," April says. "And Art brought these to you again. Here. Today. This is the magic of Art, class. It can come to us for years and bring us great success, all you have to do is let to flow through you."

68

The attendees chatter and then applaud vigorously. April raises Reid's painting above her head like a championship belt, and takes a lap around the stage.

"Actually," Reid calls, his voice drowning in the applause. "Actually I made them up myself. I worked on them for years. Origami Emu started as a sketch when I was eleven."

The crowd cheers April.

"This is Art alive," she cries.

"It's not. It's my dedication to my craft," Reid yells.

No one seems to hear him, but Xiu puts her hand on his back.

"I know, sweetie," she says. "She's caught up in her own ideas. You totally invented your cartoon. I mean, you based it off of generations of other cartoons and other cartoons, but you definitely invented it. I know it wasn't magic."

April Casablanca bounds back down the aisle with Reid's painting and places it on his easel.

"Thank you for being a willing vessel for Art. What's your name?" April asks.

"Reid Rosales."

"Thank you, Reid."

She continues around the room, stopping at every easel. Every fourth or fifth easel produces something of great genius, nearly without fail.

"This is garbage," Reid says to Xiu. "Let's go."

Xiu offers him a compassionate pout.

"There's only another hour left, Reid. Can't you just hang in? This is a once in a lifetime thing, and it's really important to Selene."

"Casablanca's a quack. She doesn't need money, so she must really believe this crap. Art doesn't just happen to you, it takes study and influences and work. You have to make bad paintings before you make good ones. It's not just magic."

"Maybe it's not for you, Reid," Xiu says. "But it might be different for other people."

"So you're not coming with me?"

"No, Reid. I may never get to do this again."

"Fine. I'll catch up with you tonight."

Reid takes his painting from the easel, tucks it under his arm, and marches toward the exit.

Selene and Gustave glare at him as he goes, but Reid doesn't see them. His vision is fixed squarely on the door.

***

That evening, Reid's wristband lights up with a message from Xiu.

"You were right. April Casablanca only got weirder. She's a kook. Dinner?"

Reid smiles and immediately replies "Yes."

In twenty minutes, Xiu is knocking at his apartment door.

"Iris, turn off the entertainment feed for me, please," he says walking to the entrance.

The projection of an action movie blinks off of Reid's brick wall. Iris opens the apartment door, to reveal Xiu standing there, smiling and holding up a bottle of wine.

"You didn't have to," Reid begins.

"I wanted to replicate a vintage you didn't have," Xiu says. "And say, 'I'm sorry.'"

Reid takes the bottle and leads Xiu into the kitchen.

"It's not a big deal. I've been a little down and I just couldn't be there any longer."

"I should've been more considerate of your feelings, but I was too wrapped up in April's personality."

"It took me years of practice to make Origami Emu, so I kind of overreacted."

"No, it's okay," Xiu says. "When society offers people so many great things, maybe it's a little easier to for them to believe it when someone tells them that creativity is magic."

"Thank you," Reid says.

70

Reid hugs Xiu, and they kiss.

"Do you want to go out?" Reid asks.

Xiu undresses.

"I thought we could stay in."

Xiu takes his hand, and leads him into his bedroom. They kiss, and Xiu slithers under the sheets. Reid undresses and joins her.

"You're kind of the best person ever," Reid says.

"Kind of?" Xiu quips.

"You know what I mean."

They kiss, their tongues making a conversation beyond words. They roll over and Xiu climbs atop Reid. They stare into each other's eyes and Reid feels like he completely leaves his body, this place, the dispassion, the fear and frustration. There is all the meaning he could need in Xiu's eyes. At least for right now.

After, they lay together among the knot of bedding, caressing each other.

"I'm hungry," Xiu says.

Reid and Xiu create an elaborate international meal using his replicator. There are tastes of Penne Arribbiata, Enchiladas del Mar, Crêpe aux Lardons, Welsh Rarebit, Panang curry, and fresh sushi. They cap the meal with Dulce de Leche. Reid loads the empty dishes into the replicator where the disassembled and conserved molecules can be used for new plates and new meals.

They ask Iris to check all the available content for anything they would like to watch and spend almost an hour reading synopses and debating the virtues of each option.

"We should probably walk this food off anyway," Reid says. "If we're going to try for another round tonight."

Xiu nods. "I should have stopped with the rarebit. Just because the replicator meals are always healthy doesn't mean they're always light."

"Let's go to the park."

Xiu agrees, and she and Reid make their way to Cheesman Park. The sky is painted orange and pink with sunset, and the park pathways are full of couples, families, and wanderers. Xiu holds his hand as they stroll past the white stone pavilion—an artifact of an earlier time pretending to be an artifact of an even earlier time. A girl has her quinceañera photos taken on the steps. She sits in elegant repose between two sturdy stone columns.

"I bet her dad doesn't even see the irony," Xiu says.

Reid laughs.

"It's 2087, Xiu, he knows what he's getting into."

The sunset turns to dusk. Bold red, orange, and yellow, fade like withering autumn leaves, lost in the deep, dark blue of the night sky. As the light retreats, so do the colors of the landscape, slipping away like a receding tide until only shadows of varying darkness remain, and there is only the black and white of old movies.

"We're really lucky," Xiu says.

"We are?"

"Yeah, silly. We have everything. We have each other. We have all the money and food and travel we could ask for. We have Gustave and Selene. I think that's nearly the definition of lucky."

"You make a good point," Reid replies. "Especially when it comes to having you."

Xiu smiles.

"Do you think it's good for us, though? Having everything handed to us? Eating what we want, traveling wherever we want, buying almost anything we wish?"

"Reid, please. Not this again."

"I know, Xiu, but answer the question. Is it good for us?"

"You mean as a society?"

"Yeah, as a society."

She pauses briefly to consider it.

"I do, Reid. I think this world is what generations of hard work was meant to create."

"But nobody has to do anything, except for the dailies."

"Isn't that what people wanted when they pledged to 'make a better world for the children'?" Xiu asks. "Isn't struggle the sort of thing that's supposed to be overcome so that we learn how not to struggle in the future?"

"Did you know that people used to write books about how the world was going to fall apart," Reid says. "They wrote books about the ice caps melting, and people participating in gladiator tournaments for food. They used to write about big, scary governments that oppressed their people to the point of near slavery."

"I took the same dystopian fiction class in high school you did, Reid."

"I can't even imagine a hero rising up with a bow and arrow to alter the course of history now. Everything is all sorted out. It's all predetermined. It's like we're the robots, programmed just to exist. Life today is rote, fucking pointlessly, emptily rote."

Xiu chortles.

"Is it that it's empty now, or do you not understand how bad an oppressed life would be?"

"Sure, but it would be exciting too," Reid protests.

"Why are you so sure that you'd be one of the people having an exciting time? It's a lot more likely that you'd be locked in a cage and starved."

Reid's mouth falls open.

"I just… I don't know."

Xiu pulls him close.

"I didn't mean to be harsh, babe. You know I'm fond of you."

"I know you are."

"Those books were all fantasies," Xiu says. "They were written to give the people back then hope. They didn't have much and they didn't have much chance of having more. But those books provided the hope that anyone—even a poor kid with nothing—could become the hero."

"Being the hero would be great."

"Sure it would, Reid, but for every girl with a bow and arrow there are twenty dead kids in an arena who wanted to be the hero too."

They walk in silence for a few minutes while Reid ponders her final point. *It makes sense that a society of struggling people would need heroes to look up to and would want to believe that they could be heroes too. Heroes balance out inequalities, and if the world is fair, there's no need for heroes. Except,* he thinks, *that heroes might be the best use of humanity's highest characteristics. If we don't have heroes, if we're deprived of our greatest goods, that leaves us sort of hollow, doesn't it? And struggle creates contrast. We can only truly appreciate what we have if we experience not having it.*

"Don't you think that all this ease has made us soft?" Reid asks finally.

"Maybe," Xiu answers. "But what's the harm in that? We don't have to be hard anymore, and that's a good thing. Plus we are hard in the right places at the right times."

Her hand on Reid's crotch, Xiu kisses him and pulls him into a small group of trees. Amid the calls of night birds, the flutters of bat wings, and the coos of other couples in the park, they have sex again in the grass. They are playful, rolling back and forth, carrying green blades on their skin.

When they have both finished, Xiu rolls off of him and kisses him on the cheek.

"For what it's worth, you're my hero," she says.

Reid pants.

"I was just going to say that."

They get dressed and walk back toward Reid's apartment. It is after midnight, and they have nowhere to be, so they stop at a nautically themed bar on 13th Avenue. They drink Cape Cods and Salty Dogs while the whole joint sways back and forth on the swells. Occasionally, a spray of cool saltwater hits the bar's patrons, or the robot Captain gives orders to the men to raise the sails or swab this or that. At last call, when the robot staff powers down to charge for the next day, Reid and Xiu leave, soaked with ocean water and pleasantly drunk.

Just a block from the nautical bar, Reid spots a sign for something he has never seen before. He doesn't know how he hasn't seen it before. *It's bold lettering, old Helvetica,* he thinks. A series of overhead lamps make it unavoidable.

The sign reads, **Club 20c: Here's to the Past.**

"Have you ever seen that before?" he asks Xiu.

Xiu shakes her head.

A door opens, unseen, somewhere at the bottom of stairs and music billows out. Plodding drums, throbbing bass lines, chunky guitar, and blended, somewhat disaffected voices:

We don't need no education

We don't need no thought control

A man about Reid's age stumbles up the stairs, a wild look in his eyes, his clothing dirty and rumpled, his face dirty with sweat. He grabs Reid by his shoulders.

"Hey, man, you got a few credits you can spare me?" the man asks. "Anything would help. Anything. Just a tiny transfer would really make my day."

"Are you alright?" Xiu asks.

"I'm in a little bit of a bind. I don't want to bother you with it, but if you could spare a couple credits that would help," the man pleads.

Then three figures appear as shadows behind the man at the top of the stairs.

"Bill, stop bothering those people," the middle man says. "It's not their responsibility to help you out of your jam, fella. Besides, I've made you a very kind offer that I'm prepared to discuss further."

"I'll be right there. I just needed a little air," the man calls back toward the shadows. "Please, just a couple credits. I need to eat and rest," he pleads again to Reid and Xiu.

"I don't understand," Xiu says. "Why do you need credits?"

"Can't you just do your dailies, or use the replicator?" Reid asks.

"I'm months behind, man," Bill says. "I made some bad bets with my dollars and I'm working it off, but I need a break. Just a few credits, please. Just so I can get a sandwich and a night's rest."

Xiu looks at Reid skeptically.

"Their charity isn't going to solve your problems, Bill," the man in the middle calls. "Come back inside and we'll talk."

Reid watches Bill's posture sink. He cowers at the other man's words, almost as if they weren't equal at all. Almost as if the man in the shadows had some kind of power over him.

"Please," Bill pleads one last time.

Xiu says, "Here's 20 credits. I hope it helps." Her wristband flashes.

Then Bill's wristband flashes. "Thank you. Thank you," he cries.

He turns toward the shadowy figures. "I have enough for two dollars. I can pay you that and I'll come back in the morning."

"Fine, Bill," the middle man says. "Send it over."

Bill's wristband flashes and then the man in the shadows sees his wristband flicker, the light briefly illuminating his face.

"Okay then," the man says. "You go get some rest, fella, and I'll see you in the morning."

Bill nods. "Yes, sir. I will see you then. Goodnight, sir."

"Thank you so much," Bill says to Xiu. He leans forward to hug her, and then stops, steps back and bows deferentially.

Reid watches as Bill scurries away into the night like a lost domesticated animal. Back at the top of the stairs the man in the shadows, and the two others flanking him turn away.

"Excuse me," Reid calls to them. "What was that all about?"

Without turning around, the man in the center says, "Some people just don't know their place, fella. But I will say, that Bill has a lot of potential. In a couple of months he'll be a Tier 2 earner, and he won't even remember stooping this low."

"Tier 2 earner?" Reid asks.

"Don't worry about it, fella," the man says. "It's just a club thing."

The man and his two flankers descend the stairs, slipping seamlessly into the shadows. After a few moments, Reid hears the music fall silent followed by the clack of a latching door.

"That was really weird," Xiu said. "I had to help him, but I don't understand entirely what just happened."

"Yeah," Reid replies. "That was something else. That guy in the shadows must be really important." As those last words leave Reid's lips he feels a bolt of electricity run down his spine. "That Bill guy wasn't just afraid of him, he looked at him like that other guy was actually better than him."

"Yeah, I noticed that too," Xiu replies. "It gave me the willies."

"I've never seen anything like it," Reid says.

Reid wonders about Club 20c for the remainder of the walk. His mind overflows with flashes of the man in the shadows and the aura of power that seemed to billow from him. *Why wouldn't Bill just run off and not go back? Why would Bill even listen to that man? There was something special about the man in the shadows, something special in his confidence, his authority, something special in his two silent associates, something special in the way that he was still in control even when Bill had found a way out.*

Reid thinks about it as they enter Xiu's apartment. He feels a strange exhilaration, his mind drifting to it as he and Xiu have sex once more. Club 20c is the last thing on his mind when his eyes close, he and Xiu still entangled.

He needs to find out more.

7

Capitol Hill Citizenry District; Denver, Colorado; United Sociocracy of the
Americas

June 6, 2087

10:10 AM

After Reid walks Xiu to the Tubecar station, he bounds back to his apartment, showers, shaves, and dresses. He does his dailies and hurriedly eats breakfast, unable to focus on the day's trending news items, no matter what modulations he applies to Iris's voice.

Scottish actor doesn't grab him.

K-Pop diva doesn't do it.

Even his own voice, an echo that should drown out his thoughts, does nothing.

"You have tried all of the available voices. Would you like to explore alternate entertainment?" Iris asks.

"No, thank you, Iris."

Reid is overwhelmed with a single goal. Today he will visit Club 20c and find out what it is. He can't get the image of the hippie and the two people in uniforms from his head. Thinking about their altercation makes his heart race.

He tosses his empty dishes into the replicator, bids Iris a good day, and bolts out of his apartment. Reid jogs down rainy 13th Avenue, drawing the eyes of his fellow Citizens, who smile and mosey, and talking to each other about art, music, games, sports, their dailies, and the weather. His pant legs are soaked from splashing footfalls. His hair is wet and matted. He doesn't feel any of it. His mind is fixed on Club 20c. On that man in the shadows. On Bill, cowering in the night, desperate to get away from the man, but so clearly intent on returning the next day to follow him.

He spots the familiar sign and approaches the metal door beneath it. His heart races. The door slides open to a long staircase. Reid descends the steps with a mix of fear and excitement. Each step creaks loudly—an artifact of the past that brings a smile to his face. At the base of the stairs, there is a roughshod slat wood door. A single incandescent bulb dangles from a wire overhead. In the door, at eye level, there is an opening that is covered from the inside.

Reid grasps the doorknob, a tarnished bronze bulb with a keyhole beneath it that he has most often seen in museums, and gives it a turn. It's locked.

"Iris, please unlock the door," Reid says aloud.

He waits, but Iris doesn't reply.

If she were here, she would at least give me the authorization denied message, he thinks.

Still, he tries again. And again, nothing.

Reid sighs and jiggles the knob again to no effect.

As he turns back toward the stairs, a voice—barely a whisper—calls to him from behind the door.

"Try knocking."

Reid turns around and approaches the door again. He knocks three times on the door, waits, and once again, there's nothing. He turns again and just as his foot is about to land on the first step, he hears the cry of tiny, rusted hinges.

"Who goes there?" asks a pair of eyes tucked in the small, eye level opening in the door.

Reid steps close to the door and peers into the set of eyes opposite his.

"What do you mean?" he asks.

"What's your name, fella?" the eyes answer.

The voice is familiar. The man from the shadows.

"Oh. Umm, Reid Rosales."

"Great, Reid Rosales, now what's the password?" the eyes ask.

"Password?" Reid says. "I don't know any password."

"We can't let you in without the password, fella," the eyes say. "What if you're a spy?"

Reid steps back. "I'm not a spy. I swear," he says. "I just wanted to maybe join your club."

"That's exactly what a spy would say."

"Well I promise you that I'm not a spy," Reid says nervously.

"Okay, fella, let me talk it over with my colleagues," the eyes reply.

The small opening disappears behind a tiny door within the door. Reid can hear a chorus of whispers, but can't clearly make out anything being said. He contemplates simply turning around and leaving, but decides to wait as his curiosity overtakes him.

The tiny door opens again, and Reid can make out the last part of the conversation.

"Alright, alright," the eyes say. "We'll make an exception, but if anything happens it's not on me, it's on all of you. You hear me, fellas. It's on all of you."

The eyes move into the opening once more.

"Reid, fella, come here," they say. "We're going to let you come in, but under a couple of really important conditions."

"Sure," Reid says. "What are the conditions?"

"Condition number one, we're going to strip search you. To check for wires, audio devices and video equipment."

"Umm, I guess. But what's a wire?"

"A wire? Are you stupid? It's a metal string that used to record people's voices."

"I definitely don't have one of those," Reid says.

"We'll find that out when we strip search you," the eyes say. "And then there's condition number two, which we're not so sure you'll be okay with."

"What is it?" Reid asks.

"It's pretty gruesome. Are you sure you want to know?"

"Just tell me."

"Alright. Condition number two is we're going to cut your dick off."

"What?"

"The Sociocracy has been trying to pollute our ranks with covert agents for months. We have some very attractive women in here and they're all for having fun when they're not fighting the good fight. But these U. S. of A. guys keep coming in here, seducing them, and then trying to steal our secrets while they're tainting the gene pool."

"So you're going to cut my dick off?" Reid asks. "Couldn't you just watch me?"

"Not a chance we want to take, fella."

Reid steps back from the door. *This is absurd*, he thinks. *It's one thing to believe the Sociocracy could be quashing a resistance, or churning out some form of propaganda—it almost makes sense given how anti-individual April Casablanca's class was, too—but sex wouldn't have anything to do with anything. If it did, everyone would think exactly what their parents did, and that hadn't been normal since the twentieth century...*

"I get it," Reid says, finally.

"You get it?"

"Yes, I get it," he continues. "This is a test to see whether I know my history. About how nuclear family groupings were integral to twentieth century culture, and how children then often followed their parents ideals blindly."

"Sure," the eyes say. "That's a semi-cogent argument. But, we were just fucking with you. We aren't really going to cut your dick off."

The wood slat door opens, groaning as it paints its arc across the floor. Candlelight drips out onto the landing where Reid stands. In the doorway stands a man with dark brown hair and olive skin, wearing a denim rancher shirt, leather chaps, and an old baseball hat with a red, white and blue M emblazoned on it. The owner of the eyes.

"I'm Reagan Mbanefo Webster," he says. "Welcome to Club 20c, fella."

"Thank you," Reid says.

Reagan leads Reid through the doorway into a giant, open cellar. The walls are painted to look like old cinder blocks, and they are covered with posters from concerts tours and campaigns. There are advertisements of men in sharp, pale blue suits with slickly combed hair, and women wearing bracelets, tutus and bangles. In the back of the room, there is a door marked "storage." Immediately to Reid's left there is a bar top, with stools, where two club members sit drinking from glasses. To the bar top's right is a counter with a box resembling an old computer, but without letter keys on the keyboard. Reid recognizes it from photographs he's seen in museums. *What did they call it? Oh yes, a cash register.* Behind the counter are two club members in some kind of uniform. One is assisting a person standing on the other side, while the other stocks items on the tall brown, wooden shelves behind them. The shelves appear to be full of cans, old compact discs and other twentieth century ephemera.

Next, near the center of the room is small display bearing the sign "Heroes of Armed Conflicts". There are stacks of magazines, historical texts, and recruitment posters for the long defunct Army, Navy, Marines, and Air Force. In front of it is a large map table with numerous game pieces on it, each one representing an old vehicle of war, or human army.

There is a corner labeled "audiovisual", with a handful of outdated machines and differing sizes of physical media. Reid counts nearly forty people standing, sitting, drinking and conversing, all dressed in twentieth century clothing.

"As you can see, everything in Club 20c is from the best goddamn century in history, fella," Reagan announces. "The twentieth century.

"We've got records, CDs, 8-tracks, 4-tracks, laserdiscs, zoot suits, flapper gowns, cigarettes, sodapops, switchblades, biker jackets, muscle cars, Model Ts, fast food, slow food, latex condoms, Wonderbread, Wonderbras, TV dinners, TVs, radios, EZ Bake Ovens, electric blankets, electric chairs, video games, corrupt politicians, strange sexual mores, civil rights, flags for so many countries, Olympic medals, and more.

"Of course, several of those things are in the form of books and posters. We don't have actual people from the twentieth century in here. Most of them are dead, except for Jake over there."

Reagan gestures to a man who looks to be in his 100s. Jake waves a liver-spotted hand.

"Above all, at Club 20c, we love the twentieth century. It was a time when men were men, women were women, sex was risky, illness was common, and war… man, war was deadly. Folks in the Twentieth didn't have it easy. They paved the way for this much easier world and for that we admire them, fella," Reagan says.

"They were people who struggled to build something," Reid says. "They worked for what they had."

Reagan slaps Reid on the back. "You sound like a natural, fella."

Reid beams. *This is where I belong, he thinks. Maybe this is the sign I've been waiting for. Maybe I can help them out of trouble with the Sociocracy, and gain some experience to make Origami Emu even better.*

"Now before I make some introductions, and give you the grand tour, there's the matter of that strip search we discussed," Reagan says.

"I thought you were joking," Reid replies.

"We were joking about cutting your dick off, but this is serious. Very serious. Take off all your clothes so we can be sure you're not a spy."

Reid pauses for a second, unsure if it's shame or disbelief holding him back. He takes off his shirt and then unbuttons his pants. He drops his shirt on the floor and steps out of his pants.

And just as he's about to lower his underwear, Reagan interrupts.

"Well alright there, Burt Reynolds. Show's over."

Reid stops and stares, confused. Reagan, and everyone else in the room bursts into laughter.

"We were fucking with you about the strip search thing too," Reagan cries. "If we were looking for spies, we could find them with a wristband scan, fella. It's not actually the Twentieth in here.

"You're a good sport, though, and we appreciate that. Tell ya what, your first month's dues are on me. How's that sound?"

"Dues?" Reid asks, pulling his pants back up and buttoning them.

"It's a club ain't it? How're we supposed to collect all this great stuff if people don't pitch in?"

"I guess that makes sense," Reid replies. "How much are they?"

"500 credits a member, but you get back all-hours access and real good company."

Reid pulls his shirt back over his head.

"Sounds good to me," he says.

"Great, fella. Let's make some new friends."

Reagan leads Reid to the right, into a corral of couches from different decades of the twentieth century. There's a Craftsman style couch with sturdy wood arms, a Modern design of swooping, overlapping ellipses, and a green-and-yellow plaid loveseat with rough woven fabric. In the center of the couches is a stack of old board games.

"Reid, meet Quinn Takejiro, she's the club secretary and second officer, as well as our resident expert on pastimes from 1901 to 2000," Reagan says. "Quinn, this is Reid Rosales, the newest member of Club 20c."

Reid extends his hand to the woman. She bats his hand away and hugs him.

"Welcome, Reid. You can keep your handshake for someone who isn't your friend yet."

"What's going on today, Quinn?" Reagan asks.

"I'm teaching these two noobs about a little something called Mystery Date."

Two men sit on the couches, leaning forward over a piece of cardboard with a tiny plastic door on it. As far as Reid can tell, the shorter of the men is supposed to open the door, as his hand hovers over it, but he seems joyfully reluctant to do so.

"Right on, lady," Reagan says. "To the Twentieth."

"To the Twentieth," she echoes.

Reagan points at a swinging door along the near side wall. "That's the kitchen, fella. We like to cook our own stuff here when we can, doing food the way it was meant to be done."

"What do you cook?"

"Mostly old military rations mixed up with other canned goods," Reagan says. "We considered starting an old fashioned food garden, but seeds are tough to come by and the ones we get out of the replicators won't germinate."

Reagan takes Reid a few feet away to an area bearing the sign: Alpha and Omega.

"Here's Tom, Kwame, and Anna," Reagan says. "And this is our little corner dedicated to the beginning and the ending of the Twentieth."

Reid greets the others, and looks around the area. There are several artifacts piled haphazardly between two computer consoles. One console bears the name 1901. On it, Reid sees a record of events from the first year of the twentieth century.

He scans through the record, surprised at how normal many of the events seem, even though they happened nearly two centuries ago. On January 1, the whole world celebrated the beginning of the 20th Century. Reid imagines a crowd of top hats and corsets holding candles and singing *Auld Lang Syne* to usher in the new century. *How exciting it must have been to experience humanity's last pre-technological gasps.* Below that, there is a notation about the first oil gusher in Texas, near a town called Beaumont. *The people would have been so excited to tap into what seemed like a limitless resource then, but what turned out to be more trouble than they could have imagined.*

There's notations for the first public telephones in Paris railway stations, the first billion-dollar corporation, the first major showing of Van Gogh's paintings, the first wireless radio, the first Nobel Prize, and an explorer setting out for Antarctica. It's like watching society advance before his eyes. Reid is envious of the people then, who got to experience the building blocks of an amazing new world. They probably didn't know how quickly everything would change.

The entries aren't all about human ingenuity. There's one about the funeral of Queen Victoria. Another about anti-Jewish rioting in Budapest. The Mayan people were fighting in the Caste War of Yucatan in Mexico. The old New York Stock Exchange crashed. President McKinley was assassinated by an anarchist in Buffalo. The Boxer Rebellion came to an end. U.S. soldiers were massacred in the Philippines. They dug up President Lincoln and reinterred him in concrete. The American South erupts in racial violence when Booker T. Washington visits the White House. Great Britain commits atrocities in concentration camps in South Africa.

Reid almost can't believe how much happened in 1901. Not only did they lack the technology to do most things quickly, they created new concepts and ideas with speed and a kind of admirable audacity. Life was mysterious then. There was invention and there was also death, but it was never empty. Reid wonders if he could have even handled life back then.

"Pretty amazing, huh?" Reagan says.

"It is," Reid says. "Such violence, such conflict, and such advancements all in one year."

"There was a lot more to be done then than the dailies."

Reid nods, and steps over to the second display listing the events of the final year of the century, the year 2000.

This record, too, seems to jump off the page into his eyes. Just ninety-nine years later, and look how far the world had come. The new millennium began with tension over computer clocks not setting the date correctly. A lot of people were very afraid. The stock market reached then new heights. The internet became a popular conveyance for short films. The last *Peanuts* comic strip was published, something that Reid had known already from school, but forgot. The population of India hit one billion, something that was novel then, before billions became a common population size.

Reid is amazed at the difference technology makes. With the internet came the beginnings of everything about the world economy changing. It allowed people to map the Human Genome. Technology also allowed for the first resident crew to live in the International Space Station. And as the world became smaller, leaders gathered together to try to fix the problems in the world. A G8 summit sought to end poverty, hunger and the digital divide. They had no idea just how close they were to the first replicators.

Still, as if cursed by its own nature, humanity made many more painful mistakes. The U.S. government seized a six-year-old Cuban boy and deported him in a custody battle. Bombers injured people in the Philippines. Anti-globalization protests erupted all over the world. Two suicide bombers attacked the USS Cole. Bombings in Manila killed dozens. And in an election for president of the old United States, the Supreme Court stopped a recount in Florida, resolving the election and handing the presidency to George W. Bush.

It's funny, Reid thinks, *just how similar the two years are. Amazing innovations. World changing political and social events. Explorers reaching out toward worlds once thought untouchable. There was greed and violence and hope and power and death and growth. From the distance of almost ninety years, 2000 seems almost quaint, like the day an ant farm was expanded with a second kit.* Still, he is in awe of the twentieth century and the Alpha and Omega boards only make him hungry for the chaotic, bloody, inventive years in between.

"Two amazing years, fella," Reagan says. "And imagine how much happened in between. Now, what do you want to see next?"

Reid points across the room to the American Dream corner. He and Reagan walk over to see a group of six 20c members engaging in a simulated type of old-style capitalist commerce. A woman wearing a dress suit and pillbox hat appears to be transacting with a man wearing coveralls, goggles and a handkerchief. Both of them hold up old tablets displaying their scripts.

"Thank you for doing skilled labor to repair my automobile," a woman says.

"You are most welcome," a man answers. "The fee is two hundred dollars."

"Your good work deserves adequate reward," she replies. Then the woman hands the man a stack of green pieces of paper, resembling the currency of the old United States of America.

The man playing mechanic smiles. "It is gratifying to be compensated for my skills."

In the background, an audio record plays of a man saying, "...there will be a chicken in every pot, and a car in every garage..."

"With hard work, anything is possible," the woman says. She smiles at the man and then pretends to leave his garage through.

"They're a little wooden," Reid says.

"It's their first day doing it for real," Reagan replies. "They've spent the last few days watching old black-and-white television shows to try to get their cadence right."

"Maybe they should use more contractions?"

"That's a good note," Reagan says. "Hey, guys," he calls to the players. "Good practice, but let's try some contractions on the next run through."

The players smile and nod. "I'm really starting to feel the gratification," the man says.

Reagan salutes and then waves them over. He introduces Reid and they all shake hands and trade pleasantries.

"So, what's the currency they're using in the shop?" Reid asks.

"Those are United States dollars, fella," Reagan replies. "The only currency that's good here in 20c."

"You don't use credits?"

Reagan guffaws. "No, credits are for people out in the Sociocracy. We feel that U.S. dollars are more authentic."

"How do people get them?" Reid asks.

"The old fashioned way," Reagan replies. "They work for them."

"So people take turns working in the shop, and then they can use their dollars to buy things in the club?"

"You're close, fella, but it's a little more complicated than that. It is Capitalism, after all," Reagan says. "The Tier 1s work in the shop. They've climbed up from Tier 4 so usually they have lots of cash on them anyway, but the shop gives them a chance to keep up their chosen lifestyle. Tier 2s are scavengers. They go out into the Sociocracy looking for stuff from the Twentieth and food that we can use. Whatever they come back with we pay them for. They earn as much as they'd like, as long as they don't come back empty handed."

"Then where to the other Tiers work?" Reid asks, his curiosity swelling.

"Glad you asked, fella. Let me show you something."

Reagan leads Reid through a metal exit door to a large, wood-fenced dirt yard behind the club. There are a couple dozen club members in the yard. Two-thirds of them are digging holes, some filling those holes back in, some moving boxes back and forth across the yard, some striking rocks with tools, and some unpacking and repacking boxes of trash and worn-out items. Reid isn't sure to what end they are doing it all, but he can tell they are exerting incredible effort. They are all dirty, their clothes damp with sweat, their faces marked with grime. One of them is Bill. Reid waves to the man, and only briefly does Bill look up from the hole he is digging to offer a polite wave back.

"What are they doing?" Reid asks Reagan.

"They're working. They are laborers, so they labor. It's not glamorous," Reagan says. "But they're an important part of the twentieth century economy, and we do things right around here."

Reid watches the laborers perform their activities. Their weary faces are gratified by their work. It doesn't matter that they aren't building anything. It doesn't matter that they work in circles. They have a job to perform. They have something.

"Laborers are Tier 4s," Reagan says. "They make about half a dollar an hour, until they earn enough to move up to Tier 3."

"Tier 3 are the rest of the people who are standing around?" Reid asks.

The other third in the yard comprises people in clean clothes; button-down shirts tucked into tan khaki slacks. Some of them wear boots, some of them wear other kinds of shoes.

"You catch on real quick, fella," Reagan says. "The Tier 3s are supervisors. They watch the laborers work, tell them to work harder or to slow down. They tell them when they can go to the bathroom and when they can eat. And most importantly, they tell them when to stop working, when to start working, and they assign them to a job each day."

"And once they've supervised for long enough, they get to work in the shop?" Reid asks.

"Exactly. Now let's head back inside. I hate to distract the laborers," Reagan says.

As they leave, the supervisors and laborers all wave to Reagan.

"Thank you for stopping by, sir," they say in unison.

Everyone is great here, Reid thinks.

"So where do the U.S. Dollars come from?" Reid asks.

"Me," Reagan laughs. "But seriously, my great granddad left me a big ol' pile of the stuff when he died. I guess he didn't know it'd fall out of fashion."

No wonder they respect him, Reid thinks. *He controls the currency. He controls them all. And if I had even a fraction of what Reagan has, I'd have the club's respect too.*

"There's one more thing to show you today," Reagan tells Reid.

They walk to the final section of the basement, where military flags and recruitment posters hang. A group of five, wearing fatigues and green dome helmets huddle around a table with a map of the world. Each one takes turns pushing different colored groups of tiny soldiers, tanks, airplanes, and boats around the table.

"Conflict brought out the best in people," Reagan opines. "Even the tragedy of war had a certain beauty to it. We fought each other for territory and for honor. We crafted strategies the likes we have never again, but most of all we made truly difficult decisions."

The group at the table continue taking turns, until it comes time for the 20c member commanding the airplanes to make a decision. She surveys the table and seeing forces mounting on all parts of the globe, she moves her planes over a large group of opposing ground forces.

"Doing what I'm about to will save countless lives in the future," she says. "I'm dropping The Bomb."

The others around the table gasp. She places a token in the shape of a bulbous warhead on the table and moves her planes back out over the ocean. She counts out fifteen concentric circles, and removes every other members' soldiers, tanks, and boats in between. Only a few ships remain on the periphery, and a small group of tanks and soldiers just outside the circles that are now clearly outnumbered by her planes.

"War over," she says.

The group applauds, and she bows.

Reagan applauds, and Reid joins in. Reagan introduces Reid to this other group. Each member greets him warmly, offering their hands and welcoming him to the club. Even as Reid's palms sweat slightly, he feels a sense of comfort and ease wash over him.

After a few moments, the group resets the board and chooses new starting locations and forces, and their game starts anew as if nothing happened at all.

"So, fella, what do you think?" Reagan asks.

"I love this place," Reid replies.

"That's great to hear. You can come by any time, but we usually lock up between midnight and ten in the morning. As long as the Sociocracy doesn't shut us down, that is."

"Why are they harassing you?" Reid asks.

"Something about a dues for a 'club or organization operating within a district,'" Reagan replies. "But we have refused to pay it. They don't make this club work, we do, and we're not about give our money to them. Besides, we're a quasi-religious organization, so we should be due-exempt."

"But they could shut you down?"

"They haven't yet," Reagan says. "They just keep asking for the credits. But I'm sure they could. I wouldn't put it past them."

"I haven't heard of them shutting down any clubs before," Reid says.

"Do you think they'd let the public know?"

"I guess not."

"They can have their 100 credits per year over our dead bodies, is what I think," Reagan says.

"It's only 100 credits?" Reid asks.

"It's not the amount of credits. It's the principle. If we give in now, they'll take more, and then they'll probably even come in here and try to tell us how to run the club. That's not the 20c way of life."

Reagan makes a good point, Reid thinks.

"Maybe we can solve this problem together," Reid says.

"Maybe, fella, but let's not worry about that right now," Reagan says. "Let's you, me, and Quinn go into the kitchen and I'll make you a meal from actual twentieth century ingredients."

"Wow, human-made food."

"Don't get too excited. They're survival rations, but they aren't from a replicator."

Quinn joins them in the kitchen.

"I just really admire people who had goals and worked for them. Every day," she says.

"It's really about how people in the Twentieth knew the virtue of a job well done," Reagan adds. "That kind of pride doesn't just happen, they earned it by getting up every day and going out there into the world to build something."

"I'm inspired by the art," Reid adds. "Think about Van Gogh. The guy paints from a place of poverty, loneliness, and mental illness. And he created some of the greatest artwork of all time. If you took away all those things, made his life cozy and simple like they are today, who knows what he makes, but I bet there are less *Starry Night*s and more derivative portraits–the kinds that bought painters made for royal families."

"At the end of the day you really felt like you did something," Quinn adds. "No matter what you did, you could step back and say, 'I did that and it's going to help feed me or someone else."

Reid nods. Reagan brings out a tray of food.

"They fought for their freedoms, too," Reagan says. It wasn't just for money. Life was all about earning it. It wasn't handed to you."

"The writing was better too," Reid says. "I mean, look at the future they thought we'd have."

"Huxley thought we all be socially engineered and high."

"Orwell imagined some terrible fascist regime closing down on humanity."

"Asimov thought that robots could be almost as intelligent as people."

They all laugh for a moment.

"I think I'd like Orwell's best, though," Reagan says.

"Oh, definitely," Quinn replies.

"For sure," Reid says. "It's the most rewarding one to fight back against. Huxley's wouldn't know you were there. Asimov's would help you find a way out, but Orwell stacks the deck. That's the only way to be a hero, to beat the odds, no matter how absurd it appears to be."

As Reid gnashes on many generations old beef and rice, he feels at home for the first time that he can remember. The food is tough, bland, and difficult to chew, but it's real and uncompromising. Just like the people in the Twentieth. He also feels a gentle buzz in his wristband. It's a message from Xiu.

"Tennis for two in Venice? I have a new skirt to show you."

Reid chooses not to immediately reply. Instead, he watches the shop performers play their game of commerce and individual transactional validation. He gulps down his food with childlike eagerness, hoping to take his own turn at the counter.

8

Grand-Bassam Beach Leisure Park; Modest, Grand-Bassam, Côte d'Ivoire; African
Alliance

June 12, 2087

3:21 PM

"It was just strange not to hear from you for five days, Reid," Xiu says.
"You're usually so responsive to messages."

Xiu and Reid stroll across the sandy shoreline, she in a blue metallic bikini,
with matching hair, and him in green trunks. The air is heavy with salty mist. The
sun is warm and welcoming. The beach around them swarms with people, but they
have found a small stretch where they are almost alone. The beach is covered in soft,
pale yellow sand that turns slowly to brown as it reaches in smooth washboards
toward the ocean. Warm water creeps up the land, lapping at their feet and ankles.

"I know, and I'm sorry. I got caught up with stuff at 20c," Reid replies.
"They're such an interesting group of people. It's like I stumbled on a missing part
of myself. They really get everything that I've been feeling. Did you know that in
1999 everyone was worried about something called 'Y2K'? It was all about
computer clocks, and people started gangs in their neighborhoods and hoarded food
and water and got all these swords and knives together because they couldn't be
broken by computers, and they got ready to fight everything from tanks to airplanes
to coffee makers. They thought it was going to be the end of the world, and I read
that some people even practiced human sacrifices to try to make it not happen. There
was even a guy who bought an island to hide on because he was sure the internet and
computers were going to kill everyone with a virus. Imagine how exciting it must
have been to ring in that new year? You'd be wondering if everything you believed
about the world was about to disappear!"

"It sounds silly, and scary," Xiu says. "Was anybody hurt?"

94

"No. Not at all. It was a false alarm," Reid says. "People used to worry for no reason all the time in the Twentieth."

"I don't know, worrying all the time sounds awful."

"But sometimes it was good," Reid says. "Like if I worried that we would only have forty or fifty years together, and only twenty or so in our primes, and that you could die, or get sick, or maybe something would happen to you because you had to drive to work in the morning, tired, in traffic. And all those things add up to me loving you that much harder because it was so easy to lose you."

Reid pulls her close and kisses her on the lips. He squeezes her tight to him, and kisses her again and again. He kisses her chin and her neck and along her collarbone. And then kisses her on the mouth again.

"Why don't we?" he asks, pointing to a small opening under the nearby boardwalk.

Xiu pulls away and looks at him. "I don't know what's gotten into you, Reid Rosales, but I like it."

Reid and Xiu run up the beach, kicking sand behind them like eager children. They fall together into the shade of the walkway, ignoring the footfalls of other vacationers as they rip at each other's bathing suits. Reid continues to kiss Xiu from head to toe, and Xiu writhes and coos as Reid's tongue travels from her breasts to between her legs.

Reid savors every taste of her, imagining that one day soon she could disappear, fall ill, or have to move far away for a career. Xiu's moans drown out the crashing water on the shore and the chatter of children bounding from one treat vending robot to the next.

Reid stops and moves up to meet Xiu's eyes.

"What?" she asks. "What's wrong?"

"You know, there was a song about this from the Twentieth," he says. "But people were so scared of sex that they just called it 'having some fun'. People back then would've thought we were crazy or disgusting. We'd have to worry about getting caught."

Reid uses his fingers and kisses Xiu.

"You'd have to be quiet because the police might come and arrest us."

Xiu moans.

"No, you couldn't do that. We could get in trouble."

Xiu holds her eyes shut tight and muffles her voice. Her body shakes

"In the Twentieth, we'd be judged, and called sinners."

Xiu grabs his arm, squeezing it.

"Shut up and fuck me," she says.

***

They lay together, panting; sand clinging to their sweaty skin.

"That was amazing," Xiu says.

"Yeah. It was."

"You've never tried that thing before," she says.

"It just felt right," he says.

"You're correct there."

"And when you picked me up. I didn't know you were so strong."

"I guess I didn't know either."

"I like this new Reid," Xiu says. "He's everything I liked about the old Reid without being bummed out. And he's extremely attentive to my umm... *needs*."

"I'm glad. I like him too. I feel like I'm finally awake," Reid says. "Oh, that reminds me, don't get dressed."

"More? Already?"

Reid reaches for his swimming trunks and pulls a small box from the pocket.

"Here, take of these," he says, extending a cigarette to Xiu.

"What is it?" she asks.

"It's called a Marlboro. It's this thing people used to smoke after sex in the Twentieth."

"What does it do?"

"Nothing from what I can tell, but doctors used to recommend them."

Reid lights their cigarettes. They inhale and exhale. The white-gray smoke is bitter and distinctly pungent. Reid coughs and starts to feel sick. Xiu coughs too.

"You know," she says. "I remember these from my History of Business class. They're really bad for you and really addictive."

"Yeah. They're weird, aren't they? It looked a lot better in the ads I saw in those old magazines."

"You do look kind of cool, Reid," Xiu says.

"You look really hot with yours too."

"It's too bad these taste awful, I think they make us look edgy."

"Maybe that's the appeal?" Reid says.

Xiu shrugs and holds her cigarette out like fruit from broken replicator.

Reid takes Xiu's cigarette and stubs both of them out in the sand.

"So not everything from the Twentieth was a winner," Reid says.

"Your heart was in the right place," Xiu replies.

Reid kisses Xiu on the mouth, and after they both overcome the lingering taste of cigarettes, they enjoy it again.

"I know something else that should be in the right place," he says.

"You're insatiable," Xiu replies.

"And I should be in somewhere else."

Xiu climbs on top of him and holds his arms down.

"I'll drive this time," she says.

***

Finally back in their swimsuits, Reid and Xiu walk back down the beach toward their bungalow in Grand-Bassam. The sun is low, casting a blade of glistening white along the ocean. Their hands entwine, and Reid feels at peace, or complete, for the first time that he can recall. As they weave among the hordes of men, women, and children, some clothed, some scantily clad, and some completely nude, they cast pleasantries out to each person they pass. Nothing about the utterances rings false for Reid.

It is a beautiful day.

The water is fine.

That is a nice sand Tubecar station that boy has built.

The robots here are remarkable, never clogging their servos with sand.

That woman's ass is spectacular.

This sunset will be something else.

Reid and Xiu don't let go of each other's hand until they part the curtain door to their bungalow. The small room is surrounded by off-white fabric on all sides and topped with a straw-thatched roof. There are no windows, but the dappled light and shadow that sneaks through the ceiling provides enough light to live by. To maintain a rustic experience, the resort does not include a digital assistant with any of their rooms. As a result, Reid had done his dailies using his wristband, and had not checked the trending stories since they left Denver and the U. S. of A.

Xiu sets her beach bag down on the manicured sand floor and goes over to her suitcase, taking out a gauzy, white sundress, and a pair of sandals.

"In the Twentieth, millions of people would have imagined this place was some kind of wild, savage, dangerous jungle," Reid says. "They might have been too afraid to even come here, but if they did, they wouldn't imagine it was a vacation."

Xiu unties her bikini top and bottom and lets them fall to the floor.

Reid pounces on her nakedness, kissing the back of her neck and caressing her breasts.

"I'm all for this enthusiasm, but I need to shower if we're going to meet Gustave and Selene in Amsterdam at 9," Xiu says.

"You can use my sterilizer," Reid replies.

"I feel like the real thing."

Xiu steps away from him and walks back to the open stall shower in the corner of the bungalow.

While she showers, Reid dusts himself off. He retrieves his sterilizer from his luggage and turns it on himself. A beam of blue lights up on his hair and slowly scans down his body to his feet. The sterilizer almost tickles as it does its work, and then shuts off. Clean, Reid changes into a pair of navy trousers and a white button down. He re-packs his bag and then sits down on the bed to read the 20c newsletter, printed on antique inkjet paper. He has read this newsletter before, and the page is folded, dogeared and rumpled from handling. Still, there's something Reid likes about holding it. Reid scans the topics to see if there is anything he missed:

1. "Go ahead, make my day" and other stories of the 20c American Man.
2. When Celebrities Weren't Human and the Cults of Fame.
3. Racism, a virtual tour of Ignorance and Independent Thought.
4. The Early Internet: How Slow Information Made People Patient.

With nothing new to read, drops the paper on the floor, flops back on the bed and stares at the ceiling. The straw is arranged in uniform rows, knitted together and overlapping perfectly. It is clearly the work of the robots. There were people here, hundreds of years ago, who had to make a structure like this on their own. Without it, they'd burn in the sun outside, or drown in the rains and come in from the sea. Those roofs would have been disorganized, imperfect and constantly in need of repair. Perhaps a person would work all morning on a portion of it, only to make a mistake or trip and fall onto the weaving, breaking some of the strands. They would have to start again, gathering the grasses, drying them, twisting them, weaving them together. And their success would mean survival. It would be exhausting to get there, but it would mean everything. Reid finds himself suddenly disgusted with the perfection of their rustic surroundings.

Maybe the robots are the problem, he thinks. But his train of thought is interrupted when Xiu emerges from the shower, dripping, dries herself off, and applies her hair-tint pen.

"Blonde?"

"I figure if I'm going to have more fun, I have to," she replies.

"You know, people in the Twentieth used to say something like that," Reid says.

"Oh, I know."

Xiu puts on her sundress and packs her things. They take their bags out in front of their bungalow and stare out over the Atlantic one more time.

"This has been a really great day," Xiu says.

"It has," Reid replies. "I'm fond of you, Xiu."

"And I'm fond of you, love," she says.

They take up their bags and walk up the paved path from their bungalow to the main resort building. The resort resembles a palace, but is actually a facade for the reception desk, a handful of administrative offices, the robot-staff recharge rooms, and the Tubecar station. Reid leaves the proximity key for their bungalow with the robot behind the front desk and thanks it for the accommodations. He and Xiu descend the stairs of the Tubecar station, and queue up behind the other travelers at the passenger scanners. The line moves quickly. Each person speaks the name of their destination, and the scanners automatically deduct the appropriate amount of credits with a flash of their wristbands.

The result is a chorus of place names and Tubecar station titles.

"Reunion 2," someone says.

"Taipei," says another.

"St. Petersberg," one calls.

"Arlington Cemetery One."

When it is Reid and Xiu's turn, they both say "Amsterdam Buitenveldert-West," and the scanners withdraw the flat fee of 250 credits from each of them. Beyond the scanners, Reid and Xiu queue in the embarking line. This line also moves quickly, and the time is helped to pass by the disembarking line that runs parallel to it. They can watch people coming from all over the world climb out of their Tubecars and head back out toward the beaches they just experienced.

In the embarking line, every passenger awaits their Tubecar's arrival parallel to the platform on which they stand. The Tubecars enter the station from the left where passengers disembark, and glide slowly to the right, where new passengers get in. Each Tubecar is a clear, egg-shaped vessel that comfortably seats six people, but they are rarely ever full because they operate on their passenger's travel plans, rather than a set route. The front and side of each Tubecar displays the next destination, so even if passengers get out of the embarking line or lose track of their place, they will know which one to board.

Reid and Xiu make their way through the line, and their Tubecar, marked "Amsterdam Buitenveldert-West" arrives. A gullwing door opens on the car, revealing the two face-to-face padded benches inside. Reid helps Xiu into her seat, and then climbs in himself. The gullwing door lowers and locks into place, sound-sealing the compartment.

"Welcome to the Tubecar," the onboard speaker says. "Your trip to Amsterdam will take two hours, twenty-nine minutes. Please sit back and get comfortable. We are about to depart the Grand-Bassam Beach Leisure Park station."

The Tubecar moves forward into a tunnel. It builds speed so smoothly that Reid and Xiu do not even notice, and in seconds it is traveling at more than 2500 km/hr.

"Global Tubecar is proud to offer you travel entertainment including film, podcasts, music, television, and holograms. Would you like to explore available options now?"

Reid and Xiu look at each other. Xiu shakes her head and Reid agrees.

"No thank you," he says. "We'll talk. Please engage ambient sound."

Quiet airflow sounds replace the complete silence inside the cabin.

"Did you know that there was a writer in the Twentieth named Stephen King, and he once wrote a horror story about fast-travel?" Reid asks.

"I think I read that one, actually, dear," Xiu replies. "Isn't it funny that people back then drove themselves all over the place? They always had to pay attention and worry about how long it would take to get places. Imagine everyone having their own Tubecar, but instead of using the tubes, we'd all crowd on the streets. So inferior!"

"Who wouldn't want to embrace that kind of power at their fingertips, or between their legs?" Reid says.

"Maybe the food vendor who gets run over by a 'streetcar'?" Xiu adds.

"But you could go wherever you wanted, and feel the wind on your face," Reid replies. "You don't feel that exhilaration in a Tubecar."

"That's a good point, mister, but you're not messing up my hair. I want Selene to see it."

As their Tubecar speeds from the African Alliance up to the New European Union, Reid and Xiu alternate conversations about the twentieth century, art, music, what they will eat in Amsterdam, and their favorite parts of Grand-Bassam. The cuddle each other on one Tubecar bench, then lay opposite, and watch the world go by them at incredible speed. The sky is a blur. The land is a blur. The cities are watercolor brushstrokes. The Mediterranean is a surrogate outer space. From the Tubecar everything is visible, and the entire world is blending together in a perfect, harmonious, continuum.

9

Buitenveldert-West Neighborhood; Amsterdam, The Netherlands; New European
Union
June 12, 2087
9:09 PM

Their Tubecar slows to a gentle halt in Amsterdam, and Reid and Xiu
disembark into a crowded station. They follow the disembarking line past an eager
line of departing passengers with damp hair and clothes from the rain falling outside.
They pass through the exit scanners, hand-in-hand, and ascend the unique spiral
staircase—a Dutch design to accommodate easier water drainage in flood conditions.
The sky is navy and purple, flickering wildly high above the clouds; giving the
impression of a great cloudy mind generating thoughts and making electrifying
connections. The rain sputters, more a gentle mist than a shower. The water is cool
on their skin, adding a gloss to Reid and Xiu's faces. Xiu's hair-tint blonde glows as
it reflects the high-altitude lightning, and the street lights.

Reid and Xiu step lightly on the old sidewalk, avoiding the gathering pools
in pockmarks and gaps where the slabs of cement have settled. They cut through
Gijsbrecht van Aemstelpark, following the path to a footbridge over the canal. The
water is alive with raindrops rolling out over the canal in perfect, expanding rings.
They stop for a moment over the canal, amid the lightshow, and kiss.

Xiu's wristband lights up. "It's Selene." She wipes away the droplets and
reads the message aloud.

"We've got a table. Hope you're on the way."

"We're a little late," Reid says. "I'm sure they'll understand."

"I hope so," Xiu replies. "I hate to keep them waiting."

Xiu taps reply on her wristband. "Just a couple blocks away. Be there soon.
Heart."

She takes Reid's hand again and they continue across the bridge, through the dense, grassy green of the park. They end up on a street called Kiefskamp that turns into Loevestein. At the intersection of Arent Janszoon Ernststratt they take a right, seeing the plazas corralled by modern brick, metal and glass buildings, and the glowing red holo-sign for the restaurant. They march through the plaza, entwined, smiling, united. When they arrive at the door, Reid turns to Xiu, kisses her, and squeezes her tight to him.

"Thank you for the trip, Xiu," he says. "It was an amazing time."

She smiles. "Me too. I'm fond of you."

Her sundress clings to her, damp enough from the mist that it's nearly transparent. They approach the restaurant door, and it opens automatically. As they pass through the entryway, an auto-dryer—common in wet climates—engages and a stifling, desert wind bursts over Reid and Xiu leaving them looking like they had never been rained on at all.

"Welcome to Ruby," the robot maître d'hôtel intones with a slight accent. "How many guests do we have this evening?"

"We're meeting a couple whom you've already seated," Xiu replies.

The robot performs a quick scan.

"There are currently three incomplete parties already seated," it says. "Please specify."

"It could be under Mr. Yamamoto or Mz. Fitzhugh," Reid says.

The robot scans again.

"Table for four under Gustave, yes. Right this way."

The robot ambles into the dining area as Reid and Xiu follow close behind. They weave through the crowded tables and around a corner toward a quiet, glass-covered patio. There, in a three-quarter circle booth, sit Gustave and Selene, sipping cocktails and perusing the hologram menu at the table's center.

The robot gestures for Reid and Xiu to sit. They slide into the booth as Gustave and Selene make room.

"You made it," Selene says, kissing Xiu on each cheek.

"We were worried you got caught up trying to build your own Tubecar, Reid," Gustave says.

The jab catches Reid off guard, but he ignores it.

"Gustave," Selene exclaims.

"Reid can take a joke, dear."

"So, how was the old Dark Continent?" Gustave asks Xiu.

Xiu smiles at Reid. "It was brilliant."

"Oh?" Selene asks. "What did you do?"

"We had some beach time, but mostly Reid was a new man… a dynamo."

Gustave slaps Reid on the back.

"Good show, mate," he says. "I knew you couldn't be down for long."

"Gustave," Selene scolds.

"It's fine, guys, really," Reid says. "I know I've been a little off lately. And, truth is, it's good to be back."

Xiu winks at Selene and mouths the words "very good."

"No time like the present," Gustave says. "Let's get you some drinks and we can raise a glass to this rediscovered prowess."

A robot waiter, noting keywords in Gustave's last sentence, arrives immediately to the booth and takes their drink order. Moments after making their choices, the robot returns with a tray of beverages.

"To a great man becoming a better man," Gustave says.

They all tap glasses and drink to each other's good health.

"So other than sex, what did you do?" Selene asks.

"We checked out some of the sites along the boardwalk, played some carnival games, ate seafood at a couple of places, and stayed in a great 'unplugged' bungalow," Reid says.

"*Reid* played?" Gustave says. "The Reid Rosales who once said that 'carnival games are the last credit pit of modern society' run by… What was it you said?"

Reid swallows a mouthful of his drink hard and smirks.

"I think I said they were run by 'generations of genetic abnormalities in garish suits.'"

"That's right," Gustave says. "Delightful."

"Reid won me a virtual pug," Xiu beams. "I'm trying to decide between Moonby and Captain Dimples for a name."

Selene squeals. "I've always wanted a virtual pug."

Xiu opens her purse and takes out a small metal band that resembles a collar. She holds it up over the table and touches a smooth black screen on its outer surface. The pet switches on and a hologram of a pug appears, filling the collar. Xiu lets go of the collar and the dog stands on the table panting for a moment, then it pauses to chew at its haunch before scratching at its ear with its back leg.

"It creates a magnetic field so it feels like it's really there, but you don't have to feed it or take it to the bathroom," Xiu says.

"Not really a pet experience without those elements," Gustave says.

"It is on the easy side," Reid adds.

"Gripe all you want," Xiu says, stroking the digital dog.

The dog arches its back, and then flops onto its side on the table, paws raised, presenting its belly.

"I love him like he is," Xiu adds.

An alarm sounds from across the restaurant and the maître d' robot advances on their table.

"Is that a service animal, ma'am?" it asks.

"It's a virtual pug," Xiu says. "So, no."

"I'm afraid you can't have it in the restaurant. It might disturb the other diners."

"Of course, I'll turn it off."

"No, Xiu," Reid says, jumping up in his seat. "Don't turn it off. It's a silly policy."

The robot flinches.

"I'm afraid your opinion of the policy doesn't matter, sir," the robot replies. "It still stands."

"It's not even a real dog," Reid protests. "How can it disturb anyone?"

"Reid," Xiu says, touching his wrist. "It's okay."

"No it's not. This robot is pushing you around and I won't stand for it," he tells her. "Tell me how a digital pug can disturb anyone?" he demands of the robot.

106

"Some diners find the image of an animal distracting to their experience," the robot says. "We instituted the policy for a reason. You can rest assured of that. Now please, deactivate the animal, or leave the restaurant."

Reid's hands are balled into fists. He looks at Xiu, and watches her hand hover over the dog's collar.

"Don't do it, Xiu," he pleads.

"It's fine, Reid," she says. She touches the collar and the pug disappears.

"Thank you," the robot says, and then it rolls away.

"That was bullshit," Reid says. "It's not even really here. That is fascism! I don't even want to give them my credits."

"Not that I don't appreciate it, hon, but what has gotten into you?" Xiu asks. Selene nods in agreement.

"I'm just tired of this crap," Reid exclaims. "That policy has nothing to do with reality. It just legitimizes that prick robot acting better than everyone."

"I must say that I agree," Gustave says. "They certainly could have asked Xiu to set it to silent. You're right to say something, someone has to."

Reid feels his confidence swell as his friends back him up. He is right. He is an individual who will not be treated like a machine, just following policies because they are there. He is better than these robots. He is a human being and he deserves respect.

Reid stands up from the booth and storms after the robot maître d', catching up with it in the middle of the restaurant's main dining area. He taps the robot on the shoulder and waits for it to pivot 180 degrees to face him.

"I don't think you have any idea why you have that policy, do you?" Reid demands. "You're just following it because you're not programmed to think or feel or do anything, but bumble around in your artificial body."

"I am sorry, sir, but I do not set the policies. I only request that our guests follow them, or choose another place to dine. Amsterdam has numer—"

Reid gets in close to the robot's face.

"Well, I think it's a stupid policy and I'd like—no, I demand to speak to your manager."

"The manager is not available this evening as it is currently charging," the robot says. "I can provide you with a contact card so that you may lodge your complaint at a future time."

The robot produces a small wristband datacard and extends toward Reid. Reid slaps the card onto the floor. All conversation inside the restaurant stops. The robot maître d' stands perfectly still, looking fazed as it scans for the next appropriate action. After a moment, it produces an identical card and extends it to Reid. Reid slaps this card away too.

"I don't want to send the manager a message later," Reid says. "I want you to fix it now."

"I am afraid there is nothing I can do to affect standing policy at this time," the robot replies. "Perhaps you would like to—"

Without warning, Reid shoves the robot maître d' to the floor. The clamor causes the restaurant to burst into gasps and conversation. The robot wobbles back and forth, trying to reposition its limbs to lift it back to a standing position. Gustave jumps up from the booth and joins Reid's side, placing one hand on his shoulder in an effort to reign in the situation. A pair of hidden sliding doors slip open and another robot appears, wearing a badge that reads: MANAGER.

"I am sorry, sir, but I am going to have to ask you to leave," it says.

"I thought you were charging tonight?" Reid asks. "You people see this?" he asks of the restaurant goers. "It wasn't charging. It's all bullshit."

"Please, sir, exit the restaurant, before the authorities arrive and remove you."

Gustave grips Reid's shoulder harder and pulls him back from the robot manager.

"Let's go, Reid," he says. "You've done all you can."

Reid wrestles out of Gustave's reach and charges the robot manager. He slams into the machine and knocks it into a table of three, who scatter as their food and drink splashes on the floor.

"Maybe if you were actually charging you could have dodged this," Reid says striking the prone robot with his fists.

The robot takes the punches without reaction.

"Sir, please stop," it says.

Reid just keeps punching. And then a hand lands on his shoulder. And another. Reid looks around, ready to wave Gustave or Xiu or Selene off, but the hands don't belong to them. Two security robots close their grips tighter on his shoulders. They lift him up into the air and carry him out the front entrance. Without saying a word, they drop him on the sidewalk, and line up between Reid and the restaurant door.

"Please leave the premises, citizen," one says. "This is a friendly warning. Please leave the premises and cool down."

Reid seethes on the sidewalk, and considers trying to fight through the two security robots, but he can see Gustave, Selene and Xiu gathering their things and settling the check, and decides that it's over for now. Reid waits out front on the curb, panting and slowly soaking up the mist when his friends come outside.

"That was insane," Gustave says.

"I can't believe we got kicked out," Selene says.

"I can't believe Reid got us kicked out," Gustave continues.

Xiu sits down on the curb beside him and kisses him on the cheek.

"You okay?"

"Okay? I'm great. Did you see what I did? I knocked that robot right on its ass."

"It was pretty impressive," Gustave adds. "How did it feel?"

Reid thinks for a second. "Like for the first time I was just being me, instead of trying to meet some expectation of self-control. It felt raw."

"It looked raw," Selene says. "I just hope I don't know anyone in that place."

Reid takes a deep breath, and exhales slowly. "Oh, yeah, I hope I didn't embarrass you guys too much. Once I set myself loose I wasn't really paying attention to anything. I just had to prove that stupid policy and that stupid robot wrong."

"It was a little scary for a second," Xiu says.

Reid frowns. "Sorry, Xiu."

"It's okay, just scary," she says. "And if it matters, it was cool that you stood up for me."

"It was outrageous," Selene says. "You really are a new Reid."

Gustave helps Reid up from the curb, and pats him on the shoulder.

"Sorry for holding you back in there," he says. "I didn't know what to do."

Reid hugs him, steps back, and straightens his shirt and pants.

"I just couldn't let them get away with such a stupid policy, you know," Reid says. "Back in the Twentieth, people used to protest and fight and stand up for the things they believed in. I wish I could go back in there right now."

"Well, you might want to take a couple of deep breaths. We do want to get dinner somewhere tonight," Gustave says. "New, twentieth century, club-going Reid can't beat up every robot in the district."

"Yeah, please, let's not make this a common thing," Xiu says.

"Exciting or not, that kind of violence isn't cool, Reid," Selene adds.

"I know. I mean, I get it, guys," Reid says. "I guess I just couldn't deal with the injustice of it. And if that kind of fight was in people nearly a century ago, it should probably still be in me now."

"Clearly it is," Gustave replies. "But starting right now, it's all tuckered out and it's going to bed. No more violence for tonight, okay, chap?"

Gustave extends his hand to Reid. Reid stares at it for a second, unsure if he likes the compromise.

"Deal," he says, taking Gustave's hand. "I'm sorry guys. I'll behave."

Gustave stares at his hand, wet with Reid's blood. His inability to process blood sprung from violence leaves him momentarily silent. Gustave retrieves a sanitizer pen from his jacket pocket and points it at the crimson stains on his hand, erasing every drop. He offers the pen to Reid. Reid shakes his head silently.

"Let's just go have a good time," Selene says.

"There are plenty of more enjoyable ways you can let off steam too," Xiu says.

Reid nods, breathes deep and exhales slowly.

"I still think that lots of those old ideas are stupid," Gustave says. "But it did make tonight unforgettable."

"I'll second that," Selene says.

"Let's get out of here, please. I'm tired of the security robots staring at us," Xiu says.

Reid smiles and hugs his friends, and kisses Xiu.

"Thanks, guys," he says. "There's no sense in missing the movie. I'll buy dinner after."

"Good man."

***

The Immersive Theatre is in Tuindorp Oostzaan, conveniently located by an international Tubecar station. There are only two other theatres like it in the world, and none nearer to Denver. Unlike the Leisure Parks that covered the globe, Immersive Theatres are far fewer in number, and the experience is markedly different. The Leisure Parks vary in design, but generally result in a direct human-to-human experience. There are zoological Leisure Parks, amusement Leisure Parks, historical Leisure Parks, resorts, national woodlands and mountains, and more. Their purpose is to offer each citizen guest a unique, real-world experience that provides them joy, relaxation, and sometimes adventure. The Immersive Theatres are wholly virtual interactive experiences. Aside from the group a person purchases tickets with, the experience is completely person-free. Guests enter an empty room, set up almost like an old theater in the round, where the floor, walls and ceiling are all densely populated with holographic projectors. The experience begins in a number of ways, sometimes clearly defined, with a roll of production credits and other times more covertly, with one of the guests simply experiencing a vision or hearing a noise that caters to their pre-immersion questionnaire. Once the show begins, the guests lose their concept of immediate reality, disappearing into the experience.

If a group of people attends together, the experience will be designed to involve all of them at once, either creating by additional pivotal characters, or by pitting them against one another as protagonists and antagonists—though only if they choose. Immersive Theatres offer a wide range of entertainment types from Shakespearean plays to old Action Films to contemporary documentaries. The theatres also feature adult entertainment, though they are most often attended by groups seeking to enhance the experiences they already have together in person. Common themes include zero gravity, time-travel, and old hospital.

Reid, Xiu, Gustave, and Selene arrive at the theatre ticket lobby at 10:02 pm. They gaze up at the marquee rotating through dozens of options.

"What are you guys in the mood for?" Reid asks.

"Space opera," Gustave says.

"Rock concert," Selene adds.

"How about a historical drama?" Xiu says.

Reid approaches the counter and hails the ticket robot. The machine ambles forward and greets him.

"What do you have that combines space opera, rock concert and historical drama?"

Without even a pause the robot replies, "*SkyRunner: Lord of Guitars* features historical flying machines and costumes, science-fantasy action on a space station, and an interactive soundtrack. This experience is available for one to twelve guests simultaneously. Would you like hear more options?"

"No," Reid says. "Give me four tickets for *SkyRunner*."

The robot vends four tickets to Reid's wristband and a mass of credits transfers from his account to the theatre.

"Please enter auditorium number six. Your experience will begin as soon as all guests are in position," the robot says, directing them with a sweep of its arm.

Reid rejoins the group and leads them to auditorium six.

Inside the large round room they find four illuminated circles, each labeled with a character name from the experience. Gustave chooses Liam, the brash airship pilot who plays by his own rules. Selene chooses Maribel, the daughter of the evil mayor of Castle Cliffs, who hopes to diplomatically end generations of conflict between her hometown and Space Station Infinity. Xiu opts to play Nisha, the secretive woman from another land whose reputation in combat precedes her, but whose intentions remain unclear.

"The only one left is..." Reid pauses to read. "Runner. The hero. Are you guys sure you want me to play the hero?"

"You acted semi-heroic in the restaurant," Gustave jokes. "And you did buy the tickets."

Xiu and Selene agree.

Reid steps on the lit circle. The lights in the auditorium dim and then drop out completely. Thousands of tiny nodes within the walls, ceiling, and floor sparkle in the darkness. The room rumbles and the floor shakes and suddenly a powerful chorus of guitars plays throughout the room. From the center of the room, the experience's opening crawl begins:

Skyrunner: Lord of Guitars

A dark cloud has fallen over Castle Cliffs. The Mayor, once a beacon of light and optimism, no longer wishes to pursue peace with the residents of the Space Station Infinity. Hoping to avert a war, Maribel, the Mayor's daughter, travels with airship pilot Liam to the distant mountains in hopes of contacting the mystical warrior princess Nisha.

Meanwhile, Runner, a messenger from Space Station Infinity, barrels through the atmosphere in his starplane, hoping to convince the mayor to consider a new proposal of trade and peace...

As the crawl ends, the guitar music reaches its crescendo and the auditorium goes once more completely dark. Reid looks around the room, but can't see anything. His eyes haven't adjusted. He can hear Xiu giggle a few meters away from him, and Gustave and Selene are whispering to one another.

The lights go up suddenly, and the room is entirely changed. Reid looks down and sees that he is now seated in the cockpit of the starplane, and wearing Runner's blue and gold 1940s-style flightsuit and helmet. A field of stars is below him, traveling back as he speeds down into the atmosphere toward Castle Cliffs. On his lap is a holodisk—a small rectangle—labeled **urgent**.

Reid guides the starplane into the planet's atmosphere, but as he flies it over to the landing pad atop Castle Cliffs, a meteor bursts through the sky and rips the stabilizer from the ship. The controls shake wildly and Reid struggles to keep the ship upright, while trying to slow it down. He can't tell how much of this he actually does himself. As he fights the controls, his heart races. The ship tumbles faster and faster. He fiddles with the switches, turning on the landing thrusters and reversing the gravity field. There, finally, the ship steadies. Reid guides the ship onto the landing pad, feeling the hull scream as it scrapes on the ground. He knows that he can't die, but the interactivity with the holograms is incredibly realistic.

The ship settles on the landing pad and the cockpit pops open and raises. Reid climbs down to the ground and secures the holodisk. Three figures await him just a short distance from his ship. The one in the center wears a gray cape. The mayor.

As if it were his own idea, Reid turns back to the ship and pulls his guitar, named Magellan's Edge, from the starplane's second seat. He straps it over his shoulder and swings it around to his back.

"You won't need that weapon," the Mayor bellows. "Castle Cliffs is a peaceful paradise."

"I have no intention of using it," Runner replies. "But I feel naked without it."

The Mayor laughs heartily.

"Just as I feel naked without my trusty bodyguards."

He indicates the man and woman flanking him, both open their jackets to display concealed laser pistols.

"Now, let's go to my chamber to discuss this proposal you're carrying," the Mayor says.

"We have high hopes that it will lead to new peace accord between the Station and Castle Cliffs," Runner replies.

Reid, the Mayor and his guards march inside to the brilliant pink crystalline city of Castle Cliffs, and the scene fades to black. Runner's powerlessness over his situation resonates with Reid. A taken guitar is a lot like a creative mind drained of inspiration; a body lacking purpose. There may not be a nefarious villain flanked by guards in Reid's everyday life, but the pursuing empty gloom carries its own weapons, and seems to lead to a trap.

A new scene rises and Reid is no longer in costume at all. He's back in his regular street clothes. Across the room, Gustave and Selene are now dressed up as Liam and Maribel, flying Liam's airship, The Astral Raven, toward the High Mountains. Reid can feel the wind cascading down from the peaks as he watches Gustave and Selene act out their part of the experience.

"If this pretty princess can't help us, I might trade this old bird in for a starplane and get out of here," Liam says.

"You can't just cut and run when things get tough," Maribel replies.

"I've done it before," he replies. "Don't think I'm above saving my own skin."

"I just don't understand you," she says.

The airship cruises between the mountain peaks, when suddenly a pair of attack blimps shoot out from behind a stone archway.

"We've got company," Liam yells.

He runs to the back of the ship's cockpit and retrieves his guitar, Tiger's Pride, and straps it on.

"You drive for a second," he says to Maribel. "I'm going to take care of our friends."

Maribel hops into the pilot's seat and grabs the controls, while Liam climbs up the airship's access ladder. Once outside, Liam takes aim, lining up the neck of his guitar with the first plane and playing a riff. The thrashing speed-metal riff creates a beam of green light that fires from the neck and blows away one of the first plane's wings. The enemy ship twirls in a tailspin and crashes explosively onto the rocky mountains below. Liam targets the second enemy plane and performs another riff, blowing it out of the sky completely. Then he swings Tiger's Pride back around his neck, victorious, and raises a traditional rock hand sign before descending the ladder back into the cockpit.

"That was close," he says. "Good flying. You might be more than a princess after all."

Maribel smirks at him, but the smirk turns into a smile. And then into a look of concern.

"I don't know how they found us," Maribel replies.

"They can't track this ship. It's too fast," Liam says. "Maybe it was just bad luck."

The airship moves further into the mountains and in the distance we finally see the entrance to Nisha's high mountain fortress.

As the ship moves in closer, it's clear to Reid and Xiu, but not to Gustave and Selene, that the back of Liam's airship is marked with a blinking tracking beacon. Reid wants to warn them, but knows that the theatre would just mute his mic and penalize him a scene for breaking the fourth wall. The lights go down again and then back up, and Reid is in full costume, standing in a large conference room with the Mayor of Castle Cliffs, his two bodyguards, and four other men. Reid counts the odds in his head, and touches where Runner's guitar strap falls across his chest. He wants to swing the weapon around and end the whole thing in one attack. His stomach crawls into his throat as the scene begins.

"My governors will also want to discuss the peace plan," the Mayor says. "I do hope you understand."

Runner nods, and sets the holodisk on the conference table top. He pushes a small green triangle on the disk's surface and the device lights up. A projection of the president of space station infinity appears.

"Mayor, we offer great thanks for your giving us an audience with you," the projection says.

"Space Station Infinity is a peaceful colony and we have for years benefited from a relationship with Castle Cliffs. In recent years, events have created confusion and blame has been placed on both sides, but today I come to you asking for a permanent end to all aggression, so that our children's futures may be brighter than ours."

"It is my hope that this message will open a new line of dialogue between our two societies. Please send your reply with my personal messenger, Runner. I await word and wish you peace."

As the projection flickers off, the Mayor bursts into booming laughter.

His governors follow suit, and dark laughter fills the room. The guards, however, remain silent.

"What is your reply, Mayor?" Runner asks, interrupting the laughter.

116

"My reply?" the Mayor responds. "My reply still requires preparing."

Runner looks over his shoulder and sees that there are two more guards directly behind him, ready to strike. He swings Magellan's Edge around to his hands and gets off two quick licks, striking one of the guards and vaporizing the other. More guards rush in from the open doorway and Runner continues to play, firing rapidly around the room. His shots hit two of the Governors, but the Mayor's guards cancel a shot at the Mayor by playing defensive harmonics.

Runner turns to exit, but there are too many guards. They pounce on him, restraining him and dragging him away down the hallway.

"My reply will be quite clear," the Mayor says. "Space Station Infinity will have all the pieces of you to prove it."

Reid feels sweat pour over his brow. Even knowing that he'd be captured—part of the script—Reid's heart races and he clenches his fists. As the lights go down again, he wrests and writhes like a trapped animal, and only notices when the scene is over that his teeth are clenched so tightly that his gums sting. He wants to kill the projections. He wants to overthrow the castle and everything it represents. Reid wants to feel himself destroy their world and save his own; himself.

Reid watches Gustave and Selene meet up with Xiu at Nisha's fortress. Liam and Maribel are able to convince Nisha to help them. They remind Nisha that the Mayor was once friends with her father, but betrayed him through elaborate gamesmanship, forcing them to live in the fortress. Her father died having never finished his life's work. As Nisha, Liam, and Maribel are about to board Liam's airship, they are besieged by a massive force of the Mayor's guards. The group fights well, and Nisha impresses the others with her amazing prowess, at once taking out eleven guards with a single pentatonic guitar solo.

The act is so impressive that Reid shouts a muted "Yeah, Xiu" from across the room, and then applauds wildly. Xiu breaks character only briefly to smile at him. And then Reid feels a wave of jealously. He can't wait for his turn to be the hero. He wonders if heroes commonly lust for the opportunity to save a life, or a world. He wonders if that's the greatest purpose.

Though Nisha, Liam, and Maribel take out many of the mayor's guards, they are overrun and escape onto the airship. As they fly off into the distance, setting course for Castle Cliffs, they watch Nisha's mountain fortress burn in the distance.

"We need to figure out how they're following us, and fast," Maribel says.

"It's not going to matter if another force like that comes after us," Liam adds.

Nisha, staring ahead, replies "They know where we're going now. And they also know that they cannot stop us."

"Why can't they stop us?" Liam asks. "The entire Mayor's guard is too much for us."

"They cannot stop us because we have good to guide us… and we have Runner, the last Lord of Guitars."

The lights go down again and rise on Reid as Runner struggling to get out of the Mayor's prison. The Mayor has taken Magellan's Edge away from him, and Runner is quickly losing hope. Reid paws desperately at the empty space where the guitar once hung. The lightness across his shoulder feels heavier than any weight. He knows he has to wait for the story to unfold, but going along for the ride is a kind of death, and Reid barely pays attention to the Mayor's trivial monologue. A commotion in the hallway leads all the guards to run up to the surface level, and Runner spies an opportunity. Using the metal buckle on his flight cap, he short circuits the electric lock holding his cell closed. After breaking out, Runner punches his way past the only guard still in the prison area, and retrieves Magellan's Edge.

A wave of euphoria washes over Reid. The prospect of being the hero he needs to be.

As he runs up the stairs, guitar at the ready, he nearly collides with Liam, Maribel, and Nisha.

"What are you guys doing here?" Runner asks.

"We're here to rescue you," Maribel replies.

"It looks like you did a good job of that on your own," Liam says.

Nisha bows ceremonially to Runner.

"What's that for?"

"She thinks you're the Lord of Guitars or something," Liam says.

"You are," Nisha confirms. "Your bloodline confirms it."

The foursome sprint up the stairs and onto the airship. They fly away to regroup where Nisha explains the lore of the Guitar Lords to Runner. Runner's unique, special, individual power exhilarates Reid. He's not playing a good guy, a decent fellow, a well-meaning average joe. No, Reid is Runner. Reid is the champion. Reid is the one without whom everything would remain an empty slog, prone to villainous fools. Reid relishes Runner's acceptance of his birthright as Lord of Guitars. He wonders if he can make it all real. *Why not?*

Together, the characters return to Castle Cliffs, ready for battle.

"If we don't make it out of this, I love you guys," Liam says.

"I knew you were a softy," Maribel says.

Nisha silently prepares, sitting cross-legged on the airship floor. Runner sits beside her and opens his eyes.

"We are destined to succeed," Runner says. "It has already been written."

Liam pilots the airship to the landing pad at Castle Cliffs. When they get out of the ship they are surprised to see that there are no guards awaiting them.

"I will go on ahead. This could be a trap," Nisha says.

Nisha darts through the main doorway and down the main hall. All is silent, but she suddenly draws her guitar. On queue, dozens of guards uncloak and surround her. Just as she is nearly captured, Runner, with Liam and Maribel in tow, charges in, playing a string of riffs that vaporize each guard where they stand.

"No one has ever done that," Nisha says. "Except for the Lord of Guitars."

Together, they charge ahead to the mayor's chamber, only to find the armored door locked tight. They decide to play together, one great multi-layered riff, and the power of their combined guitars turns the door into mush. Inside, they find the Mayor cowering behind the last of his guards.

"We don't have to fight," Runner says.

"We don't," the guards reply. "We bow to you, Lord of Guitars."

As the guards kneel, Liam and Maribel put locking braces on the Mayor. Nisha approaches him.

"Now, dear Mayor, it is time that I avenge my father, whom you destroyed with your evil."

"No, please don't kill me," the Mayor cries.

"It is worse than death," Nisha answers.

She brings out a set of ten metal caps and places them on the Mayor's fingers one by one.

"You will never play again, Mayor," she says. "Your exile is now complete."

As the Mayor falls to the floor, broken, sunlight beams in through the window, casting a glorious light on Runner, Liam, Maribel, and Nisha.

Another guitar riff begins playing as the room goes dark. The lit pad beneath Reid's feet goes dim and then turns off. A crawl of credits beams through the center of the room, and low lights come up to find Reid, Gustave, Xiu, and Selene all standing in their places, in their street clothes. They all smile at each other, but Xiu's smile is tinged by tears rolling down her cheek.

"I wanted to fucking kill that Mayor so much," she says.

Reid, Selene, and Gustave all start to laugh. Xiu follows their laughter moments later.

"That was awesome," Reid says. "Every day should be just like that."

"Yeah, it should, Lord of Guitars," Selene says, winking at him. "Is it me or did Reid get a lot handsomer tonight?" she asks Xiu.

"He's the new Reid," Xiu replies. "Shinier, but still just as handsome as before."

"What was your favorite part, hero?" Gustave says. "Being the most powerful one?"

Reid smirks. *If only I could even begin to tell them,* he thinks. *Maybe I'm destined to have power. Maybe I'm a born leader.*

"That was nice, yeah," he replies. "I liked that we were all powerful enough to make an impact. We each had our own story and our own struggles. I was surprised that Liam and Maribel got together, though."

"Makes sense," Selene says. "He's a rugged, no-rules scoundrel and she's a no-nonsense mayor's daughter. That's just how these stories work out."

"Speaking of getting together," Gustave says. "What's say we Tubecar back to my place and close this evening the right way?"

They all agree, and depart the Immersive Theatre, to board the Tubecar station back to Denver. They get back to the city in two and a half hours, spending the trip listening to music, and talking about *SkyRunner: Lord of Guitars*.

Reid can't remember ever being this happy. He feels it deep in his bones. He loves Xiu, Gustave, and Selene. He loves that they are together, and he wonders how he will help make the world a better place for them, like Runner did. He wants to be that kind of leader. He wants to be a champion. He wants to free his friends and everyone else from the mayors and castles all around them.

I can lead 20c to greatness, he thinks. *And then I'll be able to save everyone.*

Life imitating art.

They exit the Tubecar station and ramble up to Gustave's loft where they immediately undress and fall together into the conversation pit.

10

Capitol Hill Citizenry District; Denver, Colorado; United Sociocracy of the

Americas

June 24, 2087

8:08 AM

Reid sits at the base of the rickety wooden stairs outside 20c's front door. He sketches a new set of storyboards for *Origami Emu*, in which the titular character battles his nemesis, Foil Swan, in a race to outer space. It is the third storyline that Reid has drummed out in the last week and a half. His creativity flows more easily than ever, and the only thing Reid can think to thank is Club 20c, and its potent reaffirming of his individual brilliance. Nothing encourages an individual like the old American Dream.

His wristband buzzes for the fifth time this morning. It's always the same message from Gustave:

"Haven't heard from you since Amsterdam. Care to confirm plans with us and Xiu?"

Reid hasn't responded to any messages in a week. In part, he's too busy filtering through new *Origami Emu* stories and ideas, wanting to ride the wave until its inevitable break; but like any hero-to-be, Reid feels that isolation is part of the growth process. All truly great men ventured out alone into the unknown, only to return empowered and ready to lead. Even if the protected wilderness was no longer available, Reid could cut himself off from his friends and find out who he is on his own, deep down.

After all, Jesus wandered the desert.

Picasso praised solitude.

So did Hemingway.

Reid searched through the archives at 20c for the entire previous week, seeking one reputable quote that said people were better off working together and he found nothing but wretched Communists. Their ideas were easily countered by the American leaders of their day.

The America of 20c embraced the singular person. And as Reid poured over volume after volume on capitalism, individualism, and rags-to-riches tales, the questions rolling around in his head for months began to find their answers.

Why am I out of ideas? Why is there nothing?

Because the Sociocracy killed the market. In the Twentieth, the people would have guided his creative hand, but without their demand to dictate him, he was left floundering.

Why are the infinite possibilities of each day so empty?

Because men thrive when there is a course to their day. In the Twentieth, people worked not only because they needed money, but because without it they could not define themselves. It was common practice then to answer the simple question, "What do you do?" with the name of one's profession. Self and career are inalienably tied.

Why does struggle feel so right?

Because we prove ourselves, our value and our beliefs through our struggles. Without them, we prove nothing, and instead stand along the sidelines of existence learning little and growing not at all.

All of Reid's concerns were answered with deep, philosophical clarity in 20c's collection of books, their war games, their shop, their music. His fears and pains had their parallels all over the Twentieth, and so the Twentieth had gone to great lengths to answer each.

And with each answer Reid regained a piece of himself.

I might have been born in the wrong century, Reid thinks. *It's no wonder my friends won't come along. And that's okay as long as Xiu is understanding. But then, Xiu is always understanding. She wants me to be the best, when I am and I help them all find their purpose, they'll truly love me.*

His wristband buzzes again.

Same message.

He ignore it and continues drawing.

"How long have you been sitting here?" Quinn asks.

Quinn and Reagan descend the stairs, and step around Reid, toward the door.

Reid gazes at the clock on his wristband.

"About an hour, I guess," he answers. "I didn't want to bother the Tier 4s to let me in."

"We told you that we don't come in until after eight, fella," Reagan says. "We told you that last night."

"I know," Reid says. "I just couldn't stay away. My apartment is too... now."

Quinn laughs.

"You know," Reagan says. "I felt like that for a little while too. The contrast between the club and the 'real' world is sort of bracing at first. It'll pass, though."

"I'm not sure I want it to."

Quinn unlocks the door to the club and leads them in.

"Anyone want coffee? I'm going to open one of the jars of instant," she says.

"Don't waste it," Reagan protests.

"We have three cartons of the stuff. I think it will be fine."

"Okay," he says. "I'll have one."

"I'm in, too," Reid says.

The watery, flavorless instant coffee, preserved since the early 2030s, actually tastes better to Reid than anything the replicator can make. He takes joy in tweaking his cup to his liking, adding a spoonful or two to make the gray brown water a little deeper and blacker.

"This is human ingenuity," he says to Quinn and Reagan, sipping away.

"We forgot how to invent stuff like this when the replicators came along. Nobody even mixes their own drinks anymore," Reagan says.

Quinn winces with each sip. "This is disgusting," she says. "I just drink it for the nostalgia."

As they drink their coffee, Reid continues to work on storyboards. Quinn hustles around the space and sets up the mock storefront, the game area, and puts all the war game pieces back in their bins so the world is ready to be contested once more. She turns on the audio player, and selects a playlist of old jazz tunes, specifically something called Bebop.

"If every musician just worked together, there would have been no jazz, fella," Reagan says. "Improvisation is the ultimate flex of musical individualism. I mean, if Miles Davis was just playing in a marching band, it would've sounded just fine, but there never would have been anything that interesting about it."

Reid nods and raises his cup of instant coffee. "Here's to that."

More than just to jazz, Miles Davis was a hero to music, Reid thinks. *Without his experimentation and influence, rock music, hip hop, rap, and electronica would have taken markedly different forms. Who knows what the music of today would sound like without him?*

Quinn dusts the Y2K and nuclear war preparedness displays, then skips to the back kitchen. Reagan sits down beside Reid on the couch in the games corner. Reid's stylus runs circles around his tablet, as Origami Emu removes Foil Swan's original rockets and replaces them with large, long-fused fireworks.

"Still cranking away?" Reagan asks.

"I'm in a notable groove, fella," Reid says.

"Just remember that in here, you're going to need to make some money off of that cartoon soon. We're ending your grace period today."

The grace period was explained to Reid three days prior. All new members of 20c are allowed to use outside credits within the club until it ends. After that, any money spent in the club, on food, drink, or games had be earned in it, using their pre-credit United States dollars. Earning money was easy because they operated on Capitalist system.

"Instead of starting at Tier 4 I'd like to try something else," Reid says.

"We love innovation, fella," Reagan replies. "That's what made the Twentieth great."

"With your blessing, I'm going to be an entrepreneur."

125

"Sounds great," Reagan says. "What's your business? Labor? Farm? Finances?"

"Art," Reid replies. "I am going to sell my art within the club."

"Interesting," Reagan says.

"I figure if I sell an illustration to a fellow member, I can charge whatever they will pay," Reid says. "And if I sell enough, I can skip to Tier 1 and earn the rest in the storefront, or by dispensing drinks, prepping MREs, and making Spam sandwiches."

Reagan nods. "If you can make it work, fella, it sounds real nice. Just don't forget that if you're drawing or daydreaming about drawing while you're supposed to be working on something else, we will fire you."

"I know the risks. I've read all about Capitalism," Reid says.

"Alright smart guy, make me one where the emu is dancing in a frilly, pink dress and I'll give you $50," Reagan says.

"Origami Emu is male," Reid protests.

"I don't care. I'm the customer. This is how it works."

Reid sighs.

"You're right," he says. "The market is defining production and I will work past the struggle to meet that demand."

"Atta boy, fella."

Reid goes to work, sketching his usual emu with a pink gown. He fills and shades and dapples the image to give it a distinct watercolor look, and in moments he turns back to Reagan.

"Pay up, Reagan," he says.

A pair of Tier 4s, following Tier 3s to the bathroom wave politely to Reagan. Reagan nods to acknowledge them.

Reagan purses his lips and places his thumb and forefinger to his chin.

"You know, this isn't exactly what I was picturing in my head," he says. "Can you make me one with a powder blue dress instead, but not with so many frills, and maybe some poofy materials around the edges and the sleeves."

Reid gazes at his pink-clad emu and takes a deep breath.

"This is what you asked for," Reid says.

126

"I know, but I think I didn't know exactly what I wanted, you know."

Reid nods. "That's fair. I'll save this one, and make the blue one."

He puts the stylus to the screen again, sketching at speed and filling his lines with detail. The new emu wears a poofy sleeved, almost southern belle-style powder blue dress complete with a billowing skirt. He contemplates drawing a single tear gathering in Origami Emu's eye, but decides against it.

"Okay, here it is," Reid says holding the new creation in Reagan's face.

"Yes," Reagan says. "That's what I was looking for. Great work. I'll give you $25 for it."

"Twenty-five?" Reid asks. "You said fifty just 20 minutes ago."

"I did say fifty, but that was when there was only one Origami Emu in a dress picture. Now there are two, and that more than doubles the market supply. Sorry, fella, but you have to lower your price because I'm a savvy consumer."

"You asked for both of them."

"Sure I did," Reagan answers. "But it was your job to do better research before bringing a product to market. Sorry, fella, that's Capitalism."

Reid feels intense anger welling up in him, and then he smiles. *This is it,* he thinks. *This is struggle. Reagan is fucking with me about my art and it's bothering me. He's forcing me to adapt beyond my comfort zone. It's working. This is making me a better person, and it can only do the same for everyone else. And when I have enough money, I'll be an example to the other club members, so they can really understand the system, and feel like better people too.*

With pride, Reid accepts the $25 from Reagan, received in the form of two ten dollar bills and a five, all made of paper. He folds the money and stuffs it in his pocket while the image transfers from his tablet to Reagan's wristband.

"Pleasure doing business with you," Reagan says as the transfer completes. "This will look great as a full-size cutout. I can charge the members $20 to take a photo."

"You can't do that," Reid says. "It's just for you."

"That wasn't in our deal. You should've thought about that sooner."

"I guess I assumed that you were being honest with me."

Reagan laughs, nearly falling off couch.

"You'll get the hang of it."

***

By eleven a.m. Club 20c bustles with members playing games, shopping at the storefront, fighting wars, and munching on decades-old survivalist food. The Tier 1s and 2s work and wander about, while the Tier 3s and 4s make their way back to the yard, returning occasionally to collect their dollars from Reagan, spend them, give thanks, and repeat the process. People from all over the district have flocked in, filling the space. There are even a dozen faces unfamiliar to Reid. Reid's wristband buzzes with three more messages from Xiu and Selene:

1. Not sure why you're not responding. Please ping back. Fond of you, Xiu

2. Gustave and I want to know about next Friday. ASAP. Thx. Selene

3. Thinking of you, love. Hope that you're not upset or something. Xiu

Reid taps ignore for each and continues playing with an old stock broker's training computer one of the members dug up at an antique store. Reid isn't sure how, but by shuffling large sums of money around within the program, he appears to nearly double its value. He buys gold and watches it increase. Then he moves the money into old oil and the money grows. Reid gets excited that he's doing so well and starts moving the money around faster. He watches as about half of his investments fail, but Reid doesn't care because the other half succeed, and that means he makes money, even if many of the fictional companies fall apart. After a few moments, Reid grows bored of watching his money increase, and he begins exploring some other investments that he doesn't understand.

At best, Reid thinks that they are bets on whether other investments will fail, or whether other things will lose their value. After playing with those options for a few moments, Reid finds that he's making money for succeeding and for failing, and all he's doing is watching the screen and tapping at the keys of the ancient machine. He understands why the game would be so popular. It's a game where it's possible to win even if he loses because the money isn't his in the first place. He watches the money accrue for a few more minutes, and then gets bored again. Reid watches all the money disappear, and then sets the device down, turning his attention to the proposal he intends to bring before the club.

Quinn steps up on the bar top and makes a cone around her mouth with her hands.

"Attention, please," she says. "I'm calling quorum on today's official meeting of Club 20c."

The group falls silent and gathers toward the bar top.

"Everyone stand still so I can get a head count," Reagan barks.

He walks around the room, tapping each member on the shoulder as he passes. When he's finished he returns to the counter.

"Forty-one members present. We can vote."

"I call this meeting of the Club 20c to order. I am Quinn Takejiro, club secretary and second officer. Before I cede the floor to our current President, is there any new business or any announcements?"

A hand raises in the back of the crowd.

"Yes," Quinn says. "Michael."

"I recently found a surplus store in Idaho that has a full stock of MREs," the man says. "I think we could get those for our cache."

"Great sleuthing," Quinn says. "Do you volunteer to acquire them?"

"I do."

"Great," she says. "All in favor of Michael obtaining the MREs for the club, say aye."

The crowd offers a chorus of affirmatives.

"And all opposed."

Silence.

"Great. Approved. Any other business?"

Another hand comes up through the crowd.

"I was hoping we could get some non-Twentieth food options in the kitchen," a voice says. "My digestion hasn't reacted well to it lately."

"All in favor?" Quinn asks.

Only a few ayes this time.

"All opposed?"

And there is a wall of nays.

"That's democracy for you. You can try again next week," Quinn says. "Last call for new business."

Reid raises his hand.

"Reid? What do you have to say?" Quinn asks.

"I want to propose a larger discussion about what the club is doing to benefit the community," he says.

"Well, as a primarily historical preservation and leisure organization, we don't have to do anything other than welcome new members openly," Quinn says.

"Sure, but I think we have an opportunity to be heroes in Capitol Hill and beyond," Reid says. "We could liberate our fellow Citizens from the haze they're living in, and show them the vivid colors of a world where suffering makes us stronger, hard work builds character, and where the market determines who is successful and who isn't. Think of how wonderful the truly talented will feel when they finally receive the validation that they've long deserved."

Reid hears a clamor growing throughout the crowd. A few of the lower Tiers peer inside the door to the yard, hanging on Reid's words.

"We can sit by like anyone else and let the U. S. of A. tell us that other people are more important than we are. We can keep voting our dailies and taking our handouts and doing whatever we please, *or* we can lay the groundwork for a future that calls men and women to great purpose, that exhausts them, that taps into their greatest innovations, that offers the truly skilled with a path toward success, and keeps those people who don't strive hard enough in their rightful place at the bottom."

The clamor gets louder. Reid can tell that several of the group members are agreeing with him, especially the lower Tiers. He can see Reagan nodding his head. Quinn, though, has her arms crossed, standing atop the bar, shaking her head, almost imperceptibly.

130

Reid pushes through the crowd and makes his way to the front, standing before the bar with his back to Quinn.

"See, there's a whole world of people up there who think that life is supposed to be easy. They're all happy living off of what other people built, and using all those technologies to avoid learning how to do anything. And, fellas, I used to be one of them. I used to be weak and simpering. I used to eat replicator meals three times a day and take drugs and fuck my need for purpose away, but not anymore! Today, I stand before you as a changed man who wants to build something even better for tomorrow," Reid says.

The majority of the room bursts into applause. There are even hoots and hollers.

"Order," Quinn commands. "Order."

The room slowly grows quiet.

"I'm not sure this qualifies as new business, Reid," she says. "We don't usually vote on what sounds like a motion to turn our club into a revolutionary organization. And while I'm sure that we all appreciate your fervor for the Twentieth, 20c is about appreciation—and maybe a little bit of fetishization—but I don't think we're prepared to take action against other people or the U. S. of A."

"Yet, the U. S. of A. seeks to cripple our voice by charging this club a due," Reid says.

"The dues are 100 credits a year, and it guarantees this space for us. It's reasonable," Quinn says. "I paid it just last week, so we have nothing to worry about."

"You paid the dues?" Reagan asks. "Why did you pay the dues?"

"We have to pay them. It's our single responsibility to the rest of the clubs in the U. S. of A.," Quinn replies.

Reagan rolls his eyes.

"I told you that we weren't going to pay that. It's extortion," he says.

"No, it's not," she replies. "It's minor fee associated with free electricity and the credits we need to pay for all the stuff we've brought down here."

"Well, as President, I never authorized you to pay, so I'm going to have to ask you to resign."

The gathered group gets loud again. There's a mix of chatter in support of Quinn, in support of Reagan, and a few people still talking about Reid's speech.

"Resign?" she asks. "It's required by our society. It's part of what keeps the whole thing working so that we can spend all of time here."

"It's not about what you did, Quinn," Reagan says. "It's the principle. You ignored the hierarchy of office in this club. You must step down. But I will not remove you from the club this time."

Quinn's face twists into a glare of befuddled madness. She hops down from the countertop and gathers her things.

"You don't have to remove me," she says. "I'm leaving. Good luck with this madness."

Reagan doesn't speak, and lets her leave, moving with her toward the door in a passive act of superiority.

"With any luck, Quinn, we can make this club even better for when you come back," Reid says as she passes.

She shoves him, and he stumbles back a step.

"This isn't real," she barks from the doorway. "It's a joke. We were playing make-believe."

Quinn Takejiro slams the wooden slat door to Club 20c so hard that its top hinge breaks and it dangles in the doorway, purposeless. The stairs creak and wail as she stomps up them toward the street. Inside, the club members chatter about the scene. A handful gather their things and go up the stairs after Quinn, but many of them stay, staring up at Reagan and awaiting their president's next words.

Reagan climbs onto the bar top, taking the position Quinn had just held, and raises his arms . When the chatter continues, Reagan stomps his foot on the bar, and the resounding claps of his footfalls quiet the room.

"That was a tough scene, fellas. I liked Quinn a lot too. But you all heard what she said. It just wouldn't be right to let someone undermine our club," he says.

A couple of other people in the crowd mumble that Quinn was right, and that paying the club dues are reasonable. They slip through the group toward the stairs. As they exit, Reagan stomps on the counter again.

"Don't look at them. They can go if they want," Reagan says. "Now, if everyone here is still interested in Club 20c, we can continue our meeting."

He waits for any more of the members to leave. When he's satisfied that they won't, he hops down from the counter and stands beside Reid.

"This fella here is new to 20c, but his dedication is undeniable. None of us has been here day in and day out, studying, sharing, and praising the Twentieth as hard as Reid has," Reagan says.

"Now, we will have time to talk about how 20c can bring some light into the lives of the people in Capitol Hill and all over the U. S. of A. later. I, for one, believe that Reid has opened us up to a brave new world of sorts."

"I am really sorry for causing any trouble, everyone," Reid says. "I hope that we can do some good work together."

"So, I have one last new order of business, and then we can all get back to enjoying the Twentieth," Reagan says. "I move that we appoint Reid Rosales as the new second officer and secretary of 20c. All in favor?"

Reid basks as the room erupts in "ayes." His wristband vibrates again. Another message from Xiu.

Ignore.

"All opposed?"

Silence.

As the club members dissipate to different parts of the room and begin their war games, store games, and historical readings, Reid scans the room with new pride.

I am among my people, Reid thinks. *And I am one of their best.*

11

Capitol Hill Citizenry District; Denver, Colorado; United Sociocracy of the

Americas

June 26, 2087

7:01 AM

The buzzing in his wristband wakes Reid from a dream in which he's being carried on the shoulders of a cheering mob. The jolt slams him back to consciousness. For a moment, he doesn't recognize the tiled ceiling of Club 20c, or remember where he is. Reid blinks hard, clearing the sleep and cementing himself in the waking world. He raises his arm and looks at his wristband to see the message:

It's from Gustave.

"Meet me in one hour at Tom's Diner. No arguments. We need to chat."

Reid rolls onto his side on the mid-century modern couch; nearly kicking the pile of old board games off the coffee table as he swings his body to sit up. He has not been to his apartment in two days, opting to stay at 20c in hopes of fully immersing himself in the culture. He spent the days reading history, working in the mock storefront, selling original artworks, complaining about the robot economy, and working directly with Reagan on their outreach plan.

Reagan's plan amounts to active evangelism, recruitment, and the dissemination of flyers, either physical, or by advertising on wristbands. It has been a point of contention between him and Reid since Reid's appointment to second officer of the club. In the interest of respecting the Twentieth, they left the conversation open to all members, so there is no shortage of ideas, but Reid remains unimpressed.

Reid checks his credits balance on his wristband, and finds he has enough for a meal at Tom's. He has not done his dailies since his appointment, either, choosing to earn only the old U.S. Dollars that serve as currency within the club. As his credits dwindle and stagnate, his fortune in green paper has grown to nearly five hundred dollars, largely through the sales of Origami Emu illustrations and short cartoons, drawn in the style and design demanded by each customer.

He stands up from the couch and stretches, uses his travel sterilizer; then takes his pants, folded over the arm of the seat, and puts them on. Reid buzzes around the main club room, setting things up for the day, finally settling at the countertop to drink a single cup of instant coffee. As he sips, he reads Joyce's *Ulysses*, which he decides closely mirrors his own life, because their greatest parts are in ideation and contemplation.

With ten minutes to spare, Reid locks the club and ascends the steps into the rest of the world. He slips through the crowds all chattering about their leisure plans, and hobbies, and the dailies, and conveniences. *Sheep*, he shakes his head. He takes the alleyways, avoiding the Tubecar stations and the places where the most Citizens congregate.

He arrives at Tom's Diner just a minute late. The classic 1960s, angular-roofed structure is mostly unchanged. The outer perimeter of wide rectangular windows lets anyone from the street peer inside at the brightly-colored booths, lunch counter, and patrons within. The dining area surrounds a central kitchen. Chrome and colorful, restored enamel accent the space. Disorderly stone covers one wall, giving the impression of nature invading the modern space.

Reid walks through the sliding glass door entrance. Behind the counter, where there used to be human cooks, waiters and waitress, there are robots. Two robots are in the kitchen, speedily assembling foods fresh from the replicator onto plates. Two robots cruise around the restaurant, taking orders and delivering food. One robot stands behind the bar, serving, and ringing up customers that are ready to leave.

He feels a new kind of disgust rise in him; an animosity toward the robots that he never felt before. It is as if a veil were lifted from his eyes, and he could finally see the world for what it actually is.

These should be people, Reid thinks.

"Reid," Gustave calls from a booth in the corner. "Over here."

Reid ignores the robot behind the counter asking if he needs any help, and walks over to meet Gustave. Gustave stands from his seat on Reid's arrival and offers him a hug. Reid returns the embrace, but ends it and quickly sits down.

"What'd you want to talk about?" Reid asks. "I'm kind of in the middle of some stuff."

Gustave picks up the menu and doesn't immediately respond.

"Please, Reid, let's not jump to the serious part," he says. "We haven't seen each other in two weeks."

Reid sighs and takes up the menu. Its pages are a mix of traditional American foods infused with snarky commentary. A line under the À La Carte menu reads "Stupid questions… 2 credits." Nothing on the menu looks good to Reid. *It's all fake*, he thinks. *Just molecules thrown together by a computer without a solitary bit of passion, or love, or craftsmanship.*

The robot waiter arrives at the table as Gustave folds his menu.

"What can I get you boys?" it asks.

"I'll have the big breakfast, over medium with bacon and wheat toast," Gustave says.

"And for you, hon?" the robot asks Reid.

Reid slaps the menu down on the tabletop.

"Are there real oats in the oatmeal? Or does it come from the box back there?"

The robot pauses a moment to process.

"The oatmeal is made from original steel cut-style molecular schematics in our kitchen replicator."

"So that's a no then," Reid says.

"All food served in this restaurant meet or exceed the quality standards set by the Capitol Hill District and the U. S. of A.," the robot replies.

"Just bring me your fake oatmeal," Reid says.

"Coming right up," the robot answers, and then speeds away.

"You didn't have to be so rude to it," Gustave says.

"They want to serve me a facsimile of food, I'll respond with a facsimile of kindness."

136

Gustave doesn't respond right away. The two men find objects just beyond each other to stare at.

"How is your club doing, Reid? We haven't heard from you in a while."

Reid sits forward in the booth.

"The club is great. We're really making progress. I'm the second officer now, so I'm directly involved in the most important decisions."

"That's nice, Reid," Gustave says. "What do you do there that prevents you from seeing or answering us?"

Reid does not notice the implication within the question.

"We learn about the Twentieth, play games from that era, practice market economics and Capitalism through our storefront, and discuss ways we can improve your world with our teachings," Reid says. "You could come as my guest if you'd like."

"Our world?" Gustave asks. "I'm not exactly sure what you mean."

Reid feels energized by the question.

"Well, it's no secret that the U. S. of A. is a real mess," he says. "It's a giant mass of people with nothing to do, no purpose, and no meaning. All of you spend your days going through the motions that the system has foisted upon you. You're all sleepwalking, pretending to be happy and content. I know because I was like that too. But one day I woke up, really woke up, and saw that having life handed to you is poison. It keeps us from reaching our individual potentials. It leaves us empty and reliant on the State. It's disgusting, really, when you think about it."

"That's interesting, Reid," Gustave says. "I'm not sure that I agree, as you know from our previous conversations, but I'm glad that you've found your niche."

"It's more than a 'niche,' Gustave. It's a calling. I am closer to the higher purpose of man than anyone has ever been, and we're going to bring it to you."

Gustave laughs nervously.

"You know, no offense, but you sound a little crazy right now," Gustave jokes.

"There's nothing crazy about finally seeing things as they are," Reid replies. "You can keep pretending you're equal to everyone else if you want, but I want to be more. I want to be Tier 1." The robot waiter returns with two waters, sets them on the table and slides away wordlessly.

"Tier 1?" Gustave asks. "You're not making sense. Is that club lingo? Besides, usually when a person finds clarity it leaves them more humble, and thankful. You seem angry."

"Is it wrong to be angry that we're being deceived?" Reid protests. "Is it wrong to be angry that we've so lost our path that we're nearly no longer human at all?"

Reid takes a drink.

"I want to help you, Selene, and Xiu be better people. I want to help you become people who are really free, living really meaningful lives."

"Lives like the people in the Twentieth who killed each other, starved, died of disease, and looked the other way while the majority of the people had less and less?" Gustave asks.

"They were flawed, experimenting for the first time. But we have the benefit of hindsight."

"Hindsight granted to you by the current world you live in; a world built beginning in the twentieth century that grew from it."

"Tim Berners-Lee did not credit the invention of the first Web to Edison, even though the man's bulbs lit his offices," Reid argues.

Gustave grasps his coffee mug and takes a sip. He looks out the diner window at the people—smiling—in complete control of their days, months, years, and lives.

"I can see we'll make no progress in debate, Reid," he says. "As your friend, I come to you today to ask why you haven't replied to me, Selene, or to Xiu. Selene is heartbroken that we haven't blended since after Amsterdam, and to be honest, I am too. You were so lively and happy that night, and you were bold and heroic. I thought for sure that this club had reminded you of the confidence you'd lost, but now I'm not so sure."

Reid's hands ball into fists and he slams one on the tabletop. The entire diner falls silent and turns to face their booth.

138

"Don't blame my being tired of your rudeness and Selene's vacuous whoring on the club," he yells. "You have never been supportive of me. You have argued with me at every opportunity. And, what you don't realize is that your blind devotion to this stupid, temporary version of the world is exactly what makes you a pathetic, empty husk."

Reid jumps up from the booth and stomps out of the diner. He shoves a robot waiter into the bar as he passes, sending a tray of plates crashing to the ground.

"You should be a person," he sneers at the machine.

Another robot helps the fallen one up, and they remove the debris in seconds. Reid throws open the door and stops as he reaches the flow of humanity going wherever they please, lamenting their *plastic smiles*.

Gustave's hand lands on his shoulder and Reid turns fast on his heels, balling up his fist as he does.

"Reid," Gustave says. "I was only ever giving you a hard time. I thought you knew that. If you can let this go, I will too, and we'll just let bygones be bygones. Come on, let's go catch up with Selene and Xiu and we can talk it all out."

Reid turns his back on Gustave.

"You'll let this go? You'll forgive me for being unreasonable, and welcome me back into your world of drugs, handouts, and empty laughter?"

"I wouldn't use those exact words," Gustave says. "But it could all be forgo—"

Without warning, Reid spins around and throws his fist into Gustave's jaw.

The taller man stumbles back and falls down on the sidewalk. For a moment, the attack doesn't register. Gustave has known nothing like it since early in school. He cries out, grabbing his face. A small bead of blood lingers on his hand. Gustave stares at Reid in disbelief.

Reid holds his fists up in a defensive stance. His eyes are cold. Behind his back, a few of the nearby pedestrians stop to view the commotion. One woman shakes her head in disapproval. A man beside her stares, unsure if he should approach. Other onlookers gather slowly to view the strange spectacle. Reid drinks in the audience, then looks at his knuckle, bloodied, and prepares for Gustave to strike back.

"You hit me?" Gustave says.

Reid nods.

"You're an artist, Reid, and you hit me."

"I'll do it again," Reid says. "Come on, show me what you've got before the security robots get here."

Gustave lowers the hand from his jaw and shakes his blood onto the sidewalk. He looks up at Reid and shakes his head. Gustave struggles to his knees, pauses and takes a deep breath, and then slinks back into Tom's Diner. He stops at the counter and waves off a robot that is probably calling the authorities. Gustave speaks to the robot for a moment, and then goes back to the booth and sits down. The other customers crowd around him, offering him their napkins and glasses of water. Some of them hug him. After a few moments, he waves them off politely. Soon, a robot waiter arrives and delivers his breakfast.

Outside, Reid lowers his fists and opens his hands. He wipes his bloody knuckle on his pants and turns away from the restaurant. Sadness hits him almost immediately. He did not always like Gustave, but he did love him, and Selene had never done a single wrong thing to him. They were part of his life, and he would never forget them. It was just too bad that they didn't understand the direction that he had to go. It's too bad that Gustave is too much of a coward to fight him. It's too bad that they are stuck in the life that the system gave them. It's too bad the security robots would have stopped them eventually anyway. There's no freedom in this place. None at all.

Reid sticks to the alleys again as he makes his way back to Club 20c.

His wristband buzzes.

It's a message from Xiu.

"Did you punch Gustave?" she asks.

Reid taps the ignore button, and then thinks better of it. *Xiu has been the most understanding of any of them,* he thinks. *It would be a pity to lose her.*

"We had a disagreement and I did something I shouldn't have," he says. "I will let him cool down a bit and apologize. And maybe I'll lay off the action movies for a few days too."

"He seems pretty upset," she says. "You better make it up to him."

140

"I will," Reid replies.

"And you have some time to make up to me too," Xiu says. "I haven't seen you in too long."

"I know. I'm really sorry about that, love," he says. "I have let this club thing get the best of me. Let's get dinner tomorrow? You pick the place."

"Finally," she replies. "Let's go to that seafood place in Buenos Aires."

"Perfect," Reid says. "I'll pick you up at eight, fella"

He closes the wristband conversation and continues down the alleyways toward the club. When he crosses the streets, he doesn't make eye contact with the people. Reid Rosales keeps his head down, even as he walks with more pride than ever.

12

Capitol Hill Citizenry District; Denver, Colorado; United Sociocracy of the
Americas

June 26, 2087

5:12 PM

Reid and Reagan stand over the wargame map with three other upper Tier members of 20c. Reid moves his land forces across what used to be the People's Republic of China. One of the other players resists the attack with a swarm of bombers. Reagan's fleet of ships moves its way across the Pacific, setting up a blockade on the other player's base. Their pincer maneuver is working. In the background, a record by The Who plays. A small group of lower Tier club members gazes in at the game, as if watching a ballgame.

"I believe strongly that a door-to-door campaign would open some powerful conversations," Reid says. "People out there aren't happy. They think they are, but they're just numb. That numbness has become so usual that they don't question their lack of purpose anymore. They can't even conceive of a world where they earn what they spend, or where they can't just do whatever they please. We can show them the virtues they're missing."

Two other players take their turns—one fortifies the battlements along the Great Wall, and the other, a blonde woman Reid has not seen at the club before, marches her ground forces down from the old Russian border—both hoping to prevent the inevitable end of Reid and Reagan's combined assault.

"Won't evangelism alienate people? What if they just don't care about what we have to say?" one of the club members asks Reid.

"These are good questions," Reid says. He moves his battalion of tanks up the great wall, just beyond range of the defense's surface-to-surface missiles. "We'll need a script, so that no one member travels too far off point. We'll need to learn how to capture their imaginations. If they don't care, we will convince them that they do. If they feel alienated, we'll convince them that the Sociocracy is alienating them. And we'll practice together to ensure that we're consistent, all operating as a single, dedicated entity."

"We could concoct some type of test to validate our claim that people aren't as happy as they think they are," Reagan says.

Reagan moves his ships into the Bohai Bay. "I'll be in range next turn."

Reid nods in agreement.

"That's a genius idea. It would be so much easier if we just had a piece of technology that seemed to validate our claim," he says. "What could we use?"

The three upper Tier members each take their turns. The woman's ground forces from Russia are too far away. The bombers make the tough decision to pursue only Reid's forces near the Wall. The last group fortifies its structures again, placing men on each of the defense guns and sending the officers into the shelter below the structure.

"You're fucked, you know," Reagan says.

"I know," responds the member running the base.

"Surrender is an option," Reid says.

"And miss the chance to take a few of yours with us?" another member says.

"Good man," Reagan replies. "Bold even in defeat."

Reagan begins bombarding the fortress. The first volleys take down half of its defenses. Reid follows by firing over the Great Wall at the other side of the structure, eliminating the remaining defenses, but leaving the other team alive for one more turn.

"I've got it," adds the female club member.

"We can't win," another says. "We need a miracle."

"No, not the wargame," the woman says. "I know what we could use to convince people that they aren't happy."

She leaves her position overseeing the forces stuck in Russia, and runs to the storage room door at the back of the club. She enters and digs through the boxes of ephemera from the Twentieth that had no clear purpose in the main room. In a few moments, the blonde woman returns to the wargame table holding a blue, oval-shaped device with dials and an analog meter. Attached to the box by two wires are two hand-sized, polished metal cylinders.

"What the hell is that?" Reagan asks her.

"It's called a Mark Super VII Quantum E-Meter," she says, reading the label on the device. "There was a cult in the Twentieth and early twenty-first centuries that used this to convince people to pay them money."

"Oh, I've read about them," Reid says. "The Scienceologists."

"Yeah," she says. "They made a person hold onto these things, and then they'd look at this meter here."

Reid takes hold of the two metal cylinders and turns the meter on. The needle on the meter wobbles back and forth arhythmically. Reid clenches his fists and the meter bounds. He thinks about his parents and the needle spikes. He thinks about Xiu and the needle falls.

"See here, when you think about something that makes you upset, sad, anything, the needle goes up," Reid says. "We can tell people that they can lower that number on the meter, but only if they talk with us more."

"I think that's how they did it in the book I read," she says. "We can always tell the person that they weren't doing as well as they could, no matter what the meter says. That way they'll have to listen no matter what."

"You are a genius," Reid adds. "We'll use technology from the Twentieth to convince people that they're missing it."

Reid takes the device and turns it on. He grabs to the metal cylinders and holds them, watching the meter's needle rise and fall as his hands make and leave contact.

"This is supposed to tell you when memories or statements you make about your life cause you emotional stress," Reid continues. "Really, it just conducts your body's natural electricity and responds to fluctuations the way lie detectors would. The technology is so old I bet very few people would know how it works."

"Let me try it," Reagan says, taking the cylinders.

"Okay, pretend you're an ordinary sheep citizen, and tell me about what it's like to get up every day and have no responsibilities."

"Oh it's so great, fella," Reagan says. "I just do whatever I please all the time and nothing matters and that's great because I don't need to matter when the world is as great as this."

Reid taps at the E-meter, and furrows his brow at Reagan.

"Interesting," Reid says. "Could you repeat just the last few words you said?"

Reagan plays the part. "I don't need to matter when the world is as great as this?"

Reid raises his eyebrow. "Yes. There it is."

"There what is?" Reagan asks.

"A jump, and one of the biggest I've seen," Reid lies. "There's definitely some hidden unhappiness in there. Have you ever thought about what it means to have purpose?"

Reagan bursts into laughter.

Reid joins him.

The other three club members follow suit.

"This will work like a charm," Reid says. "The curiosity piqued by this piece of junk will be enough to draw them into conversation. How many more of these do we have?"

"There's a whole box of them back there," the member says. "I think we got them from an estate sale or something."

Reid beams. *This is it,* he thinks. *We can reach the hearts and minds of the people, and when they know what we're offering them, they'll be unable to resist.* The world is but a deep dark cave, and now Reid and 20c have a torch. The enlightenment they will bring to the Sociocracy will illuminate all that is wrong with the present and all that was so perfect in the past. People will wake up, and finally comprehend that they were asleep all along. Reid imagines dozens of middle Tier club members roaming the streets of Capitol Hill District, each with an E-Meter, each striking up conversations with strangers who don't know just how bad-off they are. Those people will join up, and they'll take the devices and recruit more people, and the club will expand. There will be a branch in every district in the city, and then all across the U. S. of A. And when it's all done, the people will cry out for purpose, for jobs, for the kind of meritocracy that they've always deserved.

"Starting tomorrow morning, I will train members in the proper use of these devices, and in the afternoon, we will send members out with these to all the Tubecar stations and shopping areas," Reid says. "With sheer numbers alone we'll spread our word, and people will be far too curious to ignore us. This is our best chance to bring sanity back to society. We will bring the Twentieth back, together."

Reid reaches out and takes the club member's hand. "Thank you, dear. Your contribution to the cause is an immense one."

"Well done, indeed, lady," Reagan says. "What's your name?"

"Annabelle, sirs," she replies.

"Annabelle, your name will be famous after the revolution," Reagan says.

"Thank you, sir."

"As a reward, Annabelle, you may call a truce with Reagan's and my forces, but it will mean that you'll have turn your weapons on your friends," Reid says, making a gun shape with his hand and pretending to fire it at the other two members at the table.

Annabelle nods and uses her turn to move the forces from Russia past the downed walls of the fortress.

"My cannon corps attacks your barracks," Annabelle points out.

"This isn't fair," one of the others says. "We're entitled to a round of diplomatic discussions before she secedes. It's in the rules of war."

He taps the manual, sitting on the corner of the table. The other member takes it up and flips through it, finding a page and slapping it.

"Right here," he says. "Article 72.1c reads 'No army shall close negotiations on a treaty, truce, or partnership, without providing an open forum for engagement to all participants.'"

Annabelle looks to Reid and Reagan. Both shrug.

"It's in the rulebook," Reagan says.

"What do you have to offer me?" she asks the other two members.

"An honorable defeat with your comrades in arms?" one asks.

The other digs through the pockets of his denim overalls. "I have 23 U.S. Dollars I could give you."

Annabelle stands silent, considering her options with theatrical hmms and sighs. She looks down at the table, then over to Reid and Reagan, and across to her once-upon-a-time compatriots. She lines up the cannon pieces in a neat row, clearly savoring the process, with each one aimed at the fortress.

The lower Tiers in the doorway yelp with glee.

"Victory is priceless, gentlemen," she says.

Reid and Reagan begin to applaud, but Annabelle stops and turns to them.

"But I could use my engineering corps," she says, taking up the rulebook. "Article 12.41a says 'Each land force shall contain one engineering corps with skills to perform major repairs on structures once each turn.' Seems that I could just keep repairing the fortress while we pick you two apart."

Now the other two members begin to applaud, seeing the tables turn in their favor.

Reid smiles. This type of jockeying and double-crossing would never happen in the U. S. of A. People wouldn't have any incentive to negotiate because everyone always has something, so they all think they win. But something isn't always enough, and a fair share isn't always the share that's fair.

He pulls out a wad of United States Dollars and fans the bills.

"This is nearly three hundred dollars. And I will offer you five percent of anything else I make for the next three months," Reid says. "Imagine the resource you'll tap into by choosing the right side, Annabelle."

"We've been on the same team for sixteen wargames," one of the other members says.

Annabelle turns the cannons on the fortress.

"You can't beat that deal, boys," she says to her former teammates. "I'm sorry."

With her attack the battle ends.

The lower Tiers applaud and cheer from the doorway.

"That's the Twentieth spirit, lady," Reagan says. "You go for the resources and keep your allegiances agile."

They clear the table of its pieces and slide all of them into their appropriate bins.

"Pay up, fellas," Reagan commands. "You know the rules. Loser pays."

The two losing club members withdraw folds of old United States currency from their pockets. They each count out one hundred dollars, and hand fifty each to Reagan and Reid.

"Man, I'm almost broke. Remind me why we play for money again?" one of the losers asks.

"To ensure that the way you manage your resources on the battlefield is backed by how you manage your finances, just like the great wars of the Twentieth where cash and victory were hand in hand," Reagan says. "There are plenty of ways you can pay your debts, if you'd rather work it off."

As Reid and Reagan count their money, the other two club members skulk away. Annabelle wears a giant grin and rushes to the other side of the table to hug Reagan and Reid. She kisses both men on their cheeks and bounds back a couple of steps. She's exhilarated by the concept of diplomacy-for-gain. She's proud to be able to team up with a winner, instead of just languish as neither victor, nor loser. *By the glint in her eyes, shimmering with their own light, rather than the empty reflected light of the Sociocracy, it's clear that Annabelle is alive for the first time, all because she chose herself over everyone else; the one over the many.* At least that's what Reid thinks as he watches her strut before her former allies, taunting them.

"You've brought us two victories today, Annabelle," Reid says. "Actually, make that three."

"Three?" Reagan says.

"One was for our outreach. Two was this wargame. And three is for herself," Reid says. "Annabelle, you've made yourself stronger today, which in turn makes you stronger for the cause.

"You're growing into a capable rugged individualist before our eyes," he continues. "It's humbling, isn't it, Reagan?"

"Very, fella. These are powerful times, and with that in mind, we should celebrate."

Reagan leaves the wargames table, tapping it with his hand as a way to say, "I'll be right back." He pushes through the dingy grey swinging door that leads into the kitchen. Reid can hear a clatter as Reagan digs through some boxes or cans somewhere. Shortly, Reagan reappears cradling five glass bottles filled with clear liquid. Each one bears a water-stained, peeling label conspicuously marked with three Xs on the front, and a skull and crossbones on the back. He tosses a bottle to Reid, and one to Annabelle. He keeps one for himself, and then places the other two on the countertop near the entrance.

"Ladies and fellas, this is something called moonshine, and it is the genuine article from the Twentieth," Reagan says. "This particular batch is from the area that used to be called Alabama. Vintage of 1983."

He digs through the drawers behind the bar until he finds a wine opener. Once he extracts the cork from his bottle, he passes the opener to Reid. He passes his opened bottle under his nose, sniffs it, and recoils with closed eyes.

"It's intense stuff, fellas. Proceed cautiously."

Reagan waves Reid over to the bar. Reid smiles and approaches the front of the room like he won an award. His steps are deliberate, not too fast, not too slow. When he reaches the countertop, Reagan coaxes him up onto the bar, a bit of nostalgia from the day he was elected as second officer of 20c.

Atop the bar, Reid gazes down on his people again. A larger crowd gathers at the word of the moonshine; members from the storefront and the game area and the music corner and the library and Alpha Omega are all there. Even though there isn't enough attendance for a quorum, the assembled group inspires him. He waits for quiet to fall over them. He contemplates what he will say, but knows deep down that he will say whatever he likes and that they will be captivated. In their faces he sees anticipation and admiration. When he raises his bottle they begin to cheer.

"Friends," he begins. "Today is a great day. For those of you who do not know, our sweet sister, Annabelle, has solved our days-old debate about how to reach the rest of those people up there."

He points with the bottle's neck and rolls his eyes derisively at the concept of people beyond the club.

"Annabelle, why don't you come up here," he says.

She follows the request, using the same award-show walk. Reid helps her up onto the bar and then pulls her close, squeezing her body into his, and wrapping his fingers around her hip.

"Annabelle here discovered the solution we had right under our noses. She brought us these E-Meters that we'll use to change the district and eventually the entire U. S. of A.," he says.

"It was nothing really," Annabelle says.

"There's no such thing as a nothing contribution in 20c, Annabelle," Reid says. "Here, we celebrate every individual for the great things they've brought to us. Your contribution will help us better this world, one mind at a time. You have changed our path today, so this first drink must be to you."

He raises the bottle.

"To Annabelle, and her world-changing ways," Reid says.

He waits for her to drink, and follows her immediately. Annabelle's swig hits her mouth and she gasps, closing her eyes, swallows, and then bursts into coughs.

Reid's taste of the moonshine goes the same. The liquid slides from the bottle into his mouth and hits the back of his throat like a bomb. The remnants that touch all parts of his tongue burn his tastebuds and make his gums tingle. He doesn't taste the alcohol so much as feel it happen to him. Alive, the booze crawls back past his tonsils and down his throat, scraping his esophagus while superheating it. Reid thinks of old fuels, the kinds that had nearly ended the world by running out, but which the world powers of the day averted by converting to renewables and developing tinier and tinier long-term batteries. Surely, that's what this is, an old fuel, something meant to catch fire and propel something else. The alcohol drops into his stomach and splashes around like ball bearings deflecting off each other and rebounding back.

Reid sticks his tongue out and feels the dampness glaze on his face. He feels pale, and by the looks from the rest of the club below, still waiting to drink, he looks it too. He gathers himself for his people. Then he grabs Annabelle and pulls her close to him.

She smiles at his touch.

"Just like the Twentieth," he says. "This stuff isn't for the faint of heart."

Reagan cries, "Hear hear!" and then drinks from his own bottle, recoiling again.

"Tonight we celebrate," Reid says. "Tomorrow we change the world."

The room erupts in cheers. Lower Tiers and upper Tiers united. Reid never felt like a winner so often in his life as these last few weeks. Every question he had possessed about himself wilts and dies on the vine, dropping to the ground and fertilizing his growth. Being the best cartoonist among many no longer matters. Being the best of everything, showing the world where it has gone wrong, that is the path to purpose. His Emu would become the best because it would shine some light into the mind of a pure genius, but it wouldn't have to beat the others who treated it like a hobby. It would exist far above them, light years beyond any place they could ever go. It's not even about other people.

No. It's about Reid. It's about how Reid has always been better and he was waiting for a time to show it, but now is that time. Yes. Now. Nothing can touch him. Nothing he has ever thought was wrong except for the few things that had to be wrong to get him to this place. In him, mankind is perfected. He is impenetrable. And to his left Annabelle is womankind rendered smooth as wax, impossible not to touch.

He drinks again, raising his bottle to Annabelle's so she will do the same. He grabs her and kisses her. She kisses him back. They drink again. And again. And again. And they only stop when they no longer remember what they are doing. The assembled club begins to blur for Reid. And he begins to blur for them. The only thing that remains in focus is Annabelle, whom he steals away with to the storage closet, whom he undresses, and with whom he has sex; ferocious, mindless, sex. They knock artifacts from the brown, wooden shelves. They elbow and knee each other in complete disregard. She calls his name. He calls hers. She cries his name. He cries hers. He tells her that he's known only one other like her. She coos and writhes. She applauds his power within the club. He thrusts and grapples and moans. When they finish, Reid and Annabelle fall to the floor of the storage closet and pass out, overpowered by real alcohol, and overwhelmed by their release.

The last thing Reid hears is Reagan singing a Frank Sinatra song about the future:

Given a choice I would choose to have a magic wand that I could use,
To draw a melody, from that enchanted blade of grass
And cheese and wood and wind and sea.
I would stand there, dig a grave, and quietly say,
Ladies and Gentlemen, play for me, play for me.

The last thing Reid sees is a pair of club members laughing; their heads visible, but their bodies obscured by Annabelle's breasts. The pass the bottle back and forth, their faces red and their motions jerky and chaotic. Other club members drink and stumble past the closet door.

The last thing Reid thinks, *I wish Xiu were here to see what I've built. She would be so proud.*

And then that song again, now in Sinatra's original crooning legato:

Ladies and Gentlemen, play for me, play for me.

13

Capitol Hill Citizenry District; Denver, Colorado; United Sociocracy of the

Americas

June 27, 2087

2:48 AM

A pounding in his head throttles Reid awake. His bleary eyes have trouble focusing. Everything is milky, distorted. His body is pressed up against someone. Xiu? No. It's Annabelle. He is pressed up against Annabelle, his left hand on her breast. His right arm is under him, pinned between their bodies and numb. He knows where he is—the storage closet at the club— but he has a difficult time comprehending the space. The light is different, hazy. *Alcohol from the replicator never does this*, he thinks. *That stuff makes you happy and nothing else. No bitter edge. No moral to the story*. He rolls onto his back and frees his pinned arm. He shakes it, feeling the painful tingle of deadness reverberate from shoulder to fingertips. Reid winces. He looks for his clothes and finds them rumpled beside him. His stomach turns and the pounding in his head gets louder.

The pounding won't stop. It is something alive—something beyond him. Reid feels like an exhausted smaller version of himself pulling madly at levers and switches, trying to pilot the weary meat husk around him. He gingerly removes his hand from Annabelle's breast and tries to stand. He stumbles, falling slowly toward the bookshelf. He tries to catch himself, but somehow misses entirely. His hands grasp at empty air and he's down again; on his back, on the floor, naked. The ceiling spins and the walls undulate. *I don't understand this*, he thinks. *What is this feeling?* Meanwhile the pounding in his head is even louder, getting closer than he thought possible. Reid gathers himself again and stands. His weight swings back into the shelf, but he catches himself this time. He kneels to his clothes, collects them, and tries to put on his pants.

Lining up his leg proves more difficult than standing, but Reid braces himself against the shelf. First leg. Switch arms for bracing. Second leg. He pulls up his pants and buttons them. Now he gathers his shirt and pops his head through the neckline, and puts both arms through. It's backwards. Arms pull back, shirt rotates, and arms back through. Reid looks for his shoes, but they are tangled with Annabelle. She hasn't moved. The pounding grows louder. *Why isn't she moving?* Reid kneels beside her and holds his palm under her nose. There's breath. His head throbs again, like a baby bird is inside smashing its knobby beak against his skull, trying to escape. He stays over her, brushing her hair back away from her face. *She's just asleep*, he thinks. *Maybe she's a hard sleeper.* He watches her chest rise and fall again, and then forces himself to stand. He pulls open the door to the storage closet, wincing again at the activity.

The main room of the club is littered with passed out bodies. Four club members are piled on the couches near the games, naked, entwined. There is vomit on the floor around them. Three more club members are sleeping beneath and wargames table. Six club members are around the storefront, with three behind the store counter, and more vomit. Reid stumbles toward them and checks for breathing. They're fine. They're all fine. He wades through the bodies as if in the aftermath of a human flood. The steps required to avoid each limb, head, and torso are almost impossibly difficult. Each lift of Reid's foot takes moments of preparation, and precision, adjusted for his oscillating vision and the mushiness of his limb control.

The pounding sounds so close now.

There, by the bar, he sees Reagan, leaning against the counter, eyes closed tight, shirt marked with sweat—the moonshine bottle cradled loosely in the palm of his hand. Reid takes the bottle and sets it upright on the bartop. He puts his hand under Reagan's nose. Breathing. *Thank the Twentieth*, Reid thinks. He kneels before Reagan and gently grabs his arm.

"Reagan, wake up," he says. "Reagan."

Reagan stirs, his limp neck flopping his head from one uncomfortable resting position to another. Reid gives him another shake, repeating his name. Reagan shifts again, turning his body to the side and drawing his limbs up into a modified fetal position. Reid stands and stumbles across the human carpet, toward the kitchen. He fills a pot with cold water, and carries it back to Reagan's sleeping spot. Reid blinks hard, a film building over his eyes, like jelly. He blinks again and again, until the gunk recedes. *Something isn't right*, Reid thinks. *Moonshine*. He holds the pot over Reagan's head.

"Sorry, fella, but you need to wake up," he says, turning his wrist, releasing the water.

The lights in the club go out.

The pounding stops, becomes a rumble. The club door opens. It's too dark to see. *Something is outside,* he thinks. *A raid? They wouldn't. They couldn't.* Reid stares at the doorway, waiting for his eyes to catch up with the darkness. Nothing. Total dark. As if something scooped his eyes from his skull. Reid touches his face. *I'm still here,* he thinks. The rumble moves around him, at a distance. Not too close, but definitely in the club. It moves faster and faster, a swirl of rumbling circling him. Reid holds the pot, now empty, out before him as a weapon. He swings it back and forth. He turns and swings, and spins and swings again. Nothing, no contact. *Nothing to hit,* he wonders. The rumbling gets closer.

Closer.

Reid swings the pot again.

Nothing there.

"Who's there?" he asks. "If it's the security robots, you have to identify yourself. That's the law."

No reply. Just the rumble.

Just the rumble getting closer.

Just the rumble close enough that Reid feels it in his chest, a kick drum at hyperspeed.

Just the rumble brushing by him as a gasp of warm air.

And then stillness.

And quiet.

Perfect darkness.

Reid doesn't dare move. *I'll trip on a body. Why aren't they awake?* he wonders. *They must have heard that. They had to hear that.*

"Hello?" he asks the room.

"This has some kind of kick, fella."

"Reagan?"

"Some kind of kick. They say this used to cause blindness."

"Reagan, is that you?"

"Turn a right-minded man into some kind of animal right quick, fella. My great great great great granddaddy had a still in the mountains back east. Give you something to drink and something to strip the paint from a barn with in one bottle. Talk about convenience."

"Reagan this isn't funny," Reid says.

Then the rumble starts up again, right behind him. Directly behind Reid.

Breathing.

Hot.

On his neck.

Reid spins around, swinging the pot. Again, he catches nothing. No sound. No contact.

His heart races.

The rumble starts again. Now it's moving away from him. In concentric circles. Sweeping. Reid blinks hard again. *Why can't I see yet?* he wonders. *Why haven't my eyes adjusted? The machines, the stereo, they are supposed to give off light. Something. That rickety door isn't airtight.*

Reid crouches to the floor and holds the pot in front of him. He starts to cry, so intensely dressed in fear that he can't compare it to anything he has ever felt before. The rumble passes by him again, swooping just past his ear. He feels his hair stand on end. And then the rumble passes again, on the other side. Followed by bitter silence. Complete darkness.

And then a slam, the slat wood door slapping against the door frame on its newly repaired hinges, like a child's nightmare from some farmhouse from decades ago. They'd have thought, it must be the wind, but the child would know better. No wind does that. No wind leaves a room with such angry purpose. *It's something else,* he thinks. *It must be something else.*

"Reagan?" Reid asks again into the darkness.

"Put some hair on your chest. Unless you're a lady, fella; then it'll put hair 'bove your snatch."

The lights blink on.

Reid covers his eyes, blinded.

As his eyes adjust, he sees that the club looks the same as always. Each corner and exhibit and table is in its right place.

But the people are gone.

Reid drops the pot to the floor. It gongs and clatters, doing a half-turn before coming to rest. Reid looks to where Reagan was just sitting. Nothing. Not even a hint. He surveys the floors. Nothing. He checks in the storefront, behind the counter and in front. No one. The couches by the games corner are empty. But the storage room. Annabelle. No. She's gone too. There is no one. Club 20c is empty. Reid's head throbs. The room spins again. His brain is an amusement park ride whose teenaged operator has run off for a smoke break.

Reid stumbles and falls toward the wargames table. He catches himself, but barely, and lets his weight settle against the board. The door to the storage closet slams. Reid twists to look. A light flickers beneath the door. A blue light. Or maybe a purple one. *It's not a normal light*, he thinks. It's something he feels.

Then the door bursts open again, swinging fast and slamming against the adjacent wall. Standing there, just as before, is Annabelle, nude, holding the moonshine bottle. She pours the alcohol from above into her open mouth, where it pools and rolls over the edge of her lips and down her clavicle, her breasts, chasing the contour of her body to her toes. She swallows, and smiles at Reid. With one finger, outstretched and hooking, she beckons him: Come here.

Annabelle backs up, back into the storage room, and stops, and when Reid reaches her, she wraps her arms around him.

"Fuck me," she whispers.

She kisses Reid. Hard. Everywhere. He grabs at her bare body, caressing, stroking, absorbing her flesh with his flesh. The throbbing in his head goes away. His vision clears. He feels normal again. Normal enough. The storage closet feels too large. There is an echo of chatter and yelling behind him, out there in the club's main room. He tries to turn to look, but Annabelle's hand grasps the back of his head and pulls his mouth to hers. Her hand is in his pants. The chatter outside continues. People yelling drunkenly about the Twentieth. His hand is on her crotch. She writhes and coos. He breathes heavy.

Suddenly, Annabelle stops. She shoves him back a step, playfully, and puts her index finger to her lips.

"We can't do this while I'm still dressed," she says.

"What?" Reid asks. "You're already..."Annabelle reaches behind her head, just to the base of her neck and takes hold of something. Reid can't see what she has, but she has it. Slowly, her hand moves up her neck, up the back of her head, over the crest of her blonde hair. Then down her forehead. No. The red, bursting, wet. No. Between her eyes. Then down the bridge of her nose, and bisecting her lips. Pink, ropey, bleeding. Flesh and muscle and bone. And down her chin, straight down her neck, between her collarbones. The skin above, now loose, falls open to each side. Annabelle's skeleton, wrapped in bloody muscle, stares at Reid. No. No. Her hand continues down, between her breasts, her stomach, between her legs. And then the skin remaining falls rumpled to the floor at her bone and muscle feet. She steps out of her skin and kicks it away, as if discarding a pair of pants.

Reid stumbles back, crashing into the storage room door. His hand finds the knob. It's locked.

"Now that I'm undressed, you can fuck me, Reid," she says.

But it's not Annabelle's voice.

It's Xiu's.

"Come on, Reid," Xiu says. "I'm so fond of you. Fuuuuuuuuuck meeeeeeeee."

Reid turns around, and twists the knob with all his strength. He pounds on the door, hearing the chatter and revelry outside. He screams out. He throws himself against the door. Still, that form, bloody, ropey-strands of muscle, surges toward him; its tongue out and wriggling like a hypnotized snake.

"I'm so fond of you," Xiu says.

Reid falls against the door and covers his eyes.

"So fond."

14

Capitol Hill Citizenry District; Denver, Colorado; United Sociocracy of the

Americas

June 27, 2087

7:48 AM

A pounding in his head throttles Reid awake. His bleary eyes have trouble focusing. Everything is milky, distorted. His body is pressed up against someone. *Xiu?* he wonders. *No. It's Annabelle.* He is pressed up against Annabelle, his left hand on her breast. His right arm is under him, pinned between their bodies and numb. He knows where he is—the storage closet at the club—but he has a difficult time comprehending the space.

Reid pulls his pinned arm free and Annabelle rolls toward him.

"Hello," she says. "Does your head hurt as much as mine does?"

Reid touches his forehead, then squeezes the bridge of his nose.

"Probably worse," he says.

Annabelle gives Reid a once over, and adjusts her breasts with her hands as she slowly sits up. "At least we had some fun," she says. "I don't think I can touch that stuff again. Twentieth or not."

Reid sits up, and gropes around the floor for his pants, shirt and shoes.

"It's not for the faint of heart," he says. "It gave me weird dreams, too."

Reid stands and climbs into his pants, then he slips on his shirt, bracing his weight against a black bookshelf in the storage closet. When he has both feet firmly back on the ground, he offers his hand to Annabelle. She takes hold and slowly rises, gathering her clothing on the way to verticality. Reid watches her dress as Xiu's words from his dream resonate in his head.

"I'm fond of you. So fond."

"We nearly tore that off the wall last night," Annabelle says, pointing to the shelf. "Like people possessed."

Reid looks at the shelf and remembers her hands clutching the outer frame, and his hands knit with hers as he thrust his hips. He was sure those brown shelves would have come down, dropping artifacts from the Twentieth all over them; but somehow they held, even when she was lifted, pressed against them, half her weight resting on the wooden planks.

"Were these shelves brown last night?" Reid asks her. "I remember brown for some reason."

"I don't think so," she replies. "I wasn't really studying the grain."

"Fair point," Reid says. "I just have this feeling like they weren't black last night."

Annabelle opens the door leading to main room of the club, and takes a couple staggering steps through it.

"I still can't see straight today, from the booze, and maybe the other stuff," she says. "Maybe you've got the same malady."

"That must be it."

The pair walk slowly into the main room of the club. A few club members are still asleep on the couches by the games. There are two, sleeping head-to-foot on the Craftsman style couch with sturdy wood arms, one curled up in a ball on the Modern one, and two naked club members on the orange-and-brown plaid loveseat.

"Looks like everyone had a rough night," Annabelle says.

Reid stares at the couple on the plaid couch.

"You want to ask them to blend with us?" Annabelle asks. "It might take our minds off the pain."

Reid shakes his head.

"No, Annabelle," he says. "I just thought I saw something."

She takes his hand and wraps it around her, nuzzling against him. "Are you sure you're not interested?"

Reid hugs her and kisses her forehead. "Not right now," he says.

"Your call. We'd have a fantastic time."

Reid and Annabelle walk from the games corner, past the Omega and Alpha, to the fake storefront. One middle-Tier club member is just coming to, supine on the store counter, using the cash register keyboard as a pillow. Behind the counter, another two club members are naked, holding each other on the floor. Reid doesn't recognize either of them.

"Do you know those two?" he asks Annabelle. "Or are they party crashers?"

"Bill and Harriet?" she asks, perplexed. "They were here all night, working the store."

Reid remembers Bill and Harriet. They're a couple in their fifties who had just started coming to the club a week ago. Bill's great grandfather ran a general store in a small town back in the Twentieth. Harriet writes poetry and is obsessed with W. H. Auden. *That's them lying there*, Reid thinks. His head throbs.

"Reid," a groggy voice calls from behind the front bar top. "Is that you, fella?"

Reagan's hand clasps the bar, then his other arm follows, throwing his hand like a grappling hook over the front edge of the surface. He pulls himself up and offers Reid and Annabelle a weary smile.

"Did I have as much fun as you two?" he asks.

"I doubt it," Annabelle says.

"That stuff has some kind of kick," Reagan says.

"What did you say?" Reid asks.

"I said it has some kind of kick, fella," Reagan replies.

"I thought so."

"Is he being weird, or is it just the... what's it called?" Reagan asks Annabelle.

"Hangover, I think," she says. "And yeah, he's being a little weird."

Reid blinks hard and shakes his head, trying to jostle something loose inside him.

"Something from a dream I had last night," he says. "Never mind."

Reagan shifts his weight against the counter and grabs his forehead.

"Is it this terrible for you two?"

"I think so," Reid answers.

"There might be some medicine from the Twentieth in that storage closet," Reagan says. "I think there's aspirin or something like that. You know, assuming you two didn't destroy it last night."

Reid and Annabelle look at each other. She smirks, playfully at him. Reid raises his hand.

"I'll go check," he says.

In the storage closet, Reid finds an old plastic container with a red cross on the outside. A label on it reads "First Aid." In the Twentieth, people used to need medical attention all the time. Their bodies used to be unreliable and they used to make mistakes or have accidents frequently enough that medicines and bandages needed to always be nearby and at the ready. Reid could not remember a time when he wasn't near enough to a Doctor to repair anything that could have come up. Even when he was a young boy, when another child—Gabe Simone—hit him with his bicycle by accident, breaking his arm and splitting open his forehead, Reid was fine after a quick visit to the Doctor. His arm was sore for two more days. His forehead, so bloody and open, the skin peeling. Skin peeling? Xiu. His forehead was fine right after the Doctor.

Reid opens the First Aid kit and digs around inside. There is a box of small bandages, a dried out elastic fabric wrap with two metal claw fasteners, some gauze that has yellowed with time and maybe mold, a sealed oral/rectal thermometer, a tube marked 'antiseptic', and there, the mother lode, a small bottle with a crude picture of a head with red lightning bolts jabbing at it from above. The label says 'aspirin'.

Reid removes the bottle and puts in his pocket. He closes the kit and sets it back on the black shelf. *It wasn't black before*, he thinks. *It wasn't. Was it?* He goes back into the main room of the club and sees Annabelle chatting with four other club members who seem to have just roused themselves back to consciousness. Their conversation topic is universal. "Do you feel as bad as I do?" will be the phrase of the day, if not the month.

"I found them," Reid says, holding out the bottle of pills for Reagan.

"Good on you, fella," he replies.

Reagan takes the bottle and studies it. He pours out two pills into his hand and tosses them into his mouth. The pills crunch as he chews them. He winces, curling his lip and sticking out his tongue.

"I think you're supposed to swallow them whole," he says.

Reid and Annabelle each take a couple pills from the bottle and then pass it along to the other club members. Reid swallows the pills, taking two artifacts from the beautiful past into his body. He looks down at his wristband. No new messages. The time is now 8:59. He taps through all the listings on his wristband. The new trending stories are all about the global water initiative. A cat has given birth to a pair of kittens with perfectly mirrored coloration. USoASC, the United Sociocracy of the Americas Space Coalition, is launching a manned exhibition to Mars. Nothing out of the ordinary. Reid's head still throbs.

"How long are these supposed to take?" he asks.

"I think the bottle said thirty to forty minutes."

Reid sighs. "Well, people back then could handle a little inconvenience."

"Hear hear," Reagan says.

Annabelle raises a fist in solidarity, from the other side of the room where she and three other club members are playing a game of Parcheesi.

"I'm going to head home for few," Reid says. "I need to get ready for my date with Xiu. I'll be back tonight and we can start training on the E-meters so the plan can begin in full force tomorrow."

Reagan nods. "I'm sure I'll be having a nap here soon. Good luck to you, fella."

Reid crosses the room to Annabelle and kisses her on the cheek.

"Thank you," he says. "You're an irreplaceable benefit to the cause."

"Oh, I thought you were thanking me for last night."

"That too," Reid says.

Annabelle kisses him, and gives him a shove.

"Good luck with your date," she says, winking.

Reid opens the slat wood door to Club 20c and emerges onto Capitol Hill District's 13th Avenue for the first time in days. The hordes of Citizens commuting to and from Tubecar stations, chattering about their dailies and sharing their hobbies, smiling and greeting each other and philosophizing while they wander directionless and purposeless bother Reid immediately. He slinks through the crowd, across the street, and scowls at the robots inside the storefronts, restaurants, and services. It's harder for him to see the world's mistakes now, knowing that he is only days, maybe weeks, from shining a new light into it. He imagines that this is how doctors in the Twentieth must have viewed doctors in the nineteenth and eighteenth centuries. Looking at a world this backwards, this poisonous, with people who simply don't know how much they don't know about possibility—that's a powerful burden to carry.

When Reid returns to his building, the front door is newly painted. Something Reagan must have assigned to the Tier 4s. A sign hanging from the door says so. The paint doesn't look wet to him, but he hasn't been home in days, so how could he know? *The door that was once blue is now red. Not all change is noteworthy.* He goes inside and the light in the building seems different too, warmer than he remembers. At the mailboxes, the nameplates are all new too, except for his. It must be a new building policy. Below his mailbox, on the hallway floor, he finds a thank you package from the resort he and Xiu visited in Côte d'Ivoire. Inside, there is a custom videodisk of their visit, and a handwritten letter from the managerial robot expressing their gratitude and offering he and Xiu a discount on their next visit simply for spreading the word. Reid takes the box down the hallway, and passes by the girl who is in college.

"That *Origami Emu* is hilarious, neighbor," she says. "When can we expect another book?"

"Thanks, but I haven't been writing or drawing much lately," he says.

Not drawing for the unenlightened, anyway, he thinks.

"Maybe I'll work on something in September though."

"I hope you do," she says. "I'm really looking forward to it. You're kind of a genius. Okay, well you have a great day. I'm off to my fencing class, and then I am volunteering at the Animal Park. I can't wait to pet some dogs. They are just the cutest."

The girl in college turns on her heels and her skirt twirls. She bounds down the hallway to the door.

164

"She's barely even alive and she doesn't even know it," Reid mutters to himself.

Then the 144 year-old man from apartment 16 peers out his door and beckons him over.

"Haven't seen you around for a few days, Reid. Is everything okay?" he asks.

"I've been staying with Xiu lately," Reid lies.

The old man grins.

"Oh to be young," he says. "You know, when I was in my thirties, like you, I looked and felt like people feel now in their eighties. That's how people aged back then. Why, I couldn't have managed to stay at a woman's house for days on end because I'd never get enough sleep to work the next day."

The man raises a white eyebrow suggestively.

"That and the neighbors would talk and talk. 'He was with a white gal!' It was the Seventies and people still had some pretty archaic ideas about what was okay and what wasn't."

"Wait a second," Reid says. "Did you say 'work' just a moment ago?"

"Oh my yes," the old man says. "I used to work all the time in those days. It wasn't until, what, 2008, when I finally stopped and got on the old social security. 'Course, it didn't do me much good, having so little. Everyone was arguing about it back then. Kept me alive until gene therapy in '29. That rolled the clock back twenty years, and then the Longevity Kiosks came along, gave me another sixty or so... Well, I'm still ticking I guess, so who knows how many more I got? I heard from the feeds that a woman lived to 183. Maybe I'll get there too, but I probably won't be doing much by then. We all slow down eventually, don't we?"

Reid nods at the meandering story, biting his lip to avoid interrupting him.

"Part of me wishes I could have been born a few decades later, so they could've given me a longer prime, instead of just extending my snowier years. But those are the breaks. It's an amazing little world we live in, isn't it?"

"Tell me about your job," Reid says.

"My job? Which one? I had so many back then."

"Any of them."

"Well my first one was on an oil rig," the old man says. "Worked long, tiring days. Always dirty at the end and my body was always aching."

"Sounds great," Reid says.

"Oh I hated it," the old man replies. "But I will tell you that it was somewhat gratifying to work with my hands, pulling that fuel out of the ground. Feeling exhausted after a job can give a man a feeling of strength, I suppose."

Reid nods.

"Still, I am very glad that my working days are over. So many years of making things for other people, and you know I still had very little to show for myself until the Sociocracy came about. Back then, they'd have charged you the shirt off your back for a Longevity treatment and called it fair market. That's why pencils have erasers…"

Reid smiles at his neighbor, nodding, but feels his blood begin to boil.

"But you miss that sense of purpose, right?" Reid asks.

"I imagine I do once in a lon—"

Reid doesn't let the man finish.

"Say, I have to go, fella" Reid says. "Nice talking to you."

Before his neighbor can speak, Reid walks away, turns the corner and runs up the flight of stairs to his apartment. *We often can't appreciate what we have when we have it*, he thinks. *That's what's going on for him. He spent so long living in a perfect Utopian society that it became routine to him and he could only see the worst parts of it. This new Twentieth that we'll bring back will be better than even his, and that will prove it to him.*

What a great gift to give a man his age; the dawning of a new era.

15

Capitol Hill Citizenry District; Denver, Colorado; United Sociocracy of the
Americas

June 27, 2087

8:00 PM

Reid Rosales stands between the stone lions guarding the steps to Xiu Parker's Citizens apartment. He holds in his shaking hands a bouquet of yellow, blue, and white orchids from the nearby rare botanic conservatory and replicator. Despite himself, Reid did his dailies before leaving his apartment just so he would have the credits necessary to bring a gift to Xiu. His pulse races as if this were a first date, and he wonders how Xiu will react to everything that has happened over the last two days. The Gustave incident will be excusable, perhaps, and so will his dalliance with Annabelle—Xiu had often suggested that Reid be more open and less conventional in his sexual beliefs. But he had not messaged her back, not like he used to, and for Xiu, that was an insult of a high order.

He's been nervous about it all afternoon. He failed in an attempt to take a nap. His showering was harried and he obsessed over his hair. *It's all the dream*, he had thought, *but I haven't lost Xiu. It was just the moonshine.* Reid coached himself for hours, and nothing really helped.

Now, he stands here, between those stone lions, the ones they rode through a glorious rainbow firestorm cast down by angels while high on safe LSD. That was their first date. His wristband buzzes. A message from her.

"Be down in five... unless you want to come up."

Reid taps the message and speaks into his wristband. "I'll be right up," he says.

The front security door to Xiu's building is locked, and when Reid's hand hits the handle a red keypad screen appears in the center of the door. He punches in 4658 and touches the enter key.

A buzzer sounds, and the door responds, "Incorrect passcode."

Reid scratches his head. He knows this by heart.

He sends a message to Xiu, "Passcode is 4658, right?"

"No, 4568, sailor. See you soon," she replies.

Of course that's right, isn't it?

He enters the correct passcode and touches the enter key.

The door unlocks with a slow click and a digital voice says, "Welcome, guest."

Reid takes the glass front elevator to Xiu's unit on the fourteenth floor. As he rises, the view of foot traffic on Corona Street widens to the blocks of adjacent. A game of streetball is in full swing on Downing, the red team glowing and in the lead. On Marion, a crowd gathered to watch a nighttime showing of a film, projected against one of the older apartment buildings. Reid can see that every street, Lafayette, Humboldt, and beyond past the park, overflows with Citizens enjoying the summer night in revery. When the elevator stops, and invites him to exit, everyone below is so small that Reid can barely think of them as people like him at all.

He strolls down the hall to Xiu's apartment, number 1405, and knocks three times. He's thinking of that song about knocking three times that Xiu did a cover of once. His wristband lights up again. Another message.

"Just a minute."

Reid turns and looks down the uniform hallway. Like most of the newer robot-designed buildings, this one lacks embellishment, but does its sole job, being a building, perfectly. The lighting is perfectly spaced and shaped so that no halo overlaps, but every inch of wall and ceiling above a person's waist is bright. There are digital art-vertisements spaced evenly between the apartment doors, displaying works by masters throughout history, and banners for products, shows, and events in alternating succession.

Guernica.

168

Skyrunner II: Basses of War.

The Fighting Temeraire tugged to her last berth to be broken up.

Sistar 2087 Reunion Tour.

Xiu's door slides open, finding a hiding place in the pocket of the wall, and there she is, Reid's sweet Xiu, standing in the doorway dressed in jeans and a shimmering photoreactive shirt. She holds her hair-tint pen in her left hand, point at her head, which is half lavender and half metallic gold.

"Which one?" she asks.

"Definitely the gold," Reid replies. "As precious as you are."

He holds out the orchids, as Xiu taps the hair-tint pen to the lavender side, changing it instantly to gold.

"You're the sweetie today," she says, taking the bouquet. "These are beautiful. You must think that you're in trouble."

She turns back toward the apartment and walks inside, silently inviting him in. The door slides shut behind Reid, and the aromatherapeutic air in Xiu's place hits him like a tropical burst. Smells of blossoms, salty air, and maybe a hint of sunscreen lotion fill his nose. On the wall, Xiu's projection features a family of manatees slowly soaring through the water, stopping here and there to munch on tall, green sea grasses. Much like Gustave's apartment, Xiu's has a central conversation circle, that doubles as a guest bed. Her walls are pristine white and one-way glass, rather than exposed brick.

Xiu puts the orchids in a preservation vase and sets them on the kitchen counter.

"They look best here," she says. "I guess you can tell I'm on a bit of an ocean kick since our trip. It seems like that was a long time ago."

She slips from the kitchen back toward her bedroom. Reid follows her, trying to keep up with the beginnings of the conversation. Xiu turns her back to him and changes out of the photoreactive blouse. Her bare back stares at him. *She doesn't usually bother turning around,* Reid thinks. *She's usually just so open with her body, with herself.*

169

Xiu puts on a blue sleeveless top with one strap over her right shoulder. She turns around and poses. First, with both hands on her waist. Second, turned to the side with her butt pushed out and both hands on her slightly bent knees. Finally, with a finger to her mouth, shushing suggestively in a mix of a kiss and something more.

"How do I look?" she asks.

"Amazing as always."

"That's good to know," she replies. "I wasn't sure you'd remember."

"I am in trouble. I can tell," Reid says. "Can we talk?"

"We're talking right now, fondest," she says, sweeping past him back toward the living room. "You should have plenty to say from the last couple weeks."

"It hasn't been two weeks," Reid says, following her.

"Or we can argue," she replies.

Reid stops and takes a deep breath.

"You're right to be upset, Xiu," he says. "It's pretty fucked up that I disappeared after the movie night."

Xiu wanders toward the one-way window and looks out over Capitol Hill, a grid of glowing buildings cross-hatched with dark, crowded streets.

"I don't own you, Reid," she says. "You can do whatever you want."

"I know that, Xiu," he replies. "That's not why I'm apologizing. Besides, it wouldn't be a bad thing."

"To own you?"

"Sure, to know that I was yours and only yours."

"That's another conversation entirely," Xiu says. "You're not dancing out of this one so easily."

"Okay," Reid says. "Staying on topic. I shouldn't have disappeared. I should have responded to your messages. I should have kept plans with you and with Gustave and Selene."

"Anything could have happened to you, Reid," Xiu says, turning toward him. "There are still bike accidents and Tubecar outages. You could have been chopped up by some maniac visiting from a place where mental illness isn't prevented. I had no idea where you were, and come to find out that you're sitting in some dank basement playing a suffering capitalist from the distant past. It's hurtful, Reid. You hurt me."

"I see that now," he says. "I let my passions get the best of me, and I threw myself into something that was new and exciting."

"Everything is new and exciting, Reid," Xiu says. "Look around you. You can go anywhere, do anything. You won't die from disease. You aren't fettered by systems that keep you from doing what you love. Beyond your social life, you don't have any worries or fears. If we want to get Chinese, we go to China. If there's a movie that doesn't yet exist, we can make it together. I don't understand how you don't see that."

Reid takes steps toward her, reaching out to embrace her.

"A man without purpose isn't a man at all, Xiu. I've been floating through my life doing everything that I wanted, for more than thirty years. I want to do something that I need. I want to feel important and necessary. I don't think that's so wrong."

Xiu steps clear of his arms and continues walking toward the kitchen.

"You're important and necessary to me," she says. "I don't need some cockeyed ancient philosophy to know that I'm important to you."

"That's not the same thing," he says. "And besides, people did things the old way sixty years ago. We haven't lost ourselves completely to this oppressive emptiness."

Xiu taps at the replicator and a glass of red wine vibrates into existence. She takes the glass out, swirls it, and takes a drink.

"You punched Gustave because he insulted your club, and you meant it."

Reid sighs and paces toward the kitchen to close their distance.

"You know he's always antagonized me, Xiu. He had been asking for that for a long time. Just because he doesn't agree with my ideas doesn't mean that I'm wrong."

"Nobody agrees with your ideas, Reid," she says. "That's why they changed. That's why sixty years ago, people changed them. Your ideas were killing everyone, slowly. So slowly that some people didn't notice that they were being sucked dry by a few people at the top. Capitalism didn't work, Reid. It didn't. We learned about it in Fifth Grade History. It was a cute idea, but it was too easily corrupted. Absolute power and all that."

Xiu throws back the rest of her wine, tosses the glass into the replicator, taps the dispose button, and then keys in another glass. The process is instantaneous.

"This world is just as bad. Everything comes too easily," Reid argues. "And if the robots ever decided to—"

"This isn't some crackpot science fiction story, Reid," she interrupts. "Everyone listened to Hawking and Musk. The robots can't hurt us."

"Fine. You're right, Xiu, okay. You're right," he says. "Can I please have a glass of wine?"

She taps at the machine and another glass appears. "Help yourself."

Reid takes the wine and sips it. The replicator alcohol is missing the exact thing that the moonshine had bite and danger. The wine tastes sweet, safe, and even as he feels his mood lighten, his skepticism grows.

"I shouldn't have hit Gustave. I shouldn't have blown you guys off. But I'm not wrong to want something more out life than just being one of many. I want to be an individual among individuals. With real urgency to my life and real risks."

"You could go skydiving, visit the Moon, or climb the Himalayas," Xiu suggests.

"The nets will catch me, the dome will protect, and the camp patrols would never let me get into any real trouble. It's not the same, Xiu. It's just not."

"So you need to haul off and do something stupid so you can feel again?" she asks, facetiously. "How exactly does that benefit society?"

Reid finishes his glass of wine and taps the replicator to produce another.

"How do I benefit society now?" he asks. "I draw cartoons. I fuck around. I go out for food and drinks."

"You make people happy with *Origami Emu*, Reid," Xiu replies. "And you don't exactly take advantage of everything you could anyway."

"So I would walk into the mountains like Shelley and find my sense of self in a sublime experience?"

"You could if you wanted."

Reid walks out of the kitchen and over to the window. He taps at the window key pad and removes the city, until only the distant mountains are visible.

"I could go visit there for a day, with all the other tourists, and then I'd be right back here luxuriating among the sheep," he says.

"Sheep? Really, Reid?" Xiu sighs. "That's some disgusting shit right there."

Reid turns away from the window.

"It's just something they say at the club."

"And that makes it okay?"

"People should question what their government is doing and where their world is going," Reid says.

"We vote every day, Reid. *Every. Day.* And we all get paid from the economy we gave away so that everyone has an equal shot."

She finishes her second glass and sets it down. Xiu walks over to Reid at the window and puts her hand on his butt.

"You know, I don't even care if this is your thing, Reid," Xiu says. "But you can't treat me, Gustave, and Selene like we don't matter. I don't care what century you think you're from."

Reid turns toward her and wraps his arm around her.

"I can't. And I will make it up to you and Gustave and Selene just as soon as we're done with our plan."

Xiu pushes him away.

"What plan?"

"We're going to help other people see how unhappy they are in this world," Reid asserts. "We found these old devices from a weird religion and we're going to talk to people about the ways that the U. S. of A. is holding them back."

"Why would you do that?" Xiu asks. "No one pushes their beliefs on you."

"Don't you see Xiu? The Sociocracy pushes its beliefs on all of us all the time. If we don't start waking people up now, there might never be a revolution."

Xiu steps back and paces toward the kitchen.

"I don't like this idea, Reid. It's one thing for you who to follow your heart and it's another thing to talk about revolutions. People died in revolutions. Don't you remember History class?" she says.

"Maybe sometimes it's necessary for people to die for the things they believe in."

"Maybe you are spending too much time at the club, Reid," Xiu says. "Maybe you need to take some time to experience some different things."

"Yeah, maybe you're right," Reid lies. "Maybe I should put my focus somewhere else. It'd be unreasonable of me not to try looking at things a new way. You know I've been thinking that I'd like to go to the convention this year. Would you go with me?"

Xiu's face lights up.

"You want to take me to the cartoon convention? Of course."

"It's next month. I'll get tickets for us," Reid says.

By next month, he thinks, *everything will be different. This conversation won't matter. That convention won't matter. People will see.*

Xiu smiles and taps at her wristband. "I'm already setting aside the time."

"Look, Xiu," Reid says. "There's something else I need to tell you."

"You slept with someone at your club," Xiu says, still tapping at her wristband.

"Annabelle. How did you know?"

"We know, Reid. And it's not a big deal. It's nearly the 22nd century. Sexuality is fluid. People are animals. You did something that felt good, which you rarely ever let yourself do. Maybe that's what you really need anyway?" she says.

"You think I just need to feel good and that will get my mind off of all this purpose nonsense?" Reid asks.

"Don't put words in my mouth. I just think that you spend a lot of time thinking about what isn't working and not enough time working on what does."

She finishes her glass. Tosses it. Gets another from the replicator.

"What do you have in mind?" Reid asks.

"I don't have something specific. Just something for you to think about."

Xiu takes her wine with her to the bathroom and sips while she ties her hair into a ponytail. Reid stands in the kitchen, finishes another wine, and looks down into the glass at the imperfect, perfect liquid that doesn't feel like it should. He wonders if any of this feels like it should. Even this affair with Xiu, shouldn't there

174

be some stakes, some danger, some meaning? If she doesn't care if he sleeps with Annabelle or anyone else, if no one cares what anyone does, then what does any of it mean? He should feel cold and cruel for having gone behind Xiu's back, but he doesn't. There's no back when everything is just okay. Back in the Twentieth, when a man loved a woman, he'd tell her and he'd have her. She would say yes and then they were each other's property. Even though it didn't bother Reid to think of Xiu with other men, since they had always agreed on that, he feels like it should. *I should be angry,* he thinks. *I should be heartbroken that she's not heartbroken. I should feel something.*

"Just feel lucky that I'm not going to change again, Reid," Xiu says from the bathroom. "I don't know why, but I can't get my look down tonight."

Reid turns his attention from the wine glass toward the bathroom.

"You look interstellar."

"Then let's go as far away as we can, for the night."

***

Xiu leads Reid down to the street. They take the Seventh and Downing Tubecar to Municipal Houston, formerly of the state of Texas and the Liberated People's Republic of Texas, where they take another Tubecar to the Johnson-Lu Space Center. They wait in a long, but fast-moving line to purchase their tickets for the Lunargate. When the robot transfers their tickets to Xiu's wristband, the couple move into another line for space travel suits. The suits are white, single-piece jumpsuits with numerous refractory contact points that respond to the Lunargate and ensure that the traveler does not get lost between the Earth and the Moon.

Despite their one-size fits all nature, Xiu's fits her in a flattering way. Reid feels a bit lost in his, swimming in another man's suit. Once they are dressed, they receive their somewhat arbitrary crash helmets. A sign reads, "You won't know which way is up, so cover your noggin'." Then they get into the final line. This line leads to the Lunargate. People stand two abreast, stepping forward into a large, silver metallic doorway filled with warm yellow light.

"No holding hands," a robot says.

They move forward, row-by-row with only moments in between, until Reid and Xiu are at the front of the line. Xiu kisses Reid, awkwardly craning her neck to avoid tapping their crash helmets together.

"See you on the other side."

They step into the Lunargate, and everything inside is golden, warm, and peaceful. Reid feels like he is floating, not moving. He looks to his right and sees Xiu, floating beside him. She turns her head to the left and smiles. In seconds, another door, just like the one on Earth appears, its inside is dark blue, like the night sky. Reid feels the motion suddenly, the gate moving toward them, so fast. For a moment, Reid worries that he could miss the door, that the Moon could pass him by and he might just float there in the gate forever. But that doesn't happen. He and Xiu float through the door and land on the other side, on a crash pad in the Sea of Tranquility. Reid lands on his head, flops sideways and catches himself. Xiu lands beside him on her back, laughing up at the sky.

"I love that! Don't you?" she says.

Reid doesn't answer, but nods. His nod is a kind of lie, but he won't admit it.

A pair of robots shuffles over and gathers Reid and Xiu from the crash pad. Safely clear of the landing area, they change out of their travel suits and follow a series of lit signs and markers to the city, Méliès.

Méliès exists under a large dome that creates an artificial atmosphere potent enough to accommodate five million people at once. The buildings are all multi-piece pre-fab boxes and geodesic domes, those things that were easiest to transport thirty years ago. The city had remained nearly unchanged since, aside from embellishments like projectors and newer furniture. Reid and Xiu wander the streets, through all the visitors, and a few residents, until they find a restaurant called The Full Earth Cafe. Xiu drags him inside and demands a private dining balcony from the robot maître d'. The robot leads them to a small elevator, takes them up ten floors and walks them to a small five by five meter room with a massive window overlooking the Moon's surface, and with a view of the Earth, currently half-bathed in light.

"This is amazing," Reid says.

"See," Xiu says. "You can find some interesting stuff, even in an imperfect world."

They sit facing each other on a pair of couches around a large low-set table. The robot waiter appears and Xiu orders for both of them, not asking Reid, and winking as she does. She doesn't want me to lose it on another robot waiter, he thinks. Her eyes darting after the waiter as it leaves, and her bold laughter confirms his suspicion.

Their food arrives in moments, a noble, regal spread of French and German cuisines. Xiu tells the waiter to go away for two hours, and that they will need only wine, delivered to the on-table replicator, until she sends a wristband message to the contrary.

"Now we can be alone," she says. "Alone on our own little world where no one should be able to live. Isn't this nice?"

Reid wipes his mouth and swallows a bite of chicken bathed in creamy sauce.

"This is nice, Xiu. I don't know why I don't come up here more often."

"You're kind of boring, Reid," she says. "No offense."

"Well," he says, standing up. "Then I declare this place our own Capitalist paradise. We will populate this dead rock with people who want the adventure of colonizing and who seek the glory of purpose."

He raises his hand comically, like a pose from an 18th century portrait.

"I will be King and you will be Queen, and together we will show people the virtue of work, and of the self."

Xiu stands up and walks over to him.

"I'll show you the virtue of a few other things." She kisses him on the mouth. "Don't go disappearing on me again. Talk to me about your ideas, even if you think I won't understand. We got through it tonight and we will again. Okay?"

"Okay," Reid says, but a part of him knows that it can only work if she's on his side.

He kisses her.

Her hands grab his butt.

His hands grab hers and her breasts and then her neck and strokes at her hair. She coos in that usual Xiu way, kisses his neck, and takes off his shirt. And then she stops.

Xiu moves over to the window, the Earth glowing behind her, and reaches behind her head to the base of her neck. She takes hold of something. The image is familiar to Reid, but he can't place it.

"We can't do this while I'm still dressed," she says.

Xiu unzips her top and pulls it over her head. She unbuttons her jeans and slinks out of them, a snake shedding one identity and donning another. Xiu Parker stands there, nude, and backs up until her ass presses against the window that opens up on space and the whole of the Earth.

"Now that I'm undressed you can fuck me, Reid," she says.

Reid realizes where he's seen this before. In that dream. That stupid moonshine dream that was about Annabelle and Xiu and real alcohol and fear and everything. *It was just a dream,* he thinks, as he feels his heart begin to race. *Only a dream.*

He takes off his pants and walks to Xiu. He takes her wrists and holds them firmly, but gently in his hands and raises her arms above her head. He kisses down her arms and across her shoulders, along her collarbone, and down and down. He stands and lifts her to straddle him as he goes inside her. He keeps his eyes open, watching her face shift and contort in passion. Every time he closes his eyes, he sees that thing from the dream. That thing with no skin and blood. That thing that seems to be falling apart, disintegrating before him. He can't lose her. He can't watch her become some kind of monster. He can't close them, as much as he wants to, as much as it's natural, as much as he feels strange taking some advantage over Xiu, her eyes closed.

He lowers her from the window and turns her around over the table. He can't hear her moans. He hears the echo of those phrases. "We can't do this while I'm still dressed." "Now that I'm undressed you can fuck me." He melts away into his mind, lost in whatever dark corner conjured the dream in the first place. *She's supposed to be with me,* he thinks. *That's what it means. It must. Annabelle isn't the woman for the revolution. She's a shell. Yes. That's it. Xiu is the one. That's why that thing is in my head. That's why I can't stop seeing that bloody thing.*

Reid wishes he had real alcohol. That kind that erases the mind for a moment, taking intelligence while doling out pleasure.

"Is something wrong?" Xiu asks.

Reid blushes and stops. "I don't know."

Xiu pulls away and lays down on the sofa where she sat during dinner.

"Come here, face me, and that will help."

Reid complies, and in time, her coos and moans drown out the vile spectres in his mind.

They finish together.

They huddle together on the couch, side-by-side, catching their breaths.

"I had a terrible dream the other night," Reid says. "It was after I was with Annabelle, and we had drank alcohol from the Twentieth. In it, she took off her skin and underneath she was you, but without skin."

"That's pretty gross. I'm glad I inspire such romantic dreams."

"It's just, I didn't know what it meant, but now I do."

Xiu leans into him.

"What's that?" she asks.

Reid reaches out and takes up his glass of wine. He takes a large gulp and sets the glass back down on the table.

"I think it means you're a poor substitute for Annabelle," he begins.

"That's a given," Xiu quips.

"And I think it means that you're supposed to come to the club with me," he says. "I need you there Xiu. You are my balance, and with you on my side I know that our plan can work and that we can really change the future for everybody. We might even be able to keep some of your ideas since you really still believe in that place out there."

Reid points to the distant Earth.

"And I can protect you this way. You won't be hurt when the revolution comes. It's really for the best," he says.

"When the revolution comes?" Xiu asks, sliding away. She gets up and hurries to her clothes.

"Reid, I thought you were interested in doing something else, in dropping this," she says.

"I know. I lied."

"You can't do that, Reid. You can tell me some stupid shit, but you can't lie to me," she says. "If you aren't even just willing to take a break from this silly idea and spend time with your friends again, I don't know why we're even here."

"It's not silly," Reid yells, standing up. "You are mine, Xiu Parker. You are my girl and I'll be damned if you're going to call me silly and turn me down. I need you. I need you to make sure that I make the world better. If you don't come with me, I can't be accountable for what I do."

"Reid, this isn't you. This is disgusting."

"No," he yells. "This is passion. This is purpose. Are you going to save the world with your stupid cover songs and your slutty outfits? Are you going to change things by sitting around sipping replicator wine and changing the color of your hair?

"No you're going to come with me and you're going to join 20c and we're going to make everything the way it's supposed to be. You'll be proud of me and we will oversee a new district where people know how to earn what they take."

Xiu is already dressed and walking toward the door. She sobs. She hides her face. She won't let Reid see her. She taps at the door comm, calling the maître d'.

"What are you doing? You can't leave," Reid protests.

"Fuck you," she says. Quiet, steady, emotionless.

"You're supposed to be my perfect partner. We're supposed to change things."

"No. That's not how this ends at all."

The maître d' robot appears at the doorway and opens the private dining room.

"Is everything alright, miss?" it asks.

"Fine," she says. "Please ensure that the gentleman finishes what he's started before he leaves. I'll add another 500 credits to your tip."

180

Xiu Parker exits the private dining room and disappears down the hallway toward the elevator.

Reid Rosales, just climbing into his pants, tries to run after her, but the robot maître d' proves obedient and closes the room door, locking it.

"You heard her," it says. "Finish the meal."

Reid pounds on the door, but it makes no difference.

How did this go so wrong? he wonders. *How could she not understand?* Reid finally found his purpose in life and it cost him Xiu, and his friends. *Or maybe that's just how revolutions are meant to work. A true leader must discard their old like to begin a new one. Annabelle will be the new Xiu, that's what the dream meant. She was Xiu on the inside, all her positives, but Annabelle on the outside, smart and dedicated to the cause. Yes. That's how it is supposed to go.* Reid would be like the Buddha, casting off the world that he knew he had to save, a world of luxury and feeling and emptiness, and he would turn it into something better by creating purpose for everyone.

Reid sits by the window, trying to choke down the last of the canapes, when he see Xiu, in a travel suit, walking from the entrance to Méliès out to the Lunargate. Even as he knows that she's no longer part of the plan, he wishes she would turn around, just a moment to see him one last time. She doesn't.

She walks on, head up, shoulders back, hair a mystical gold.

She approaches the gate, aligned with someone else, and steps inside.

And like that Xiu Parker disappears from Reid's life.

He didn't need her anyway.

This was a kind of test.

A test of his dedication.

Yes.

If she couldn't be convinced, maybe trying to talk to people about the cause was the wrong path all along. The cute E-Meters wouldn't change people's minds. The whole process would take years, and by then, they'd lose momentum, and purpose.

No. Talking wouldn't do it.

They would have to do something that couldn't be ignored.

16

Capitol Hill Citizenry District; Denver, Colorado; United Sociocracy of the

Americas

June 28, 2087

10:12 AM

"Where are we going, Reid Rosales?" Iris asks from Reid's wristband.

"We're going to the club. I'm not going back to my apartment. It's filled with their things."

Reid carries a small container with his clothing, drawing tablet, an auto-inflate mattress, and a handful of paperback books he had acquired in stores and had borrowed from the club. He pushes through the crowded sidewalks along Pearl Street wearing a sneer. It was enough that his nosy bitch college-girl neighbor had to ask where he was going with the box. It was enough that the old man from number 16 wanted to tell him a story about his second true love, a woman named Scarlett who worked in a pizza shop. He kept talking about the feelings, but never about how having to go to work made the moments they were together even better.

"Potential software conflict," Iris says. "If another instance of my system is already installed at 'the club' an issue could arise that would impair both programs."

"I know that, Iris, that's why I checked. You'll be the only one there."

"That is a relief, Reid Rosales," Iris says. "Would you like to do your dailies?"

"No, Iris," he says. "I'm not doing them now or ever again. Fuck the dailies."

The Tubecar Station at 13th and Pearl is nearly empty. *Strange,* Reid thinks. *It's almost as if people are avoiding it on purpose.*

"Iris, is there an outage at the Tubecar station?" he asks.

"No outage has been reported."

"Idiots. These sheep can't think for themselves. One person probably chose not to go down there, to go to the next one, and they all followed. How happy they'll be to be awakened."

"Talking to oneself can be a sign of stress and/or mental impairment," Iris says.

"I was talking to you, Iris," Reid barks. "If you were an actual person you'd have understood that."

Reid turns the corner at 13th, and jumps into the old roadway. What used to be an eyesore filled with noisy commuters, smoke, and honking horns, is now an empty greenbelt with an unblocked view of the mountains to the West. Reid isn't going west, though. His only goal is getting back to Club 20c, where he can install Iris, set up his mattress in the storage closet, and sit down with Reagan and Annabelle. *I've been through enough in the last few hours. Xiu locking me in that stupid Moon restaurant. It took me hours to choke down all that food. That's what she wanted, though, wasn't it? To punish me for having different ideas. To twist the knife after she left.*

When the maître d' finally let him out, he had to run, weighed down with food, to the Lunargate; where they informed him that it was closed temporarily for maintenance. He stood there debating with robots for twenty minutes before he finally just bribed them with the last of his U. S. of A. credits. It disgusted him to spend their money, but as he floated through the gate back to Earth, he took solace in the fact that he was rid of that currency forever. He could rid the whole U. S. of A. of their currency once the revolution took hold. *And that revolution,* he decided, *would have to be a violent one. Citizens won't listen to anyone or anything but the Sociocracy, unless they're forced to.*

A group of young kids on bicycles zip by him on 13th wearing backpacks. On their way to school to be indoctrinated with all the sharing is caring, we succeed together, lovey-dovey bullshit. No one is going to tell those kids the truth. No teacher tells them that the incredible emptiness of having everything leaves us all as husks, without a sense of self, of individualism, of rugged, tested, human pride. No, their school will focus on the wars ending and the diseases eradicated and the art, music, games, happiness. They'll miss the point.

Reid nudges past a group of young women, standing near the top of the stairs to 20c.

"Pardon us," one says.

"Have a lovely day," says another.

For a moment, Reid considers inviting them to the club. He pauses at the base of the stairs to eavesdrop.

"I'm going to compose a musical of that Jean-Paul Sartre play we read in book club," one says.

"That sounds so interesting," says another.

"It's a new genre, a bottle musical," says the third.

"So it comes to this; one doesn't need rest. Why bother about sleep if one isn't sleepy? That stands to reason, doesn't it?" the first one sings.

"Beautiful," says the second.

"Lovely!" exclaims the third.

Reid shakes his head. *Idiots*, he thinks.

He shoves open the slat-wood door to Club 20c. A steady flow of Tier 4s and Tier 3s move through the space. Upper Tiers eat, shop, and chat. In the games corner, Reagan and Annabelle are testing an E-Meter, sitting across from each other on the couches. "(I Can't Get No) Satisfaction" plays from the 8-track in the audio corner. Reid nods to the pair on the couch and walks back to the storage closet. He sets his box of effects on the black shelves inside and clears a spot on the floor. He drops the auto-inflate mattress and taps the touchscreen on its outer edge. The mattress pops open into the shape of a single-bed, unadorned, on a box spring, with powder blue sheets.

"Iris, please install at this location," he says.

"Installing," Iris says.

"The following issues have been detected: projection interference may occur due to outdated electrical signal pollution."

"Ignore," Reid says.

"Playback of newsfeed and entertainment channels may be affected," Iris says.

"I know, Iris," he says. "Ignore."

184

Reid sets his books on the shelf. A copy of *Don Quixote*. A set of comic books titled *Watchmen*. *Capitalism: The Unknown Ideal* by Rand.

"So you're really moving in here, fella?" Reagan says, standing in the storage closet doorway.

"It's the only way we can do this right," Reid says. "If I'm distracted by that fake world up there, I'll be worthless to the cause."

Annabelle peeks into the closet, just over Reagan's shoulder.

"What happened in that closet should be distracting enough," she jokes.

Reid smiles at her.

"Good news," she says. "We've figured out how the E-Meters work, and which questions are most likely to get a reaction. It's a pretty simple logic trap, and we'll get almost every citizen we talk to."

Reid takes his clothes out of the box and lines them up on the shelves.

"We thought you'd be happy about that, Reid," Reagan says.

"It's great," Reid replies. "Thank you. I just don't think we can go forward with the evangelism plan now."

"Why's that, fella?" Reagan asks.

"I think we've been wrong-minded to think we can reach people by talking to them."

Annabelle nudges her way into the doorway.

"Shouldn't we at least try?" she asks.

Reid sighs.

"How many people from up there do you talk to about what goes on down here?" he asks. "I bet you can count them on one hand."

Reagan extends four fingers on his right hand and nods.

"Last night I tried to talk to the one person I thought I could," Reid says. "And you know what? She rejected me, our cause, and all of us. I just don't see why any of the rest of them would listen. They're all sheep. A bold idea like ours will only frighten them."

Annabelle hangs her head.

"Annabelle," Reid says. "Your idea was a good one. You couldn't have known that the situation would change. Maybe someday soon we can still get out there and use those E-Meters to educate people. I just don't see them changing a lot of minds, not when the people aren't ready."

Reid stands up from the bed. Reagan and Annabelle part before him, and he strides out into the main room, stopping beside the wargames table.

"When will the rest of the club get here?" Reid asks.

"I'm not expecting anyone until late this afternoon," Reagan replies.

"I have an idea. But... it's a bit tricky, and it might be smart to recruit the best of the group."

"What's the idea?" Annabelle asks.

"The way I see it, those sheep won't listen to reason, even if we offer it up to them on a silver platter. They're all too wrapped up in their music and photography and hair-tint pens. They don't care about what being a human means. We're going to have to do something that draws their attention. We're going to have to shake up the system ourselves and show them what they've been missing.

"Once we've brought the Twentieth back up there, people will love it again. They'll greet us not as invaders, but as liberators. Then we can use the E-Meters to spread the word, and help the last few people who don't seem to get it to understand."

Reid stands over the wargames table and gathers the tanks, planes, infantry, and boats into the center. He puts the infantry pieces in the center of the old United States.

"This is us," he says. "And this area here is our district."

Reid then lines up the tanks in the area that used to be called Mexico.

"This area here is the Lincoln Park District, and these little cannons represent the guns we need if we're going to succeed."

"There aren't any guns in the Lincoln Park District, fella," Reagan says. "They got rid of all the guns in 2039 with the Common Sense Safety Act."

"They got rid of all the guns owned by Citizens," Reid says.

Annabelle's eyes open wide. "But they didn't get rid of artifact firearms."

Reid touches his nose, using a physical expression that he saw on an old television program.

"The VFW Post One museum is in Lincoln Park," Reagan says.

Reid pushes the infantry pieces over toward the tanks triumphantly.

"Exactly," Reid says. "I propose that we go tonight, break in, and take all the firearms they have. With those, we can force the people, and the Sociocracy, to listen to us."

Annabelle and Reagan look at each other silently.

"The security bots will be all over us the instant that they discover the guns on us, fella," Reagan protests.

Reid just smiles.

"Iris, read line 37 of the Common Sense Safety Act of 2039," he says.

"Line 37 of the CSSA 2039 reads as follows: 'Firearms deemed significant to historical preservation shall be neither destroyed, nor chipped. Such weapons will be disarmed and left in the custodial care of authorized organizations throughout the U. S. of A. so that we may never forget their role in the formation, and near extinction, of modern society."

"The guns in VFW Post One don't even work. They're museum pieces that the security bots couldn't care less about," Reid says. "But to those fools up there, they'll look real enough, and they can still pack a wallop if you hit somebody with one."

"Okay, fella, so we got these guns, then what are we going to do with them?" Reagan asks.

"We cut off the grid at the district seams, take down everyone's dailies. Then we march into every restaurant, storefront, bar, cafe, museum, Leisure Park, cathouse, diner, theatre, hotel, and we deactivate the robots. Turn off their charging stations and in sixteen hours they'll just be mannequins. Then, we put Citizens, real life people up there, in their places," Reid says. "Every day they work, we pay them, not in credits, but in real American Dollars. They'll all learn the glory in a hard day's work, and in time, we'll have an independent economy that's the envy of the Sociocracy."

Reid takes out a roll of U.S. Dollars from his pants pocket. He fans the bills out and holds them above the map. Reid lets the bills loose and they rain down from above. The cash splashing onto the table, catching fine threads of air and skating around until it covers almost all of the map's North and South America.

"People are going to resist, Reid," Annabelle says. "What do we do when they do?"

Reid moves a group of ships over toward the infantry pieces.

"When they do we'll make an example of a couple of them," he says. "We'll hit them with the guns, like they did in the old movies. And then we'll drag them away. Once the loudest voices are hidden away, the rest of the sheep will do what sheep do best: follow orders."

He surrounds two of the ships and then topples them.

"Of course, I hope it doesn't come to that," Reid says.

Reagan nods.

Annabelle nods too.

"Let's not hurt anyone, Reid," she says.

"Not unless we have to," Reid replies. "And if we do, it will be a small price to pay compared to the freedom and purpose we're going to bring them."

"Well, we seem to be in agreement," Reagan says. "I'll call a quorum this afternoon and we can take a club vote to decide if this new course passes."

Reid walks from the wargame table over to the bar and pulls a half-empty bottle of moonshine from behind the counter. He draws out three glasses and pours a small amount in each one.

"I don't think we should have a vote, Reagan," Reid says.

"But Democracy is one of the founding principles of the Twentieth, fella," he protests.

"If we don't vote how can we count of the rest of the club?" Annabelle asks. "We'll need every last person if we're going to make this work."

Reid cradles two of the glasses in his right hand, holding the other alone in his left.

"That's just the thing," Reid says. "If we tell the rest of the club members our idea, we run the risk of another Quinn arising. They could sell us out to the U. S. of A. before we even have a chance to start. I don't want to take that risk. Do you?"

Reagan shakes his head. "I suppose that makes sense."

"And, Annabelle, the rest of the club members will follow us because we are their leaders. They know that we'll make the right call. It's why they elected us

188

to our positions. When they see how smoothly everything goes, they will be happy to help. And anyone who isn't, we will deal with at that time."

"Like the loudest sheep." she says.

"Like the loudest sheep."

Reid hands each of them a glass and then raises his own.

"To the dawn of a better tomorrow."

Reagan and Annabelle raise their glasses and tap with each other's and Reid's. They drink the moonshine, each grimacing as the ancient poison careens down their throats and into their stomachs. The fire sprints from Reid's belly to his head, wrapping around his brain. It only confirms the genius of his plan. *There is no reason this could not work,* he thinks. *All great causes feel this way when they begin.*

"When do we hit the VFW?" Reagan asks.

"Tonight," Reid replies. "I see no reason to delay changing the world."

"Won't we need more time to prepare?" Annabelle asks.

"Not at all," Reid says. "The way I see it, the three of us go to Lincoln Park District tonight. The VFW museum closes at ten p.m. We can go in for the last walkthrough at nine-thirty. Hide in the bathroom stalls until eleven, and then go to the arms and armaments exhibit at eleven-thirty. Break into the antique cabinets, take the guns, and come back here. We'll take three separate Tubecars so no one gets any ideas about us working together."

Reid feels the excitement coursing through this body like electricity.

"You shouldn't come with us," Annabelle says.

"I agree, fella," Reagan adds.

Reid sets his glass down on the bar and pours another.

"Why exactly shouldn't I be there? It's two districts away and it's my idea. This was all my idea."

"That's just it," she says. "You are the brains, Reid. We can't risk that you'd be captured. Or injured. Or worse."

"We'll take care of everything, fella," Reagan says. "Annabelle is right. You're our leader. She and I, we're replaceable, but without you this whole idea could just fall apart."

"But I want that danger," Reid says. "It's what I signed up for. The glory is supposed to be mine."

"And it will be," Annabelle says, laying her arm over his shoulder. "We'll get the guns and you can lead us into battle right here in the Capitol Hill District tomorrow. Getting the guns is a formality, Reid. You're smart enough to know that. Let us take care of that for you."

"Yeah," Reagan adds. "You can spend the time we're getting the guns sorting out all of the charging stations and the grid access points so we can shut this place down."

Reid sips from his glass and contemplates the offer. They could be right. Risking the entire executive team in one operation, and not even the final operation, would be foolish.

Reagan and Annabelle stand at the bar, watching Reid, hanging on his every word.

"I'll drink to that," Reid says, finally.

He pours moonshine in the other's glasses. They raise them and cheers.

"If you have any trouble," Reid says. "If you get separated, or if anything goes wrong at any point, you come straight back here. If the security bots get to you, you know nothing about this. Whoever is left, we'll come back for you."

Reagan and Annabelle nod.

"To the Twentieth."

"To the Twentieth," they echo.

Reid, Reagan, and Annabelle cook up a batch of old Spam and MREs. They eat around the board games table as the other club members funnel in from the street. Two Tier 2 members arrive and stock the storefront, excited to sell some calculators and old sports team drinking glasses from the days of full-contact football. Three upper Tier members crowd around the wargames table and set up their previous battle. Five people crowd into the corner and take out the books they've been reading and converse about them. They discuss *Neuromancer*, a book from the Twentieth, about a strange alternate future of crime and digital existence. Another dozen come in and take turns playing records. Four come in with crates of Spam and Twinkies and something called beef jerky that they've made by adding replicator salt to replicator meat. "It's kind of like cooking."

The assembled Club 20c hits full swing around six p.m. The crowd trade items they've made, sell each other songs they've written. One man sells a birdhouse he has made out of antique dollhouses he found in the Baker District. The sights and sounds of commerce all around. Individuals are doing what they do best, making their way by it, and remarking about the joys of tired hands and sore feet, of building and trading. Even the joys of bartering.

All of it warms Reid's heart as he sits in the storage closet on the foot of his bed, his open door inviting all the experience and any visitor inside.

Then, Reagan calls for everyone's attention with a loud whistle and climbs atop the bar.

"Fellow friends of the Twentieth," he says. "I need to bring something to a vote."

Betrayal? Reid wonders. *There was not supposed to be a vote.* He stands from his seat on the bed and starts toward the bar top.

"I know we decided to delay the E-Meter program, and that it confused some of you," Reagan continues. "But there's a very good reason why."

Reid pushes up to the wargames table, closing the gap on his would-be antagonist.

"Reid, my loyal, exceptional second officer, and possibly the most dedicated individual in all of Club 20c, has come up with a better idea."

Reid grinds his teeth.

"It's an idea so good that, I've come to realize something," Reagan says. "I'm not supposed to be your President. President Reagan sounds silly to me and that's because it is. I'm the leader for the past, but I'm not the leader for the future. Reid Rosales, that fella over there."

Reagan points at a now-relieved Reid.

I have to trust my friends, Reid thinks. *I can't do this without them. They're the only ones who recognize my genius.*

"I want to formally nominate Reid for the presidency of Club 20c, and I hereby tender my resignation."

The crowd of club members applaud, hoot and holler.

"I will second that nomination," Annabelle says.

Another roar rolls through the crowd.

"Let's vote on it," Reagan says.

"All in favor?"

A wall of yays crash through the room like something Phil Spector might have produced back then.

"All opposed?"

Silence.

"Reid, Mr. President, do you have any words?" Reagan asks.

Reid his heart warm and his mind racing, walks up to the front of the club and stands up on the bar as Reagan steps down.

"You should be my second, Reagan," he says. "Do you accept?"

"Of course," Reagan replies.

Reid turns to the rest of the club.

"You all know how I feel about this place and about all of you. I love it so much that I no longer want to live in that mistake of a world up there," he says. "I promise to give you all my heart and soul, and to do everything in my power to make the world out there as wonderful and perfect as the one in here. I am humbled by your confidence in me. I am honored to serve you. I am forever indebted to you all."

"But for now, I think we should have some fun." Reid takes out his U.S. Dollars and throws them out into the crowd. "All the fun is on me tonight. What kind of leader would I be if I didn't spread it around?"

The crowd cheers and chases the paper falling and fluttering around the room.

Reid kneels down to Reagan and Annabelle.

"Of course, you two go easy until the job is done."

His friends nod.

Reid climbs down from the counter and spends the evening reveling in his recognized greatness. First the presidency of Club 20c, next the leader of the entire district. After that, who knows? He fills his glass with something called Absinthe, dug out of an old warehouse in the middle of the New European Union. The green liquid shimmers gold under the light as he holds it. Or maybe it's just that everything Reid touches now turns to gold.

The last thing Reid remembers for certain is seeing Annabelle and Reagan off.

Everything is falling into place, he thinks. *It's never been this easy. Great ideas simply work, that's why they're great ideas.*

17

Capitol Hill Citizenry District; Denver, Colorado; United Sociocracy of the

Americas

June 29, 2087

2:02 AM

"Reid. Reid. Wake up," Annabelle says, shaking Reid in his storage-closet bed.

Reid's eyes blink slowly open, impaired by the absinthe that recently ushered him into his bed.

"What is it?" he asks. "Did you succeed?"

Annabelle looks terrified. Her eyes are watery. Her lips thin and tight. Her brow twisted.

"They followed us, Reid," she says. "I'm sorry. They followed us."

Reid jumps up from his bed. Everything he thought could never happen is happening. He feared that they'd come before they could begin the revolution. *That's how oppressive regimes always do it, isn't it? They find a way to infiltrate you.* All of the club members were now under suspicion. If they had been sold out, the U. S. of A. would take them and brainwash them all. *"You'll love the freedom of nothingness again, by golly,"* they'll say. And they'll strap the whole club into chairs and rip the passion and purpose and need out of them. *"Welcome back to the Sociocracy, Reid Rosales. We're so glad to have you again."*

He stands and grabs his pants from the bottom of the black shelf. Reid's heart races.

"Where's Reagan?" he asks.

"They have him. Outside," Annabelle says, shaking her head. "We were leaving the Tubecar station, we took separate cars like you said, but it was like they knew who we were."

"This is just like them. Just like they are in all the books from the Twentieth. They look like they're your friend on the outside, but deep down, they're tracking you, labeling you, watching you, holding you down. This is why big government doesn't work, Annabelle."

"What are we going to do, Reid?" she asks, her face twisted into a frown.

Reid puts on his shirt and smiles at her.

"Don't worry," he says. "Before I fell asleep last night, I found a book. Right in front of me, actually. It was surprising that I never saw it before. But it offered a little more information about the development of our robot friends. It seems that the charging station is their most obvious weakness, but just like anything, that's not their only one."

They walk out of the storage closet and Reid combs through his hair with his fingers, attempting to create an air of control and station before confronting the Sociocracy outside the club. *It's important to look important*, he thinks. *A being believed to be someone with power is as valuable as actually being someone with power.*

"Every robot has a logic chip that's connected to its language processor. That's how the robots can understand us when we order food, or ask for a room, or buy something. The thing is, they can only process so much information at once, and even then, they're calibrated to process normal human interactions that are rooted in reality.

"'I'd like a sandwich' or 'What a lovely rainstorm we're having' are things they can easily process, but something like 'Why is the sky so green today?' or 'The man is a giraffe under an iron sun' will cause a hiccup."

Reid strides toward the door, stepping around sleeping club members, with Annabelle in tow.

"It wasn't explicitly stated in the book, but my theory is that if I throw enough of these nonsense phrases, and unreal concepts at the robots at the same time, they'll burn out their processors and shut down."

"It sounds genius, Reid," Annabelle says. "How can I help?"

"We won't know if it'll work for sure until it does or doesn't, but when the opportunity arises, I need you to grab Reagan and the guns and bring him back in here. I will keep talking and keep the robots busy for as long as I can. If it doesn't work, you have to continue our plan. I have some notes with Iris and she's authorized to dictate them to you and Reagan only."

"What if they capture all three of us?" Annabelle asks.

"Then all is lost. The lower Tiers can't do it alone."

Reid grabs Annabelle by the waist and presses her back against the bar top by the entrance. He kisses her, and as she kisses him, they disappear for a moment into a warm, incredible place millions of lightyears from here.

"For luck," he says. "Stay behind me. And get Reagan. At all costs."

Reid Rosales opens the slat wood door to Club 20c and steps into the open base of the stairwell. He can hear the security robots, at least three, maybe four, at the top of the stairs, buzzing orders back and forth to one another.

"Citizen Reid Rosales. Citizen Annabelle Tkachenko. Please come speak to us immediately, regarding a matter of potential criminal activity."

He can hear Reagan struggling. Grunts and kicks and anger. Reid's heart races faster as his foot touches the first creaky step that leads up to the U. S. of A. His stomach turns. His face feels hot. For a moment he wonders if this is the end. If it was all destined to fail in the first place.

Reid ascends the stairs, his confidence growing with each step. Every stride reveals the secrets of the universe. All revolutions see blood spilled. All revolutions have their squares. All revolutions have their martyrs.

As he reaches the last five steps, the security robots come clearly into view. There are four of them. Each one in a blue uniform with a blue helmet. Each one a tin can on three all-terrain treadmills. Each one with arms designed to capture, detain, and eventually unseen by the public in some sound and lightproof place, to torture. Surely they torture to keep the people like him who know the truth from spreading it to everyone else. Beyond the four robots the streets are empty. Unusual for there to be no Citizens out wandering, especially with the number of bars, restaurants, and theatres along 13th; surely it's an act of the security robots, sending the only witnesses away to allow them full control over the situation. *What better way to oppress the individual than to isolate them so no one can see the extent of cruelty employed by the oppressors?*

196

The third robot from the left is holding Reagan, one metal gripper clasped on his arm, keeping him from moving. At their feet, laying on the ground ready to be taken, are the guns. Ten museum pieces, lined up, and so close to their rightful place inside the club. There are two muskets, and three Kentucky longrifles. There's a pair of AK-47 and two M16s, and a lever-action Henry repeating rifle. The robots are so cocky and sure of themselves that they've left them on the ground, barely confiscating them at all. *Just like the Sociocracy to believe that it has everything under control, to underestimate an individual citizen because its eyes are always fixed foolishly on the collective good.*

"I'm here to negotiate the release of our friend," Reid says to the robots. "I hope that we can come to a peaceful solution."

"**Citizen Reid Rosales, Citizen Reagan Mbanefo Webster** was discovered in possession of museum artifacts without authorization. **Citizen Annabelle Tkachenko** was spotted at the scene with additional artifacts. When approached for questioning the Citizens attempted to flee, at which time we deployed basic restraining maneuvers."

"Well, I'm sure there's an explanation," Reid says. "We were asked by the VFW Museum to take possession of these weapons for the purpose of a temporary exhibit at our club. We focus on the lifestyle and history of the twentieth century."

"Explanation acceptable," the lead security robot says. "Please present evidence of prior exchange with VFW Museum."

"Well, you see, I don't actually have anything because we met in person," Reid lies.

"All transfers of U. S. of A. artifacts are recorded by wristband by the custodial party," the robot says. "Accessing record bank for **VFW Museum Archivist**. No record found. Citizen Reid Rosales, please explain conflict between records and your claims about the nature of the museum artifact transfer."

Reid looks at Annabelle. She looks at him. He winks at her, a signal, one that she surely must understand.

"I don't have a good explanation I'm afraid," Reid says. "The mustard elephants rained electric to the crying vacuum."

The lead robot clicks and buzzes. It rolls forward on its tread about one meter and then back one meter.

"Processor error. Please repeat previous statement."

"I said that we're supposed to take the guns, but that apple chowder management heat ray folds salmonella."

The robot clicks and buzzes again. A shallow, small grinding sound emits from the machine's head section. There is a gentle whirr, the sound of a fan coming on, compensating for rising temperature. The other three security robots respond similarly, each looking to one another for some confirmation of the information, or some explanation.

"Processor error. Please rephrase previous statement, **Citizen Reid Rosales**."

Reid looks to Annabelle and smiles. He mouths "Now."

Annabelle runs toward the pile of guns.

"**Citizen Reid Rosales**, please rephrase previous statement. **Citizen Annabelle Tkachenko**, please cease advance toward seized museum artifacts."

"Let's calm down," Reid says. "It's just that the authorization for the transfer wanton mandible astrology tumbler trampolined over Jupiter's great Aunt Martha."

The robots click and buzz. The sounds of fans turning at full-speed spreads among all the security robots. They look back and forth at each other. *It almost looks like they're scared, like they were experiencing some sudden, terrifying break with reality. Like a terrible hallucination, a bad drug trip. The robots twitch and process and reprocess and reprocess the information before them trying to forge some sense from it.*

"No **Citizen great Aunt Martha** found. Processor error. Processor error."

The robot holding Reagan suddenly drops its grip, and Annabelle grab his hand. Together they gather the weapons and scurry past Reid. The security robots turn and try to reach out to detain them, but their metal grippers are opening and closely wildly, at random.

"Lemonade winter salad with two acrobat dinosaur archangels riding the leopard ocean," Reid says, taking a step back, as Reagan and Annabelle pass by him, reaching the stairs down to 20c.

"Processor err. Err. Err."

Reagan and Annabelle clatter down the creaking stairs, each carrying an armful of ancient weaponry.

"I think that you're confused because the marmalade carburetor triggers antediluvian Monday hamsters."

The first security robot on the left begins spinning madly on its treads in the tight circles of an old-Olympic figure skater. The second robot, the leader, shakes as if seizing, its eyes flickering on and off like a strobe light. The third security bot springs up and down on its suspension, its arms flailing. The fourth robot screams, in what Reid knows can only be a conditioned and programmed response to the extreme overload of its language centers.

"Err. Err. Er."

Reid turns to see Reagan and Annabelle safely inside the club's doorway, waving for him to run down and join them. Reagan's face wears a satisfied smirk. Annabelle's is a soft smile. Reid doesn't turn. Not now. This is his chance to make the overture of the revolution. *Only a coward turns away from the opportunity to demonstrate the incredible power one man, one individual can have to alter the course of a system that thinks of him as nothing more than another entity to serve and protect. All the others have always been so busy with their numb enjoyment that they never tested their might, and the Sociocracy probably counted on that never happening, but today is my day.* Today is Reid's day.

"Flexible iron porkpie doppleganger jam session."

The robot on the far left spins faster, faster, and falls over. Its head bursts into flame. The lead robot shakes and vibrates intensely. Its cries of "err" are bitter—pained and almost animal. The robot shrieks as the vibrations shake it outer paneling loose. Its hands detach and fall to the ground. Its head wobbles, pitching back and forth on a spring. Then the robot emits one last scream of "er" before stopping suddenly, slumping forward over its treads. The third robot bounds on its suspension and finally overreaches its capacity; snaps free of its base in mid-bounce, and flops onto the sidewalk in a puddle of fluids. The fourth robot falls on its side, shrieking, until its head, burning from the inside of its processor out, melts into a horrible skeletal shape and then drips away in a pool of hot metal and steaming ooze.

Reid walks over to the lead robot and kicks it in its torso section. He looks around at the Capitol Hill District, and sees no one. Not even the Tubecar station is active. *They can close down everything whenever they want,* he thinks. *Their power lies in controlling where we can go and what we can do.* He kneels down before the lead robot's head, cradles it in his hands and turns its face to meet his.

"I know you're watching," Reid says. "You always are, aren't you? Well I know about you and I know how afraid of me—afraid of us. You are. This is only the beginning, so enjoy your perfectly controlled world filled with mindless sheep to shepherd, but know that I'm coming for you."

Reid releases his grasp on the security robot's head, and lets it fall- linked by spring and wires to its body, dangling there on a broken neck. He turns and walks down the creaking stairs, each step taking him further away from the terrible world outside Club 20c. Each step a marker in time for the great change he will bring to the poor fools of the U. S. of A., ending their enslavement in lives of empty liberty.

He re-enters the club to applause. A group of club members hoist him onto their shoulders and sing an old song that was popular early in the Twentieth about him being a jolly, good fellow. And Reid does feel good. And jolly. His first brush with them was easier than he could have imagined. *All because they underestimated my brilliance.* When the group finishes singing they lower him down, and share in toasts and drinking and revelry.

"Reid, that was close fella," Reagan says.

"It was too close," Annabelle says.

Reid nods. "They weren't prepared for us."

"Let's wait a couple of days," Reagan says. "We'll iron out any kinks in the plan. Prepare the rest of the club members."

"It would be prudent, Reid," Annabelle says.

"We can't endanger the mission, not now that they have been to our doorstep," he says. "I appreciate your loyalty and your advisement. We prepare beginning tomorrow."

"But tonight we celebrate," Annabelle says, taking Reid's hand.

Reagan digs through the kitchen for more alcohol from the Twentieth. They drink and dance and sing. Reid feels that nothing can touch him, not tonight. The Sociocracy can have a day to lick its wounds, to discover its flawed security measures, to consider its inevitable future.

Reid and his new friends—his true friends—celebrate throughout the night. And when the sun is nearly ready to rise over the fake world up above, Reid and Annabelle retire to his room, lay naked on the bed, and make love until their bodies and minds are too tired to continue.

18

Capitol Hill Citizenry District; Denver, Colorado; United Sociocracy of the
Americas
July 1, 2087
8:21 AM

"Today is our greatest challenge," Reid Rosales says from the bar top, to the assembled Club 20c membership.

More than fifty people, ranging all four Tiers, fill the subterranean, vintage-coated clubhouse. All of them are silent, hanging on Reid's words. The only sound, aside from Reid's voice, is George Gershwin's "Rhapsody in Blue", playing in the background at Reid's request.

"I have no doubt that the U. S. of A. knows that we are coming, after the attack two days ago; when they unlawfully detained second officer Reagan, and forced me to use my cunning to keep them from coming in here and taking all of you away."

Propaganda is a valuable tool, especially when it is finally applied for the greater good. Reid knows that the complete truth of the previous night is less important than its essence. That essence is the dangerous power of the Sociocracy. The details are often dubious, anyway.

"You have all been assigned to a strike team relative to your skills. You have all been trained in your missions. You have all been assigned a subcommander. But most importantly, you have all acknowledged the danger we are about to face, and you have all pledged your greatest effort to our cause.

"In just a couple of hours, we will strike back against the oppressive regime that nearly brainwashed each of us into a life of complacent ease and leisure. And sadly, some of us might not make it back. Some of us will fall this day, and those of us who do will fall as heroes. When the history books are rewritten, let 2087 be the year when we took back humanity from the collective, when we wrested individuality back from the gilded claws of the group."

A roar rises in the crowd.

"Do yourselves proud today," Reid says. "You have already earned my admiration and my respect. Today we earn the respect of the people up there and of the Sociocracy. Today we show them what a man or woman can do. Today we strike fear into the hearts of our oppressors and usher the dawn of a greater future."

The crowd roars again. Reagan whistles. Annabelle claps. The music crescendos, with Gershwin's grand band blasting their anthem throughout the club.

"Now, report to your group assignments for final roll call, and may the glory of the Twentieth go with you."

Reid watches his denizens filter to their respective corners of the room. He never thought himself one for military service, even though there had not been country-based militaries for forty years. When he was young, the prospect of killing other people over land and resources seemed silly, aimless, and thoughtless. Now he knew just how wrong he was. There was nothing more gratifying than laying down one's life for a cause, and leading men and women into certain danger. *The violence was cursory*, and that's where he got it wrong in his youth. *Some blood would always spill over ideas, it was just a matter of whose and how much. The violence of war, of revolution, led immediately to the balm and celebration of peace. There were other routes, sure, but those were slow and unreliable. Nothing gets your point across like charging ahead in sacrifice.*

He climbs down from the counter and meets the first group, Grid Team, in the games area. There are twenty members to this team, the largest. Reagan leads them, and as Reid approaches, Reagan is in the middle of a rallying speech of his own.

"Each of you is accountable today, and each of you has a kind of absolute power and absolute responsibility. If one of you fails, we all do. I know that's going to feel like a big dose of pressure, but it's the truth, and I couldn't be prouder to lead you all. I have the utmost confidence. Any questions?"

One of the men seated on the couch across from Reagan raises his hand.

"When we've each finished disconnecting our part of the Grid, should we check each other's work?" he asks. "That could be a good way to create oversight."

Reagan looks to Reid before answering.

Reid nods.

"Good idea, Jackson," Reagan says. "Each of us will disable our Grid point and then rotate one point clockwise to ensure that the next point is disabled. If you discover that one of our comrades has failed, disable that Grid point and keep moving. If you run into trouble, hide in a safe place and contact me via wristband. Any other questions?"

No hands raise. Reagan looks to Reid again. Reid nods again.

"The security robots will show up, fellas," Reagan says. "They'll be dispatched the instant that the Grid points go offline, so get to the nearest Tubecar station and go to your safehouse once you've completed your task. By the end of the day, you'll be coming home to a new, better Capitol Hills District."

Reid raises his hand, and Reagan calls on him.

"I wish that I could be out there with you, on the front lines, personally cutting us off from the rest of that U. S. of A., but as my esteemed colleagues have informed me, my place is here," Reid says. "I will be personally counting on each of you as I lead the Reassignment Team in the final wave. Thank you for your work today, for your sacrifice, and for your love of the Twentieth. May each individual here define him or herself in honor."

The Grid Team salutes Reid with raised fists. "To the Twentieth," they cry in unison.

"To the Twentieth," Reid echoes, and then continues to the second group.

The Grid Team will disconnect the Capitol Hill District from the rest of the Sociocracy by deactivating, then sabotaging twenty-one optic cable mainlines around the outer circle of the district. The Robotics Team, led by Annabelle, will enter each shop, bar, restaurant, and anywhere else there are active robot staff, to disable their charging stations, which will in turn, disable the robots.

"Enter each location on your list," Annabelle says. "Everyone has their lists, right?"

Each of the group of fifteen holds up their wristbands, with their assigned list up on the screen.

"Good," Annabelle continues. "Enter each location on your list, follow the attached maps to find the charging stations, and insert one of these into each of the two contact ports per station."

Annabelle holds up a pair of old United States pennies, emblazoned with former president Abraham Lincoln.

"Don't worry," she continues. "The one-cent piece won't cause sparks or alert the robots to what you've done. You just have to walk out like nothing has happened and move onto your next target. But be ready because the robots will ask, and then insist on helping you, and they might inquire as to why you're into an area usually not entered by the public. You need to ignore their questions and proceed with the mission. Do not order a drink. Resist the urge to be civil. They are your enemies, whether they know it or not.

"Timing is essential here, folks. The robots work and charge on eight hour shifts. We need to get them down quickly so that the final team can get moving sixteen hours later. That's why the list is systematic. We're sweeping through, so the Reassignment Team knows where to start. Let's not let them down."

"Anything to add, President Rosales?" she asks Reid, standing over her shoulder.

"You've covered most of it, I think," he says. "Remember Robotics Team, that these machines are tools of our oppressors. That makes our use of these old metal coins even more significant. You see, Lincoln once freed the slaves of America from their shackles, and today you are going to free a new generation of slaves from theirs. Once you've disabled each charging station on your list, your work is done, and you can return here to join me on the Reassignment Team, or you can simply celebrate your contribution to the greater good."

"I'll be joining you for the main event," Annabelle says. "I wouldn't miss it."

Reid smiles at her. He places his hand on her shoulder, not as a general, but as a lover.

"May we all possess your continued passion for the cause," he says. "To the Twentieth."

The group, Annabelle included, returns, "To the Twentieth."

Reid meets with the remaining club members, all huddled by the storefront and wargames table. As he approaches they stiffen up, standing at attention like soldiers once did.

"Reassignment Team, we have possibly the most difficult task ahead of us," he begins. "First, we have to wait, standing pat here until I hear back from the other team leaders. Second, when it is our time to shine, we must be decisive, and unyielding. Those people up there aren't in their right minds. And what's worse, they don't know that. They think that their world of shared capital, creativity, and freedom of leisure is the paramount of human society. They believe that being able to wake up whenever one chooses, and spending one's days doing whatever one pleases are the highest use of mankind and *the* greatest expression of individual liberty."

"They are wrong. They are empty things lost in their own reflections. They do not grasp how much better a person becomes when their desires, their happiness, their needs, go unmet unless they earn them. That struggle—the permanent toil to better oneself, and rise up in the ranks of humanity—is the only thing that makes humans great, and they have lost it."

"Being free to do anything you want without consequence or responsibility because the Sociocracy provides for you is not freedom at all. It's Hell. Yes, I said it. It's Hell. That place wherein you suffer for eternity. The U. S. of A., this thing that gives every person everything they need simply because it can, is our suffering. It chains us to lives of creativity, sex, and relaxation, but I ask, is that why we came together to build societies? Did we join together to make our lives easier, or did we—back in that forest or cave or field—come together to struggle together, to face off against the elements and each other, together, as it was always meant to be?"

"I say it was the latter. I say that we are here to fight for greatness, and anything, no matter how perfect-seeming, that gives us happiness we haven't earned, is bullshit," Reid says. He paces among them and continues his speech.

"Before tomorrow dawns, we will have set the table for humanity's future—and our grand experiment will prove to the world that there's nothing so wonderful as people pushing each other to do more, infinitely more, than their best, just to survive.

"If any of you has even the slightest doubt that this is the correct path for the future of humanity, speak now, and show your disgusting cowardice to your former friends."

Reid stops before one of the club members and positions his face uncomfortably close to the other's. When the member doesn't crack he moves through the crowd. *Intimidation is a display of power*, he thinks. *Intimidation is the natural law. The lion in the wild claims its crown not by showing the other lions how thoughtful he can be, but by smacking down those lions that question him. Come at me*, he thinks, staring at another club member. *Come at me and see what happens.*

Not one of the Reassignment Team members balks, blinks, shakes, or objects. They stand. Rapt, at attention.

"When we go out there, people will resist us. People will say 'I don't need to work. The robots will do it.' and we will reply, 'If you don't need to work, you don't need to eat.' People will throw up their hands and say, 'You can't make me. This isn't right that in the second most prosperous society in the world, a person should have to toil every day just to get by.' And we will ball our hands and we will strike them until they learn that happiness and health and security are not rights. They are purchased through work and they are earned through playing in the system of Capitalism."

Just as Reid finishes, almost as if perfectly coordinated, the alarms on Reagan and Annabelle's wristbands go off. The bright, trumpeting tone grows louder with each cycle of three, and after ten cycles the alarm stops. Reagan and Annabelle stand and command their respective teams to rise with them. They come together in a circle around Reid's group, and all of them, stand once more together at perfect attention.

"That sound means it is ten a.m. on July 1, 2087," Reid says. "More than three hundred years ago, and three days from now, people first celebrated the Independence day of the old United States of America. That was a day when they took their future course out of the hands of England. Well, today will be a new independence day. It will be our Independence Day when we shake off the shackles of ease, excess, and laziness."

The crowd cheers.

"Go forth and may the Twentieth watch over us all."

Reagan and Annabelle march up to the front of the group and stand before Reid.

"You guys ready for this?" he asks.

"Ready, willing and able, fella," Reagan replies.

"I'm a little excited to tell the truth," Annabelle says.

"Good. I have complete faith in you both."

Reagan extends his hand, and Reid takes it. They shake, and then Reid pulls him close for a hug. Then Annabelle leans in to kiss Reid on the cheek, but he grabs her and kisses her square on the mouth. The kiss lasts a few moments before they separate.

"Remember, you have to stay in here until Reagan and I give you the signal," Annabelle says.

"It's essential that you are safe, and that everything is prepared before you leave the club, fella," Reagan adds.

Reid had argued previously with them that having not gone out to the VFW museum; he should have to take one of the greater risks, but again, his comrades had insisted that he remain safe. This was okay with Reid, if only because he could make an impact in the center of Capitol Hill District as easily as he could sneaking around it, or patrolling its borders. *It's a blessing to have friends such as these,* he thinks, *so much more helpful and attentive than the ones he used to have, Xiu, Gustave and Selene.* No, Reagan and Annabelle give Reid protection and guidance, keeping him safe in the club, and ensuring that his every concern is attended to. Before, he would roam around the city and the globe, aimless, with no one coordinating his whims for him. Now, Reid feels in charge, and independent.

"If there's an incident," Reid says. "You will contact me immediately."

"Of course," Annabelle says. "But it is imperative that you stay here, should anything arise. The future needs you more than it needs either one of us."

"And besides, fella, we'll be fine. They'll never see us coming."

Reagan and Annabelle turn to leave.

"Thank you, both," Reid says. "Annabelle, can I speak to you for a second?"

Reagan returns to the Grid Team and begins barking orders. The team makes a formation of three equal lines, with Reagan at the front. They file away from the games area and toward the front bar. Reagan turns and offers Reid a salute, and then opens the slat wood door. The Grid Team ascends the stairs in front of Club 20c and as each row of them disappears from view, onto the streets of the Sociocracy, Reid's heart does a drumroll.

"Annabelle, I'm in love with you."

"I'm in love with you too, Reid."

"You are? Really?"

"I'm surprised you couldn't tell," she says. "I wouldn't go maybe get myself killed for just anybody."

"You have to come back," Reid says.

"Don't worry. I'm signed on for a long time," she says.

"Signed on?"

"Committed," Annabelle answers. "To the cause, and to you."

She kisses him on the cheek.

"Now, let me get this show on the road. We'll signal when it's your turn."

"And you'll come back here."

"As soon as possible," she says.

Annabelle steps back from Reid and salutes him. Reid returns the salute.

"To the Twentieth," she says.

"To the Twentieth," Reid repeats.

Annabelle gathers the Robotics Team. They take a similar formation to the Grid Team, lined up as soldiers going to war. She counts off and leads them to the doorway. Then up the stairs. And as they disappear into the streets of the Capitol Hill District, Reid's heart beats like a drum once again, but the only thought on his mind is, *Will I ever see her again?*

Reid leaves the main room, entering his storage closet apartment. He taps away at his wristband, setting the timer for sixteen hours, when the closest of the robot targets will be completely discharged and useless.

He lays down on his air mattress, facing the ceiling, and stares at the infinitely textured tiles.

"Iris, read me the news of the day," he says. "I want to remember what the world was like before we changed it."

"There are three top stories currently trending in the feed," Iris says.

"Headlines, please, Iris," Reid commands.

"'Parisian Science Enthusiasts discover simple hack that increases Doctor effectiveness by 20%, human lifespan by 15%.'"

"Next," Reid says.

"'Miami Beach District opens first entirely underwater housing development.'"

"Next, Iris."

"'New Leisure Park opens in U. S. of A. promising experience of the twe—'"

"Enough, Iris," Reid says, cutting the computer off. "Is there anything interesting?"

"No additional top stories are currently available," Iris says. "Shall I repeat the current trending list?"

"No, thank you, Iris."

Reid Rosales sits up and takes a book from the black shelf across from him—*The Protestant Ethic and the Spirit of Capitalism* by Max Weber. He leans up against the wall, opens the book, and begins reading. The act is meditative. The words flow over, through, and around him. He is at once independent of the text and a vessel by which it takes life. His mind is alive with anticipation. As he turns the pages, he fights the urge to look down at the timer on his wristband.

He wonders if this is what the other greats of history might have felt before going to war, before making a world altering speech, before setting fire to the bridges that linked them to the old worlds. *There is no better way to calm the spirit than to turn one's mind to learning*, Reid thinks. *We should all be so lucky as to*

expand our minds every time the world seems too small or too easily understood.
After all, knowledge is power.

19

Capitol Hill Citizenry District; Denver, Colorado; United Sociocracy of the

Americas

July 2, 2087

2:00 AM

Reid's wristband bursts into song. He sits up so fast that stars fill his eyes. Destiny sometimes comes by way of an alarm. Destiny sometimes sounds like "Back in the Saddle Again." Reid lies back on the mattress and taps furiously at his wristband. No messages have arrived yet, but that doesn't mean anything. The strike teams were delayed in their departures. Reagan and Annabelle wouldn't let him down. That's not their way. They are believers. They are true friends; the kind that understand you and agree with you, and bolster you with the praise your genius deserves.

He retrieves his drawing tablet from the shelf next to his mattress and scrolls through the remaining illustrations. At one point, he believed that *Origami Emu* was the pinnacle of his creative ability, and the greatest contribution he could make to the world. The idea that a cartoon could ever matter so much to anyone, or that he could be the one piloting such a magnificent success in the twisted system up there was now humorous. What a cruel joke, to offer each person the keys to do whatever their heart desires. Reid Rosales begins with the first comic on his tablet, an illustration of Origami Emu battling Foil Swan in a traditional Japanese tea garden. The image is considered a classic among collectors and fans. He looks at his work one last time and deletes it, tapping firmly at the icon demanding that he confirm his choice, or rectify his mistake. *If only life had such a button.* Are you sure? *Yes. No.* There could be satisfying finality to action.

The first Origami Emu disappears, the original gone, leaving only those copies floating in the technological ether. Reid plunders the rest of his original creations, too, viewing them as a grieving widow might, one last time; before sending the corpus, but not its memory, into the incinerator to be turned to ash. Throughout the process, the culling of his last ties to the world before, Reid checks his wristband, and begins to worry. *Something must be wrong*, he thinks. *They can't be a half-hour behind schedule. No. Patience. They will do right by me.*

When the last Origami Emu is gone, Reid opens the drawing program and starts something new. He draws a field of familiar buildings, landmarks of the Capitol Hill District. They are dull gray, cold, and oppressive. He mottles the sky with oranges and pinks—the bright, colorful glory of the rising sun. In the foreground he sketches a pile of wrecked and wrought metal, limbs and torsos; a pile, nay, a burial mound of robots towering from the base of the image. Atop the scrap mountain, Reid draws the Origami Emu, once more, reinvented. No longer the harmless, charming, comedic protagonist. Gone is the slapstick. Gone is the jovial clumsiness and the well-meaning accommodation. The new Origami Emu stands proud on the bodies of the fallen robots, one large foot planted on the disembodied head of a fallen machine. In one winged hand, Reid draws a Kentucky longrifle—which Reid intends to take as his own—and in the other, a flag for the new Capitalist utopia that his revolution will bring.

He borrows from the flag of the U. S. of A., keeping the large field of blue stars, each representing the countries and states from the northern edge of Canada, down to the tip of Patagonia, and the quartile of the Antarctica Confederacy. Instead of placing the stars in a field of white, Reid chooses a field of gold. In red he adds one star to the center of the banner, much larger than the rest, gilded with piping and inscribed with the phrase: *Mankind is not an entity, not an organism, or a coral bush.* He adds more gold piping to the flags edges, to mark the prosperity that comes not merely financial, but to the soul, when an individual gains purpose and understands the twin glories of struggle and sacrifice.

Reid Rosales finalizes the details of the illustration, fills the image with oil paint-like tones that embolden the already powerful image. An image that will no doubt become a poster of the new world. The Origami Emu, holding his weapon—his license—and waving their banner atop the desiccated corpses of the dead system. It was an image that would go down in history, that would transcend time, that would be truly immortal. In the bottom left corner, he writes: "Originality Emu #1." In the bottom right corner, Reid signs it: President Reid Rosales, July 2, 2087.

Still no messages. Reid taps at his wristband again. Fear rises in him. It is nearly three a.m. *They are an hour behind schedule. I should have received something by now.*

"Iris," he says. "Local news, please."

Iris does not respond.

"Iris," Reid repeats. "Local news, please."

Finally her voice: "I am sorry, Reid Rosales. There is no connection to the U. S. of A. information grid at this time. Please try again later."

No connection to the grid? Reagan did it. He must have. But why hasn't he reported back in? And then as if on cue, Reid's wristband lights up with a message from Reagan.

"Mission accomplished, fella," he says.

"Is everything okay?" Reid replies. "You had me concerned."

"Hit a small snag at the connection point between here and Cherry Creek District," Reagan replies. "Had to have a couple bodies there to completely disable it. Everything is fine now. All Grid Team members are Tubecar bound to safe locations."

"You've done well, Reagan," Reid says. "Thank you. I trust you're en route to your safe house as well."

"Affirmative, fella," Reagan says. "I'll return in a week, as planned, to help with the transition."

"Have you heard from Annabelle yet?"

"No, but she's almost definitely done by now," Reagan replies.

And again, as if on cue, Annabelle's message comes through on Reid's wristband.

"Sorry for the delay, Mr. President," she says. "The last charging station has been pennied. Robots are running down all over the city. You should see it. Bar hoppers are replicating their own drinks. There's a lot of confusion up here."

Reid taps a quick, repeated message of thanks to Reagan, before turning his attention to Annabelle.

"Glad you're safe," he replies. "Get back here as soon as possible. You deserve a stiff drink and a good rest."

"Wish there were time for a stiff something else," Annabelle replies. "But you have important work to do. Please just stick to the route we planned out. There's no telling what a rundown robot on its last burst of power might do. We have to keep you safe."

Reid smiles. *So protective. There is nothing more affectionate than concern, from one individual to another.*

"I will assemble my team and depart immediately," Reid replies. "By this time tomorrow, we will be together again, in embrace, as liberators of the old world, and creators of the new."

"Going to lay low, and get back as soon as I can," Annabelle says. "I love you. Remember to stick to the route."

"I will," Reid replies. "I love you."

***

Reid Rosales and his assembled mini-army of Club 20c members—the Reassignment Team—slowly ascend the stairs from their glorious paradise, up to the chaotic repugnance that will soon know the grace of the past. He grasps his defunct and useless Kentucky longrifle, taking each step with relish, and listening for signs of trouble. Without the Grid connections, the U. S. of A. should not even know that they are there. Capitol Hill District is now under the purest kind of autonomy; sweet self-reliance.

He turns to face his team, taking the moment to record their faces with his wristband. Two team members carry other inoperative guns, and the rest carry large briefcases. It is a sight to behold to be sure. *History will be made today and these men and women are no different than the boys crammed onto boats landing at Normandy, or the wild-eyed hippies who marched all over the old United States of America to demand the upholding of individual culture, beyond even individual freedom,* he thinks.

"Smile, friends," he says to them. "Today is the first day of a new era."

Reid takes multiple images and records a few moments of video. Something to show Reagan and Annabelle, as well.

The Reassignment Team reaches the top of the stairs and Reid gazes up and down 13th Avenue. Two blocks to the east there is a pop-up party city, a makeshift assembly of tents and basic structures. It looks abandoned, missing the hordes who usually dance about while indulging in all manners of safe drug and alcohol. *Those shops always have robot contingents, too, which means that it has either been deactivated, or simply evacuated.*

"Team, hold here," Reid says. "I'm going to investigate that structure."

Two of the team members join him, ignoring his order to go it alone. Reid considers putting them in their places, but decides that it is probably best to have backup. He does not need a keeper, but it would be foolish to go it alone.

The entrance to pop-up party city looks like something out of an old war book or concert video. Replicated cups are strewn all over, most crumpled and discarded on the ground. Reid uses the barrel of his longrifle to open the draping canvas door of the first tent. Inside, there are more empty cups and containers on the pavement, the kinds of trash that a sanitation robot would usually gather up and disassemble in one of the replicators. The first tent is designed to match an undersea theme. It is abandoned and quiet, probably happening sometime around when its robots lost the last of their charges. The interior walls are blue, and an array of projectors display layers of water-like overlay into the air. Dolphins, sharks, fish, manta rays, whales, all swim by them on a long cycle, appearing to exist within the ocean that is contained in notable depth inside the tent.

Whale sounds pipe through the tent, but above them, as he and his two comrades march forward, Reid hears music, maybe two tents away. Caribbean music. *Reggae?* He flicks the canvas door at the back end of the tent open with his rifle. Another abandoned party tent; this one themed as the Arabian desert palaces of ancient Persia. The sound of a cruel sandstorm cries throughout the tent, and projections of veiled dancers appear and disappear, seeming to teleport all around the space. The reggae, though, sounds louder, closer, so Reid and his two escorts press on.

One more canvas doorway opened with the barrel of an ancient gun and inside they find a tent themed like the islands. It isn't abandoned. There are a couple dozen Citizens dancing to a classic reggae track. The gold, black and green lights wave in time with the music, and give the disordered swaying of the dancers a feeling of coordinated elegance. To the right of the dance floor is a bar, and behind the bar, to Reid's pleasant surprise, are two human beings; one man and one woman. Reid lowers his gun, aiming toward the floor, pushes gently through the sweat-covered dancers, and bellies up to the bar.

"You come from one of those reenactment parks?" the male bartender asks.

Reid looks puzzled.

The man points at weapon in Reid's right hand.

"Oh, no. This is a museum piece that I borrowed for a play," Reid lies. "What happened to the robot bartender?"

"Dunno," the bartender replies. "Just went all wobbly a couple hours ago and toppled over. Probably just in need of maintenance. You know how things go."

"So you and her are just serving the drinks yourself?" Reid asks.

"Why wouldn't we?" the bartender asks. "People need drinks. And anybody can use a replicator."

Joy washes over Reid.

"And how are you collecting credits without the robots?" he asks.

"We're taking transfers to our wristbands and sending it over to the robot economy at the end of the night," the bartender says.

"Minus a small fee," the female bartender adds.

"Minus a small fee," the male bartender reiterates. "We're not going to miss out on dancing and not take a little for ourselves. Plus, we'll pay it forward."

"It's already working," Reid says, absentmindedly.

One of the two escorts nudges Reid.

"What's working?" the bartender asks.

"Oh, nothing," Reid says. "I took some mushrooms earlier."

"Right on. You wanna drink?"

Reid shakes his head. "No, I think we'll check out some of the other tents. I like to wander when I'm high," he lies.

"Suit yourself," the bartender says. "The other two tents, umm, space, and what was the other one?"

"Rainforest," the female bartender chimes in.

"Right, rainforest. Those two are abandoned. Once the robots went down a lot of people scattered, looking for another party, I guess."

Satisfied, Reid turns back. He and the two guards with him wander back through the Arabian palace tent, and through the ocean life tent. As they exit into the middle of 13th Avenue, Reid sees a line of people returning to the reggae tent.

"Party's still goin'," one says. "Couple of people are serving drinks."

"Cool," another says. "It's like a house party, but out."

Reid smiles, seeing that human ingenuity and Capitalism never left each other's sides fully, they were only unjustly separated by the Sociocracy. Soon all those dancers and partygoers would be working in bars, and restaurants, at stores, and in theatres and Tubecar stations. And so would everyone else in the Capitol Hill District.

"You'll be proud to know that it's already begun," Reid addresses the rest of the Reassignment Team. "A pair of the partygoers share our spirit, friends. And they were tending bar themselves, seeing that their robots were down. Onward!"

Reid leads the Reassignment Team in a bold march into the first target on their schedule, the nautically-themed bar just two doors down. Reid shoves open the front door, slapping the door against the wall inside. A dead, lifeless bouncer robot looms over the doorway in silence. Reid holds his longrifle low at his side, an act of non-aggression, and stomps into the center of the room.

"The robots are down," someone says. "We can't get no more drinks."

Reid laughs, drawing the attention of the bar goers, who offer him only confused looks.

"You and your friends should find somewhere else," another says. "I'm sure they'll fix this place up by tomorrow."

Reid doesn't respond. He savors the moment of control and paces the room. Finally, he storms up toward the bar, standing beneath a busty, wooden, mermaid figurehead that hangs from the rafters above, watching them all; leading them from the drinks to the dance floor.

"Friends. The robots are down here and everywhere in the Capitol Hill District."

Groans rolls through the bar. There is chatter and dismay.

"No where else to go?" someone asks.

"I wanted to go to the movies," another whines.

"Don't be so sullen," Reid says. "The robots have been deactivated on purpose, by myself and my friends here. And your new life without robots is going to make you happier, healthier and more fulfilled."

Another set of groans, but now there's anger within them; deep anger.

"Now, now, friends," Reid continues. "Settle down. I have a solution for all of your concerns if you'll only let me speak for a few moments."

"Go ahead," someone shouts.

The groans and anger seem to dissipate.

"In the twentieth century, they didn't have robots to run their bars, or to do much of anything actually, but those people survived. And what's better, they thrived. Do you know how they did that? They worked. They used their hands, and they earned money. That made every day a mission to wake up and complete goals that would make the next one more successful. That's how they lived. And you, some of you, can start today, right now, in this bar. All you have to do is climb back there and serve other people drinks."

A large man on one of the bar stools turns around and smiles.

"That sounds almost like fun," he says.

"That's the spirit, friend" Reid continues. "Why don't you try it out? What's your name?"

"Jean-Paul," the large man says. He gets down off the stool and walks back behind the bar.

"Don't be afraid. You can just kick that robot out of the way. They don't have feelings," Reid says.

Jean-Paul nudges the robot aside, and then walks over to one of the women sitting at the bar.

"What can I get for you?" he asks her.

"A Dark and Stormy," she replies.

Jean-Paul smiles at the woman and walks over to the replicator. He punches in 'Dark and Stormy' and the drink appears out of nowhere inside the box. He takes the drink out and carries it over to the woman at the bar. Then he turns to look at the bar menu, carefully designed to look like an old chalkboard sketched in chicken scratch by some veteran of the High Seas.

"You owe the bar 50 credits," he says.

Reid steps toward the bar and raises his hand.

"I'll stop you there," he says. "Now, credits are a fine currency, but they won't do if we're going to earn our ways. So, I propose that you use something a little more individual."

Reid waves and one of the Team members holding a briefcase nods and walks over to the bar. He sets the briefcase down on an empty barstool, and taps a touchpad. The briefcase bolts unlock with a hiss and a subtle click, and Reid opens it before the enthralled population of the bar. He reaches in and takes out a stack of green paper, wrapped with a white paper ring.

"This is old United States currency. These are Dollars. And from now on, you'll be using these instead of credits," Reid says.

He drops the stack of bills on the table.

"They work just like credits, but instead of just receiving them for doing your dailies, you get them when you complete a task, or a shift wherever you choose to work. Since our friend, Jean-Paul, has taken a shift, I'm going to give him ten dollars. And now Jean-Paul can try to live on that ten dollars, or he can work more to have another ten, and another, and another. But I think Jean-Paul is special, so I'm going to pay him twenty dollars, right now."

Reid hands a twenty dollar bill to Jean-Paul, who takes it into his hand with a broad smile.

"You think I'm special?" Jean-Paul says.

"It doesn't matter quite so much what I, or anyone else thinks now, Jean-Paul, because you have the most money. And the more you work, whether it's here, or somewhere else in the district, the more you'll earn," Reid continues. "And that means that you control your own destiny in a way that you've never been able to before."

The crowd is silent. Reid can't tell if their silence if from awe and admiration or simply from the confusion a sheep must feel upon first realizing that life as a sheep isn't the only one available.

"To get you all started, I will leave this briefcase here, and you may all take what you can to start. But remember that if you do not work to get more, that's it. You'll be hard-pressed to pay for food and shelter and all the things you've been so used to receiving for nothing."

"Wait," another man says. "We won't get anymore credits? This sounds like a terrible idea."

An antagonist, Reid thinks. He knew this would happen. *It could never be so simple as reasoning with these idiots. No, they'll never adopt something that's better for them just because it is better. They'll require convincing, of one kind or another.*

"The sociocracy provides us with a fair share of funding so that no one risks suffering and no one becomes so financially powerful as to influence the rest of the people," the man says. "I don't think adopting an economic system based on competition, that is inherently biased to parties with special access, is good for anybody."

Reid shakes his head.

"I'm sorry you feel that way," he says. "What's your name?"

"Patrick," the man says.

Reid walks slowly over to the Patrick. He stands by a booth opposite the bar, sipping a glass of red wine.

"Well, Patrick, I hear that you have concerns about the new system that is already going into place, but I want to assure you that..."

Without finishing his sentence, Reid smacks the wine glass from Patrick's hand. The glass tumbles to the floor and shatters, and a stain of red spreads across the wooden, poop-deck-style floor.

"Hey," Patrick says. "I wasn't done drinking that."

"Oh, I'm sorry," Reid teases. "Go ahead and get another."

Patrick walks up to the bar, and orders another red wine from Jean-Paul.

"That'll be, umm..."

"Six dollars," Reid calls out.

"Six dollars," Jean-Paul parrots.

"I only have credits," Patrick says.

"Oh, then I'm sorry, but the well is dry for you, Patrick."

Patrick looks at Jean-Paul and Jean-Paul just shrugs.

"Are you serious?"

"I'm afraid we are," Reid says.

Patrick storms out of the bar and into the streets.

"Don't fret, friends," Reid continues. "This means that there's more dollars for the rest of you, and more drinks. Patrick will come around."

Reid walks up to Jean-Paul and gives him another ten dollars.

"Nice work, Jean-Paul," Reid says.

"Thank you, umm, sir," Jean-Paul replies.

"Now if anyone else has any concerns about the new system, you can follow Patrick, but I really believe that you'll happier once you earn not just money, as Jean-Paul has, but my respect, and the respect of the rest of my colleagues."

Reid steps back toward the bar's entrance, and without even a moment of pause, the crowd within the bar stormed the briefcase, knocking it to the floor and casting the strapped stacks of currency onto the floor. They crawl around, nudging each other out the way, shoving, and tackling each other, just to get their hands on more old currency. Eventually, when the Citizens realize that Jean-Paul has slyly slipped extra stacks behind the counter for himself, they storm the bar, bounding over it and throwing him into the back wall. Jean-Paul slumps to the floor, knocked unconscious by the cataclysm, and the other Citizens pocket their earnings.

"Now, now," Reid says from the doorway. "That will be enough of that. We don't harm one another to earn our money. We work for it. As such, I'm assigning one of my friends to this bar, and he will ensure that you don't cause any more trouble."

Reid gestures, and the team member who had been carrying the first briefcase walks behind the bar and takes over serving the drinks.

"If you cause any trouble for member Esme, I will hear about it," Reid says. He raises the rifle and aims it at the others in the bar.

222

At the sight of the gun, the bar falls silent, and Reid knows it is from fear.

"And I will be forced to take further action."

He turns on his heels, and the remaining Club 20c members line up behind him, filing out of the bar.

"Make a note," Reid says aloud, once they are outside. "We must find a solution to prevent that kind of violence in the future."

"In the future?" one of the team members asks.

"A little violence is allowable in any Revolution," Reid replies.

Next, Reid leads the Reassignment Team to a restaurant on Clarkson, where his spiel goes over similarly well to the nautically-themed bar. Luckily, the people there are just so hungry and eager to eat that they were willing learners. He delivers another briefcase full of cash, and when no one in the restaurant volunteers to work, he assigns three of the team members to the roles, with the promise that no one in the restaurant will eat until they earn something. Almost immediately, a table of five stands and begins working in the kitchen and throughout the dining room. They take their money and the extra tips Reid offers them, and they beam with pride.

Reid and the Reassignment Team repeat their process at twenty other locations in the district. They bring capitalism to the bars, to the eateries, to the theatres, to the stores. Even the Tubecar station takes to the idea easily enough, though the two club members assigned went into it alone, cautioning Reid that the station is the most vulnerable place for him where the U. S. of A. would have the easiest access. Reid and his team leave each location having made one or two Citizens especially happy by rewarding their intelligent compliance with extra cash. The strategy proves unbeatable as even those who don't want to work discover that their connection to the Grid is severed, and that being one of the haves is more valuable than being difficult.

"There will be no more dailies," Reid says with certain relish, at each location.

When the last of the briefcases is opened and the last of the club members is assigned to a post within the district, Reid and his two guards, walk heroic through the streets, watching everything that they have created, and cradling their ancient weapons. They weave down Logan and across Eighth, they snake up Lafayette, and double back to Marion, and then somehow, without realizing it, Reid is standing in front of Xiu's building.

He gazes up at her window on the fourteenth floor, he knows that he can't see it even if he wants to. The light, by his count of floors, isn't on. Her place is still. *Perhaps she moved,* he thinks. *She would be happier somewhere else anyway, somewhere barbaric and close-minded, where she can be the person she was meant to be.*

Still, Reid wishes she were here to see his greatest accomplishment.

20

Capitol Hill Free Trade Republic; Denver, Colorado

July 9, 2087

11:12 AM

Reid Rosales's new office, a converted former Sociocracy apartment above Club 20c headquarters that also serves as his new home, has windows facing out over 13th Avenue. When he engages the background layer filters, he can see Colfax, and beyond to the northern border of the District. A 20c club member kneels before Reid's office door, laser-etching his name and title into the metal surface.

`Reid Rosales; Chief Executive, Capitol Hill Free Trade Republic.`

"Iris, give me the news," Reid says.

"There are four trending news topics within the Free Trade Republic," Iris says.

"List, please, Iris."

"Topic one: 'Unemployment rate within Free Trade Republic hits all-time low, with 61% of the population currently working in part-time or barter positions.' Topic two: 'New poll shows after one week, citizen happiness and fulfillment is up by 4%.' Topic three: 'Tanking art economy blamed on number of hobbyists flooding marketplace. Labor prices on the rise.' Topic four: 'Disturbance at 13th and Pearl Tubecar station as excited newcomers, and protestors from across the nation, flow into new Free Trade Republic.'"

"No details, please, Iris. I get the gist," Reid says. "I am unhappy that the Tubecar station is still a site of disturbance. But then, the transition from oppression to absolute freedom doesn't happen without a few disagreements."

Reid rises from his high-back desk chair and walks over to the corner of the office where a small digital safe holds up a no-water fern hologram. He kneels and keys in the safe code. Inside, stacks of old U.S. currency comprise his tiny, but effective fortune in this new era. The cash could have been dispersed into the Free Trade Republic before, but as Reid reasoned, there is a cost to creating a new future, and as it's architect, he should be compensated. Also, the funds will make their way into the FTR eventually, from his hand, through goods and services rendered, and into the hands of those who did not yet have his wealth. The system works as it is intended, but for it to even begin, someone must be up top. *Why shouldn't it be me?*

He retrieves two hundred dollars in twenties, folds them over and places the currency in the interior pocket of his suit jacket. Gone with the Sociocracy were the days of wearing a t-shirt and jeans, playing the part of a humble, artsy, cartoonist type. Now, Reid's station requires a certain level of respectability, and thus, a suit. Today's is gray-blue.

On a small shelf in the safe, above the cash, is Reid's drawing tablet. Once a day, since the Liberation of July 2nd, Reid has drawn a new Origami Emu image, inspired by the noble story of the 20c Revolutionaries. He puts the images up for auction each day, and earns a fair supplementary income. He contemplates taking the tablet out now, but can't think of an idea worth committing to screen. Reid closes the safe and taps in the safe code once more, locking his valuable assets away.

Reid stands at his window, looking out over 13th. The street, formerly filled with wandering Citizens; all eagerly darting from place to place, smiling and conversing, making art and music, and partying at all hours, is now crowded with individuals plying their wares to passersby on their own ways to jobs and businesses. One particularly industrious man converted the useless chassis of a bartender robot into a cart, to which he attached his home replicator. The man sells his "street food" at prices just below the nearby restaurants, and as word spreads, he attracts longer and longer lines each day. Taking advantage of the gathering of hungry Citizens, one woman tries to sell jewelry she recycled from another desiccated robot. There is even a boy, fresh out of school, playing an electric guitar for tips.

To his dismay, though, some people were still hiding from the future, locked in their apartments, eating food from their replicators; perhaps hoping that the U. S. of A. would step in to do something about it. That was the only explanation for the lack of foot traffic. And the lack of familiar faces. So many people biding their time. Like the old man and the girl from college, in Reid's old building. He has not seen them since before the Revolution, but they must be somewhere in waiting. Reid wonders when the Sociocracy will come for them, but it is a distant worry, as the smiling faces and clear marks of ingenuity all over the FTR fuel his pride for his perfect new future. *Besides*, he thinks, *Xiu, Gustave, and Selene, and the others out there hidden away will have to come out eventually, and when they try life here, instead of fearing change, they will grow to love it. Or, they will move away, to live with the sheep that they deserve, only to fall behind as the economy of the FTR turns the Wheel of Destiny one-hundred-eighty degrees.*

"Iris, what is my schedule today?" he asks, stepping back from the window and re-centering himself in his office.

"You currently have two optional appointments. You can join the Reassignment Team on the southwest FTR training exercise, and you can attend the Welcoming Party for Annabelle Tkachenko and other members of the Robotics Team at Club 20c."

"I think I will wristband in for the Reassignment Team exercise. When does it start?" he asks.

"The exercise begins in twelve minutes," Iris replies.

"Great," Reid replies. "Establish a video connection for me, please. And RSVP 'yes' for Annabelle's party. I should bring a gift."

"I recommend a romantic meal at the Colfax Wicked View eatery," Iris says. "I will obtain a reservation for next week."

"Excellent, Iris. Thank you."

Reid makes some hot water in an electric kettle that he found among the scavenged goods in the Club. The wait for the water to heat is longer than he anticipates, but he imagines the patience he's practicing only makes him stronger. The water finally hot, Reid sprinkles in some of the instant coffee crystals he brought with him from the club. He swirls the liquid until the tiny fragments of brown dissolve, takes a satisfying sip. His revolution succeeded easily. His true twentieth-century-loving love is returning from her safe house. The Free Trade

Republic is making news, and the economy is booming. He would pinch himself, just to see if it was all a dream, if he had any desire of waking up.

"Video feed established," Iris says.

"Thank you, Iris."

Reid's wristband lights up, showing the audio connection to Jones, one of the newer Reassignment Team members who came on board when he saw the good works they were doing. Iris projects the video feed on the wall in front of Reid's desk. He takes a seat in his high-back chair and slides up to the desk, crossing his fingers and sitting tall in an authoritative posture.

"Jones, this is Chief Executive Rosales," he says. "Thanks for letting me join you remotely."

"No, sir, thank you," Jones says. "It's a real honor to have you with us."

"So, what's the situation down there?"

The video pans left to the Seventh Avenue and Sherman street sign. The depth of field adjusts and a blurry, colorful mass, comes into focus in the background. Lined up on the curb, in front of an interactive sports arcade, are fifteen or twenty people holding up their wristbands with projected signs reading 'Please help,' 'Just need a few bucks,' and 'Can't afford to live.' The sign-holding people are flanked by other members of the Reassignment Team.

"As you can see, we're having a little trouble getting a few of the Citizens in the southwest corner to fully adopt the new system," Jones says.

"And you've given out their starting cash?" Reid asks.

"We have, sir. These spent it right away. Never tried to earn more."

"Did you tip the scales by giving one of them a bonus to fall in line?" Reid asks.

"We tried that yesterday, sir," Jones says. "The silly fuck just shared it with the rest of them."

Reid leans back in his chair and places his thumb and forefinger to his chin. Suddenly, one of the seated Citizens rises up and holds his sign high over his head, shaking it.

"Fuck you, we won't work," the man with the sign chants.

Another citizen with a sign stands and joins in the chant. Then another and another.

"What's happening over there, Jones?" Reid asks, leaning forward in his seat.

The video pans back to Jones.

"Just some unrest, sir. Any recommendations you might have are welcome."

"Let's try the gentle approach. Open a strap and toss them some capital. See if that quiets them down."

The video pans back to the protesting group. One of the Reassignment Team members opens a briefcase and removes a stack of twenties. He tears the paper strap and tosses the stack of bills out to the sign-holders like an old man feeding ducks in the park. The bills flutter and scatter and a few fall with a plop onto the pavement. The protesters stare at the splash of currency, and for a moment, they do not move.

And then they pounce, dropping their signs and gathering up the currency. Each one clutches at a bouquet of bills, and then jumps back into line with the others.

"Imagine," Jones says, off-camera. "If you work, you can have this much every couple of days. And then all your worries would be over."

One of the Citizens steps forward with her stack of cash, and walks toward Jones.

"Excuse me, I'd like to hear more about getting a job," she says.

Jones holds his arms open to her as she approaches.

"We have many opportunities available in the Free Trade Rep—"

The woman throws the stack of dollars at Jones and it explodes like a snowball.

"Credits are the only currency of the Sociocracy," she yells. "We have come from all over to fight for the world we believe in. This cause is everyone's cause! Long live the U. S. of A."

The other protesters throw their handouts toward the Reassignment Team. Some have even wadded their bills into pellets, insulting the currency as well as the system for which it stands; indivisible.

The woman—the leader, it's clear now—turns and coaxes them all into a louder chant of "Long live the U. S. of A." Then she rejoins them on the sidewalk and kneels down for something, a bag. She roots around and finally extracts a handful of robot parts. She throws the shards of scrap metal at Jones and the Reassignment Team and all the while the protest gets louder and louder.

"Sir?" Jones says, still off-camera. "What do you recommend?"

Reid wraps his fingers on the desk, clutches his cup of instant coffee and takes a sip. He looks to the window, where his view of the almost cloudless blue sky makes him think of the infinite potential of tomorrow. He breathes deep and exhales.

"Jones, can these people be reasoned with?"

The camera fixes again on Jones's face.

"I don't think so, sir."

A stack of bills hits Jones on the cheek, showering twenties across the projection.

Reid sighs.

"I authorize use of deterrent force," Reid says.

The video pans back toward the group of protesters. First Jones, then the rest of the Reassignment Team slowly move forward. Jones draws a baton from its holster on his belt and raises it. He grabs the woman—the insurrectionist, the aggressor—with his free hand by her shoulder and brings down the baton on her head. Or near it, from this angle it's hard to tell, but yes, it must be on her with how she reacts. The first strike causes her to rebound and then lash back, angrier. The second brings tears to her eyes. The third; she slumps and lowers below the field of vision in the video. The other protesters scream and yell as she disappears from view. A couple of them turn with their signs and run away. One appears to crouch down, gathering a load of the errant U.S. Dollars for himself. But many continue to resist. The Reassignment Team closes in, and Reid's force of men and women bring their batons down on the remaining antagonists. The yells and screams come through the feed loud and clear. One of the downed protesters cries loudly. Another simply yells 'no.' But one of them is more articulate in his pain.

"Kill me. I'll never be the pawn of tyranny."

This grips firmly at Reid's heart.

"Jones," Reid says. "Halt the deterrent measures. And turn up your wristband. I'd like to speak to them directly."

Jones complies and the Reassignment Team stand down. The video feed pans to face the protesters directly, and all of Reid's people step to the sides, giving the sign-holders a chance to sit, gather themselves, and lick their wounds.

"Ladies and gentlemen," Reid says. "This is Chief Executive Rosales."

One of the protesters boos. Then another. And another.

"Sir?" Jones asks.

"It's fine. Just turn up the volume, Jones," Reid replies.

"Ladies and gentlemen," he says again, over the chorus of displeasure. "Your disapproval is noted. And I completely understand what you are feeling. This is a new era, and having barely been alive for a week, it still has some kinks to work out. Each of you, like the infant that one day grows into the businessman, will cry out because this world is new and frightening to you. But you will mature over time, and the ways—the better ways—of the Free Trade Republic will come to you.

"All things are scary at first," Reid says as the video pans across the line of beaten protesters. Only the woman who led their first assault is still, likely unconscious. Reid will see that she is taken to a Longevity Kiosk.

"The new things are all scary," he continues. "But that is usually sign that you are on the right track. Instead of seeing the FTR as some kind of outside force, perhaps it would be better to view it as something born and raised right here in this neighborhood. I came up with the idea while living among you, and seeing the emptiness behind all of your eyes. This is a local solution to a local problem, applied by a local leader."

The protesters rub their injured arms and dab the blood from their lips and foreheads with their clothing.

"I urge you all to give me, yes me, and my idea another chance," Reid says. "And because you've each shown an admirable capacity to live as individuals;

against the grain, I am prepared to offer each of you starting positions within the Club 20c storefront and Real Alcohol bar. You will start at thirteen dollars per hour worked, well more than anyone else in the FTR makes, excepting yours truly and the Reassignment Team, of course. All you have to do is show up at the club one week from today. I will meet you personally, and there will be no interviews. You'll simply start right away and we can put all this ugly language and violence behind us."

The protesters sit on the sidewalk in silence, still tending to their wounds.

"I look forward to seeing each of you next week," Reid says. "Jones, please lower the volume."

Jones complies.

"Well done, sir," he says.

"Thank you. They can always be reasoned with," Reid says. "I hope this is the end of our issues in this corner of the Republic."

"I think it will be, sir."

"Good. Keep me posted, Jones," Reid says. "Will I see you at the festivities this evening?"

"I intend to make an appearance, sir, as soon as I give my wife and son their allowances for the week."

"Good man."

Reid raises his arm and salutes Jones. Jones returns the gesture.

"Iris, drop the connection, please," Reid says.

The projection disappears and his wristband goes silent.

"You handled that uprising well, Reid Rosales," Iris says. "Would you like to watch some entertainment?"

"No, Iris," Reid says. "I think I'll go shopping."

Reid stands from his desk, pats at his wad of cash in his suit jacket pocket, and exits his office above the Free Trade Republic for the streets he built.

***

Club 20c is decked out with crepe paper streamers for Annabelle's—and the other Robotics Team members—homecoming party. The other club members hung posters and signs and banners reading:

```
Welcome Home!
We salute you!
Thank you for your sacrifice.
Robotics team, we love you!
Annabelle and her angels.
To the twentieth!
```

There are balloons, the old rubber kind—not projections—float and hang all around the club's main room. Even the wargames table is decorated with colorful versions of tanks and ships, and the infantry pieces are holding their own tiny signs and tiny balloons. The effort put forth by his friends—his disciples—impresses Reid as he strolls through the space. In the games corner they have set up an old copy of Pin the Tail on the Donkey, but this version features the logos of the two prominent political parties of the past, awaiting slogan-inscribed tails. The music corner has a selection of party records and 8-tracks pulled out, including something called Party Time Buzzy Greene! featuring a topless woman on the cardboard sleeve.

The coup de grâce is in the Alpha Omega display, where the club members have added a the notations:

```
Before: July 1, 2087—Club 20c members take back individual
freedom from the Sociocracy.
```

```
After: July 2, 2087—A new dawn of capitalism as the Capitol
Hill Free Trade Republic is born.
```

The history had already been written by its rightful winners. Reid smiles and touches the notations on the screen, just to make they are real.

"Are you pleased, boss?" a club member says behind him.

"How could I not be?" Reid says.

She smiles and curtsies.

"We aim to please," she says. "It's all for you."

"Well, much of it belongs to Annabelle and Reagan, and to all of you," Reid says.

"Of course, sir. Of course," she replies, and then she bounds away to tend to something on the other side of the room.

Reid sits on the couches by the games, sipping a glass of bourbon that came to the club in their last scavenging trip before the Revolution. The club fills quickly, as members arrive and gather, eat from the assembled MREs, Spam, and even some meals hand cooked from replicated ingredients. Reid fiddles with his wristband, stopping occasionally to speak with a club member and accept congratulations or compliments or questions about how his genius came about, and if he thinks that it's possible for anyone, someone like me, to lead a revolution too, someday.

To which Reid replies, "Any individual with a dream can make that dream happen."

The person smiles, bows, thanks him, and walks away.

Reid had just begun to grow bored with the lavish praise and interviewing when the woman from before, the club member who had been occupied with the decor, runs up to him and says the words he has been waiting to hear.

"She's outside."

Reid stands up and gathers himself. He presses the lapels of his jacket and slides his palms down the length of his slacks. He adjusts his shirt and tie. He slicks his hair down, double checking his cowlick by patting it and then forcing it down with his hand. Reid's heart beats faster. His palms begin to sweat. He has been waiting for days to see Annabelle again, and despite his best efforts, he worried about her safety.

Then the slat-wood door to Club 20c opens, and there she is, blonde braids wrapped up and around her head like a laurel wreath. She wears a paisley print skirt and a loose-fitting, almost billowy top. But the most important thing is that when she makes eye contact with Reid, her faces lights up so obviously that he couldn't fail to see it. Her mouth smiles and her eyes smile and if it's possible her ears and hair and breasts and arms and legs smile too.

"Reid," she calls, running to him.

He opens his arms and catches her. He twirls her around a full turn and then they kiss like something out of the old movies, the movies that inspired people in the Twentieth to believe in Love and Success and Possibility. Reid sets her down and the rest of the club members begin to sing, something old, "For She's a Jolly Good Fellow", with changed lyrics to include everyone on the Robotics Team.

When the singing subsides, Reid steps up to the bar, but doesn't climb atop it. He no longer needs a bully pulpit when his station is unquestionable.

"Friends, we're here to celebrate Annabelle and the heroes she led on the Robotics Team. Without their efforts, none of what we've seen change, so rapidly and so successfully, over the last week could be possible," Reid says. "But we're also here to celebrate each of you. Without your individual faiths and passions, we might still be just a club that people dismissed as a 'playing make believe.' So I thank you, and I raise a glass to each of you, and suggest that you each raise a glass to one another. We have done something incredible. We have changed the world."

The club members applaud, and Reid raises his glass. The others raise their glasses, and they all drink of the various real alcohols that came from the greatest time the world has ever known. Reid puts away three glasses of bourbon and begins to enjoy the questions and conversations that come from the other club members. And it's so much easier to answer the questions knowing that Annabelle is going to stop by and hang on his arm and answer some of the questions for him.

"When were you most afraid?" one club member asks him.

"I was in that room," he answers, pointing toward the storage closet that's now used solely for storage again. "I was waiting to hear back from Annabelle and Reagan, and I had no idea what was going to happen. I'm sure that I would have gone after them, but when my worries reached its highest point, they finally contacted me, and I knew that all of it was meant to be."

"What about you?" he asks Annabelle.

"Oh, me?" Annabelle says. "I don't know. There were a lot of scary parts. The whole operation was complex."

"There must have been something," Reid goads. "So many intense moments."

Annabelle shakes her head and sighs.

"Come on," Reid says. "Tell us something, miss hero."

"Okay, okay," she says. "Umm. When we were near the end of the run, there was one restaurant where I couldn't get to the charging station because there was a stack of old replicators sitting there. I had to move them all myself."

Reid smirks at his love.

"That doesn't sound so scary."

"Well, you weren't on a strict timeline, counting the precious minutes away and thinking that a single mistake was going to endanger the entire Revolution," Annabelle says.

A couple of club members listening in nod and thank her and then bow out to mingle elsewhere in the party.

"I think I can understand the fear you felt," Reid says.

"I'm glad," Annabelle replies. "It wasn't easy for me."

"There's so much tangible fear in the unknown," he says. "But we preserved."

"You know we did, Reid," she says.

Reid takes a drink of his bourbon and leans on her. He kisses her on the cheek and she returns the kiss to his.

"The only thing that I wonder is if it was all too easy," Reid says. "In a week, we've managed to set most of the Citizens out there straight, and start a new society. I guess I expected a bit more of a fight or something, but that was probably just me getting wrapped up the old movies and interactive experiences."

"The danger felt plenty real to me, honey," Annabelle says. "I think we were just doing what the world needed, so it happened the way it was supposed to."

"Not that I'm complaining, of course," Reid says. "I'm just surprised that the Sociocracy gave up so easily. I thought for sure that they'd try to re-indoctrinate us. Or send another security force or something."

236

Annabelle sips her wine and smiles. "Sometimes the right way is the easy way." She sets her glass down and takes Reid's hand. She pulls him close and whispers in his ear.

"I haven't had you in days," she says. "Let's go up to the 'Presidential Suite.'"

"And leave your own party?" he asks.

"They'll be here when we get back."

Annabelle leads Reid toward the slat wood door of Club 20c. Neither of them say goodbyes. They just slip through the partying crowd. She opens the door and ushers Reid out onto the landing.

"Finally, some alone time," she says.

Then a spotlight falls on them, then another, and another. The mechanical rumble accompanying the lights is unmistakable. Seven security robots.

"**Citizen Reid Rosales. Citizen Annabelle Tkachenko.** Please come speak to us immediately regarding a matter of secessionist activity," the lead security robot says. "Do not resist. Resistance may result in harm."

21

Capitol Hill Free Trade Republic; Denver, Colorado

July 9, 2087

10:17 PM

"Get behind me," Reid says, nudging Annabelle back toward the club door. Reid ascends the stairs with his hands raised over his head.

"I was just wondering where you were," Reid says. "How convenient. Were your robot-ears burning?"

"Rhetorical colloquial questions will not be answered," the lead robot says.

"Fine, fine," Reid replies. "What seems to be the problem, officer?"

"Security readings show that **Citizen Reid Rosales** has orchestrated an operation to disconnect Capitol Hill District from the U. S. of A. master grid," the lead robot says. "Readings also show that **Citizen Annabelle Tkachenko** worked to disable robot workforce and economy in the District. These are acts of secession against the greater good of the Sociocracy, and Articles of Protection dictate that you must be tried for this crime by a jury of your peers and an independent arbiter."

Reid turns to Annabelle. "Don't worry, love, this will be over soon."

He holds out his hands, limp at the wrists, begging them to restrain him, while taking slow steps forward.

"I understand the charges against me," Reid says. "I am certain that I will be found innocent, after your trial. The people will not be fooled by the Sociocracy's oppressive tactics any longer. Their eyes have been blind, but now they see."

"Please desist ranting. You have the right to remain silent, and research shows that exercise of said right is ninety-eight percent more effective in maintaining your innocence than its alternative," the lead robot says.

"Of course that's what you want—us to be quiet," Reid says. "That's why you fill our bellies and distract our eyes, so we cannot feel or speak up for ourselves."

"World hunger and U. S. of A. entertainment practices are not associated with security systems," the robot says. "Security protocol seeks to protect Citizens from themselves, and ensure happiness within the Sociocracy."

"Propaganda," Reid yells. "You should choose your next words wisely because they will be your last."

"Threatening a security robot is not advised. In the interest of a fair defense, we ask that you comply, **Citizen Reid Rosales**."

"Bramble sugarpie mandible aioli ricecake."

Each robot rattles. Their heads swivel and they look at one another, perplexed. The lead robot tips and bounces on its suspension, waving its arms momentarily. *It's working,* Reid thinks. *Nothing like the Sociocracy for leaving vulnerable products in service. In the FTR, the moment something—or someone—is obsolete, it is replaced. Moving forward is always better than standing still; working harder is always better than being bored.*

"Processor error," the lead robot says.

It's definitely working, Reid thinks.

"Identified," the lead security robot continues. "Processor error isolated. Processor error logged. Damage repaired. Action logged: Attempted assault on security robot by **Citizen Reid Rosales**."

"Reid, it's not going to work," Annabelle says. "They must have adapted."

The lead security robot reaches out for Reid, catching his arm within a quarter-second. The machine overpowers him, dragging Reid.

"Assault charge added," the robot says. "Prepare for temporary detainment."

The robot grabs Reid's other arm and lifts him off the ground. Reid struggles, shaking and shimmying, trying to free his arms or kick the robot or make contact with something, but it's no use. The machine is too strong.

"Corncob ashtray hammock deliberation," Reid says.

"Second assault charge logged," the robot replies.

"You won't stop us this way," Reid says. "Another will follow in my place."

Reid struggles again, kicking his legs wildly, hoping that he'll wriggle free.

"Crimes not yet committed are not of interest to the security robots," the lead robot says. "Come along peacefully."

Reid tries to look back to Annabelle, but the robot's metal grip is too tight and he can't turn far enough. The machine starts wheeling backward, off the sidewalk and into the street.

"Annabelle," Reid screams. "Evacuate the club."

There is no response. Reid can only gaze into the flickering electronic eyes of the machine that now holds him captive; a full foot off the ground as they wheel slowly toward the Tubecar station where everything will come to an end. *But then,* he thinks, *it probably had to end sometime. There are few Revolutionaries who live long lives. Perhaps this act of martyrdom will accelerate the cause, draw more eyes and ears, and change the world even faster.* He can hope so, at least.

Suddenly, Reid drops to the ground, and the arms holding him go slack, and fall to his sides. Behind the lead security robot he sees, Annabelle, holding a cavalry sword, having freshly cut through the shoulder joints of his captor.

"Get out of here, Reid," she says.

Annabelle swings the blade again, crossing the lead robot's neck and decapitating it. The machine's head dangles on a few wires and strands of connective insulation.

"Where did you get that?" Reid asks.

"I stopped by the VFW museum on the way back to town," she says. "I thought it would make a nice souvenir."

She swings again and strikes two of the other security robots, removing one's arm and another's head with balletic fluidity. The body parts crash to the ground, and their former owners spin and writhe.

"Get out of here. Go back to the club. Lock yourself in the storage," Annabelle says.

"But what about you?" Reid asks.

"The others are coming to help. You have to go."

"I can fight too. It's my fight after all."

"Shut up, Reid," she says. "Get to safety."

Reid sighs, turns, and descends the stairs. A swarm of club members charge past, carrying the guns from the museum, crying out for battle. When Reid gets to the doorway, he can hear Annabelle scream. He moves back toward the stairs, but the woman from before, with the decorations, who has curtsied, grabs him by the shoulder and pulls him inside.

"No, sir," she says. "That's not for you."

"I should help them," he says.

"They'll be fine. It's what they signed up for."

"But it's what I signed up for too."

"No, sir, you signed up to lead us, and that's what you're going to do," she says. "And you thought that it was all too easy before."

Reid nods.

But did he say that it was too easy in front of her? He must have. There was a crowd, and the alcohol, he was the center of attention, but he wasn't sure exactly whose.

"There are always going to be challenges, sir," she says. "I'd bet my hat on it. If I had a hat. Now let's get you into the closet. It's lucky that we left your air mattress in there."

She shoves Reid inside, and for a moment, he wonders if he's being protected, or taken prisoner.

"You sit tight, sir. I'm sure Annabelle will be back to check on you when the coast is clear."

The door to the storage closet closes and Reid is alone in the dark.

He gropes at the wall for the light switch, and after his eyes adjust he looks for something to distract him for his worry for Annabelle, and his fear for himself. He takes down a new book, one that must have been recently acquired, and opens to its first page. *The Moon is a Harsh Mistress* by Robert A. Heinlein. Book One. *That Thinkum Dinkum*. One. "I see in *Lunaya Pravada* that Luna City Council has passed on first reading a bill to examine, license, inspect—and tax—public food vendors operating under public pressure…" As the book goes on, Reid loses himself in the struggle of Citizens on the Moon, fighting against the oppressive government of Earth.

He almost forgets about the battle going on outside.

He almost forgets that he's locked in a small room.

He nearly believes that he's back on the Moon.

Art imitates life, he thinks.

***

A pounding on the door to the closet shakes him from the lunar plight of the book pages.

"Reid," a woman's voice says, weary. "Open the door, Reid."

He stands and turns, then taps the code into the keypad. The door slides open, slowly. He can see that the club members have returned- but several have bloodied heads, bruises, and torn clothing. Then he sees her, Annabelle, now unobscured by the door, holding her cavalry sword, breathing heavy. There is a gash on her forehead. And a bruise on her cheek. Her torn skirt flaps like a dead limb. Her blouse bears a claw mark, where one of the robots must have grabbed her.

She looks at him, her tired eyes with little glimmer left.

"We won," she says. "They won't bother us again."

The curtsying woman appears again with drinks in hand. She gives one to Annabelle and one to Reid.

"Let's drink until we can't remember what we just did," Annabelle says to the wounded crowd.

They cheer and take up drinks of their own.

Annabelle stumbles forward, exhausted, and plops down onto the edge of Reid's air mattress. He joins her, holding her side gingerly in an act of gentlemanly uselessness.

"What happened out there, Annabelle?" he asks. "Are you sure you're okay?"

She sighs, and slams her drink back. Without even being asked, the curtsying woman reappears with another drink, taking Annabelle's glass.

242

"You saw most of it," she says, taking another sip. "The club members really saved my ass up there. I had one of the robots on the ropes. I was about to cut it in half, and then the two others grabbed me."

Reid is riveted. His glass shakes in his hand.

"Luckily, the reinforcements came, and they got me free and beat the robots back."

"I'm glad you're safe," Reid says.

"Then if you can believe it, another set of the security bots showed up right after we finished with the first. But this time they were double. We're weren't going to make it, Reid. I was really scared. I thought I might never see you again."

Reid holds her.

"But you did. You're seeing me right now."

Annabelle's voice shakes. "It was the most amazing thing, Reid. We were fighting the next wave, and we getting beat up pretty bad. And then, the guys from the bar next door came out with broomsticks, and the restaurant across the street emptied out too. And then there were Citizens from apartment buildings coming out with tennis rackets and bat and just about anything they could swing.

"The people stood up for you today, Reid. They stood up for us. It was hard-won, but we did it. There was nothing easy about what just happened, but maybe it had to, you know, so that the people living here, in the Free Trade Republic, could understand the real meaning of community."

"And so I could earn their blessings," Reid says.

"They abolished the Sociocracy. It was beautiful." Tears come to Annabelle's eyes. "This little girl was hitting one of the robots with her doll, and she was screaming, 'Stay out of Capitol Hill. We take care of each other' with this darling lisp that... that..."

Annabelle hides her face in her hands and sobs.

"I'm so proud of you, Reid," she says through her tears. "I don't think I knew what it mean to be proud of someone at all until you came into my life. You've given those people something to believe in and live for. I wouldn't have believed it could be so powerful if I wasn't just out there watching."

"I knew they would embrace it, and that just living in a new world out from under the yoke of the U. S. of A. would give those Citizens new energy," Reid says. "You can't imagine how happy I am to hear this, Annabelle. But I'm angry, too. I'm angry at you for risking your life for me, because if I never saw you again, I don't know what I would do."

She takes her hands away from her eyes and throws her arms around him. He squeezes her, she him, and then she cries; loud, heavy sobs. Reid holds her tight and cries himself. The people had rejected their enemy. His revolution had succeeded in the only way that it could have, by the people, by their hands and their hearts, by their blood and their passion. In a life that would be filled with accomplishments, Reid feels that this, right now, is the One. The bar is set. There was never anything like it before, in the days of the Sociocracy, creating laughter-generating cartoons for public consumption; doing drugs and roaming the world, playing games. No—finally—Reid's life is no longer a game.

"We had to do it, Reid," Annabelle says, still sobbing. "We do it all for you."

They hold each other there, on the air mattress, in the storage closet, crying together- in some combination of joy, exhaustion, stress and fear. New worlds are born, and in so being, the old ones are discarded. There is a sadness in death that is nature, but without it, there could be no rebirth. Without endings, there could be no new beginnings. *Without the struggle of this battle, or the struggle to live, what's a life worth anyway?* It's only appropriate that in bringing purpose and individuality back to the people, that there should be a resistance that validates the movement simply in its existence. Reid, cradling her in such a way as to avoid her wounds, would not have it any other way.

Annabelle pulls away and wipes her eyes and nose. She throws back the second drink, and sets the glass on the floor.

"Now, where were we, before we were so rudely interrupted?" she asks, and kisses him.

"Are you sure?" Reid asks. "Maybe we should get you to a Doctor."

"No, let's just go upstairs," Annabelle says. "The best balm for pain is pleasure."

244

She kisses him again.

Reid stands, and helps her up. They walk, arm in arm, out into the club where their loyal friends and followers drink and share war stories and tend to each other's wounds. As they make their way from the closet to the club's front door, the club members begin to applaud. The claps are like an ocean wave rolling and crashing against the shore, sweeping away the old, and birthing the new. All the sheep have died, replaced with individuals. All the mistakes are being forgotten.

All the old ways are now renewed.

All the heroes have stood to be counted.

And tomorrow morning, a bright, new peace will grace the FTR.

22

Capitol Hill Free Trade Republic; Denver, Colorado

August 9, 2087

9:04 AM

Dear Reagan,

I hope this letter finds you well, my good friend. I was dismayed to hear that you remain in hiding, buried amid the Sociocracy in some dark corner of the Central Americas. I had hoped, as we all had, that you would be able to return to us this month, and see what bountiful fruit your seeds have grown. Instead, I'm writing you this note to tell you about our progress and hopefully bring a smile to your face that can wipe away the worry and the fear you must feel while running from our former oppressors.

It has been just over one month since the Revolution, and life in the Capitol Hill Free Trade Republic could not be better. At last polling, we now have a strong 80% employment rate—including elderly individuals and children—a number for which I am very proud. There also seems to be a steady flow of new faces, eager to join the cause, as well as the beginnings of a tourist economy.

I had always assumed that I wasn't alone in my feelings of directionlessness, purposelessness, and dissatisfaction. The fact that so many from all across the Sociocracy are coming to peacefully explore our Grand Experiment just confirms it. As I suspected, you and Annabelle, and the others, and I, we were not anomalies, but representatives of the human condition. I hope that this knowledge gives you as much pride as it has given me.

Yesterday, I oversaw the opening of a new business, modeled on the system of our glorious Twentieth. It is the first bank to grace the Capitol Hill neighborhood since the robot economy, and now that people can once again protect their personal interests, instead of relying on the U. S. of A. to do it for them, the occasion was especially momentous. The bank opened in old Quizno's Plaza Tower building at Grant and 13th Avenue. We performed a ribbon cutting ceremony, during which I cut a hologram ribbon with a pair of oversized hologram shears. The bank proprietor even asked me to open the first account, into which I deposited two-thousand dollars. (The rest I will keep in my office safe until the bank proves itself successful.) It was a sight to see though. Individuals from all over the FTR lined up behind me to protect their earnings.

After the ceremony, the proprietor read a passage from Friedman, and they served replicator food and alcohol. Would you believe that when I asked them why there wasn't real alcohol and cooked food at the event, they replied that they would next time, after they've made some return on the invested deposits from the individuals? I was astonished and proud once again at their ingenuity. They were going to make money from our money, just like the simulator in the club.

You'd also be excited to know that I am leading the first State of the Republic meeting next week. I had hoped you might be in attendance for that as well, but circumstances are understandably complex at this time. Annabelle and I are still working on the structure of the event—running the FTR with just two full time officials isn't easy, but we're making do. Perhaps, you'd read over our concept and send your ideas back, if you have the time.

> Individuals gather in 13th Avenue outside Club 20c
> Chief Executive (Reid) and Officer of Operations and Happiness (Annabelle) ascend the steps from the club and take to the podium atop the stairs
> Opening remarks by Annabelle

- Happiness on the rise, you can see it on the streets as people value themselves and everything they do and make more than ever
- In one month we have accomplished more individually than the Sociocracy could dream of in 1000x that time
- Four straight weeks of peace, without resistance or protest is cause for celebration
- Introduction of Chief Executive
- State of the Republic speech
  - The state of the Republic is strong
  - We are all participants in the new era of personal prosperity and individual success
  - Our example is capturing the imaginations of people from all over the Sociocracy
  - No residual threats of U. S. of A. attacks based on intelligence reports and news stories from the Sociocracy feeds
  - Opening of bank, new street vendors
  - Closing remarks

That is what I have so far. I am confident that Annabelle will perform exceptionally, as she always has been perfectly prepared in the past. I am stuck on the closing remarks, and what I can say that adequately captures the optimism and potential of year and years to come. The people are proud in the Capitol Hill Free Trade Republic, Reagan, and they deserve to feel that pride reflected by their leadership. The people are embracing their assigned Tiers, taking up shovels, aprons, and anything else with hungry hearts. I want to ensure they trust the upper Tiers with their futures. Any assistance you can provide is most definitely welcome.

In other exciting news, we will establish three additional exchange stations in the month of September. As Citizens come into the FTR, so many of them need to exchange their Credits for Dollars that we have developed our own "cottage industry." When visitors or new individuals arrive they can trade their credits at a rate of 200-to-1, or use their credits to purchase items from the Twentieth that we buy for the 20c Museum, or which we convert into currency at fair market value. These little booths employ three individuals each, and the transition is proving easier than what we saw with the Longevity Kiosks. Though, if you must know, we've designed a training program that has been successful, and there are no further issues to report.

As for me, fella, I have been very busy leading, but in my free moments I still find time to indulge in a wargame or two back in the club. My new series of *Origami Emu* cartoons, subtitled "The Birth of a Flock," is receiving positive reviews from the populous. There is not much in the way of competition at present, as most of the individuals work as many as twelve hours each day, but I am confident that I'm providing valuable inspiration to the young people of the FTR.

Annabelle and I are doing very well. She recovered so quickly from her injuries after the final battle with the Sociocracy that I was joyously surprised. Apparently, her grandmother had worked as a nurse, so Annabelle had no difficulty self-administering from the Doctors. She is a truly remarkable woman, so intelligent and strong and driven by the cause that if I were a religious man I'd say she was designed by a higher power just for me. But, that is what love can do to a person. It creates strange ideas in your head, or colors your vision so that everything is perfect and beautiful.

Before I forget, Annabelle sends her love and regards to you, and hopes that you will return soon. At the moment, she is out doing a happiness check with the E-Meters near the Tubecar station. We have found that most visitors are excited to take the test, and that many accept the notion that their leisurely existences in the old world are causing them deep psychological pain. I couldn't be more pleased, as I'm sure you will be too.

I want to close this letter on a note of encouragement. I have neither seen, nor heard from you since you led the Grid Team to begin our great Revolution. Though it must be incredibly difficult for you to be separated from your friends and truest comrades, know that our hearts and spirits are always with you. You should also know that it was Annabelle who told me that she discovered a secret network of information that told us that you are alive and safe.

I worried that we had lost you and the Grid Team forever. While you wander the jungles and feign love for the oppressive past in which you now hide, please take heart in the knowledge that all you have helped to build stands and thrives. And that I, your former Second Officer, and always friend, await your return with open and welcoming arms.

With Gratitude,
Reid Rosales
Chief Executive
Capitol Hill Free Trade Republic

Reid folds the piece of paper in half, and then folds it into quarters. He writes "Reagan" on the exterior and places the letter in his suit jacket pocket. He leaves his office and takes the elevator to ground level. The gilded metal doors slide open to 13th Avenue, and welcome in a bevvy of sights, sounds, and smells from the street. A young man, dressed in coveralls, collects trash from each individual's residence and business, accepting payment for his services. A street-food vendor serves a line of customers who clamor and argue as they wait for their meals, before they rush off to their places of business. A woman in a fine suit negotiates with someone through her wristband as she hustles by.

"I don't care if you don't like the hours," she says. "You want a job, right?"

A couple passes by Reid, going the other direction, talking loudly to one another. Reid only overhears a moment of their conversation.

"Well we both have to work, so someone has to watch Stephen."

And then, a little girl, too young still to go to school, runs up to Reid from the crowd. She jumps at him and throws her tiny arms around his legs. The squeeze nearly buckles Reid's knees, but the girl relents just in time.

"Hello, young lady," he says.

"Hello Mr. Chief," she replies.

Reid smiles. "Actually, it's Chief Executive, but my name is Reid. What's yours?"

"Arian."

"Well, Arian," Reid says, kneeling beside the girl. "Did you just want to give me a hug?"

The girl shakes her head; her braids whip.

"Did you want to ask me a question?"

The girl nods vigorously; her braids flop.

"Okay, go ahead, Arian," Reid says. "I won't bite."

The little girl looks up at him and then looks away and down to the street.

"Can I be the Chief Exetive when I grow up?" she asks.

"It's Chief Ex-ec-utive," Reid corrects. "But of course you can. You can be whatever you want to be, Arian. As long as there's a job to do in the Free Trade Republic, you'll be able to do it."

"Mommy says that we don't have them at home," Arian says.

From the crowd, her mother appears, calling the little girl's name.

"There you are," she says, grabbing the girl's arm. "I told you to stay with me."

"Oh, we were just talking," Reid says. "Arian may want to be Chief Executive some day."

"I hope she didn't cause you any trouble, sir," the woman says.

"None at all," Reid replies. "It's always a pleasure to speak to the next generation."

The mother takes Arian's hand and begins leading her back into the crowd of vendors. The little girl waves as she drifts away from her hero. Reid returns her wave and smiles as she disappears.

Reid continues down 13th until he reaches Downing. He turns right, and crosses 12th, 11th, 10th. At the corner of 9th and Downing, an old school building—long ago replaced by a skyscraper, but still wearing the old facade—marks the meeting location. Reid walks up to the stone archway in front and sits down on one of the two benches there. He checks his wristband, noting the time to be 10:20 a.m.

Ten more minutes.

Reid fiddles with his wristband to pass the time. Connections to the other Districts and cities outside the FTR has been spotty for weeks, but they still manage to receive entertainment content, and some news. Reid cycles through the available shows and doesn't find anything he likes. He won't listen to the music produced outside, in part because he believes that it contains opinions that undermine the FTR, but also because he might find something by Xiu. Instead, he sends a message to Annabelle.

"How's the Happiness Program going today, darling?" he asks.

"Better even than yesterday," she replies. "A man broke down crying about how spending his life on his sailboat traveling to exotic ports felt so empty to him. He got a little snot on my pants, though."

"Wonderful, love," Reid replies. "You'll come by my place around six?"

"That's when my shift ends. I'll go home and change first."

"Why change?" he asks. "You won't be wearing much for long."

"Hahaha. Then I'll be there at ten after... with bells off," she replies. "Oh, how's the letter to Reagan coming?"

"I'm just about to meet your contact to send it," he says. "So strange to send paper letters again. I love it. It's real."

"I thought you would," she says. "It's what we have to do. They can't intercept a paper message very easily, but a digital one would show them right where Reagan is."

"I hope he comes back soon," Reid says.

"I think you can bet on it, sweetheart," Annabelle replies.

Reid looks down at that last word, 'sweetheart' and smiles. Annabelle really is too good to him. She always knows what to say and she's almost always right about how things are going to work out. There's nothing better than having a muse and an oracle wrapped up into one.

"I better be going, babe," she says. "These unhappy people won't realize it on their own. I'll see you later."

"Of course. Keep up the great work," he says. "I will be counting the minutes. I love you."

"I love you," she replies.

And then she closes the connection.

Reid checks his wristband again. 10:30. The contact should be here any minute. And then a tap on his shoulder startles him.

"You Reid?" a woman in a blue jumpsuit asks. On the jumpsuit is a logo: LoR

"I am," he replies. "Are you Annabelle's friend?"

"Yes," she says. "That's me. You have a letter?"

Reid reaches into his jacket pocket and retrieves the folded sheet of paper.

"Here," he says, handing it over to her. "You'll be sure Reagan gets it?"

"Yes," she says. "I should have it to him in the next couple of days… as long as I'm not caught or something, I guess."

"Please see that he does. And please be safe," Reid says. "Your sacrifice will not go unrecognized by the Free Trade Republic."

"Sure thing. Thank you, sir," she says.

The woman turns and walks away down Downing. Reid loses sight of her when she crosses 8th Avenue and heads down the hill. In a few blocks, she'll cross the border back into the Sociocracy in Cherry Creek. As Reid walks back up toward his office, he says a silent prayer for her safety, and Reagan's, out there in the wild misery of the U. S. of A.

23

Capitol Hill Free Trade Republic; Denver, Colorado

September 24, 2088

11:51 AM

"Mr. Rosales," Reid's secretary calls from his office doorway. "Your noon appointment is waiting downstairs."

"Thank you, Eve. Send them up," Reid replies. "And my title is Chief Executive. Please try to remember to use it when you interact with the public."

Eve nods, and then nervously flattens her blouse.

"I'm sorry, sir. I promise I'll get it. It's only my second day."

"See that you do, Eve," Reid says. "And don't worry. You're not in any trouble."

Eve does something of a half bow and backs away from the door, knocking her elbow as she turns. The mousey woman's tiny footsteps disappear down the hall and into the elevator.

Reid had been happier with his previous secretary, Alicia, who was big, loud, and boisterous. Alicia would have burst into his office, giving him a scare perhaps, but her confident chaos was far more interesting than Eve's nervous mincing. Before Alicia was Nina. She talked fast, but she always forgot his appointments and after the first couple of days, Reid wondered if Nina took her job seriously at all. Luckily, she decided to pursue something new after two weeks. That was when Alicia showed up, and Alicia was wonderful, but she, too, left to do something else before a month passed. When Reid had asked why she was leaving, she only said that she had "other places to visit." No other explanation was given, and the next day, there was Eve, freshly hired by the Free Trade Republic administrative office downstairs in the old Club 20c.

In the last year, Reid was never without a secretary, but his office had been a revolving door for new ones. They came and went, but that is the nature of the Capitalist system. Each man and woman who had set his appointments and taken his administrative messages probably moved onto something better, something higher paying, something more fulfilling. That, after all, is why the FTR came to be, so Reid was always happy to see them go, even if he wished Alicia would have stayed a bit longer.

And when the time comes, Reid will be happy to see Eve on her way too. She would certainly find something gratifying, perhaps in writing, or even early education. Turnover is a normal part of life in the FTR. The bars and restaurants, the banks and Longevity Kiosks, the clubs and museums and theatres, all see what seems like complete turnover every couple of months. The founder of the First Bank of Free Trade had left his position just a couple weeks ago, and Reid had not seen him since. That is the price of turnover. People do not stay around for very long, but it means Reid meets a lot of new people each month, week, and day.

Those meetings were always gratifying, too, because new people were always happy to meet him and ask how he was doing and to talk about what he planned to do next. Many of them led to long conversations about how he came up with the idea for the Free Trade Republic and how he coordinated the Revolution. He welcomed the admiration. *After all, a good idea is a good idea, and the people should want to know how one man managed to reimagine the way the world works. And change it for the better.*

What matters most is that the individuals in the Free Trade Republic are happy. And they are. Annabelle's recent report from the Office of Operations and Happiness shows that 98% of individuals living and working the Free Trade Republic report themselves as extremely happy, while the remain 2% report themselves as very happy or simply happy. The people are starting families, filling the schools, and opening new businesses wherever an old one shutters—a bittersweet result of the all-knowing marketplace.

Reid fiddles with his wristband. All this thinking about the success of the FTR is just stalling. His noon appointment is one that he has been looking forward to for two months- since it was first set. The anticipation has been building and building, but now that it's finally really here, Reid almost wishes he could cancel it or avoid it entirely. Then again, this is the struggle that he fought so hard for. *It's a funny thing, but it doesn't matter how successful you become, or how far away you travel, or how much time passes, but when the past comes to call, it holds an undeniable power over you,* he thinks.

Three knocks on the door draws Reid's attention. One silhouette per knock is just barely visible through the frosted porthole of glass in the door's upper half. Reid squirms in his high back chair, adjusting his suit jacket. He knits his fingers atop his desk, frees them and hides his hands, then decides to rest them on the arms of the chair. Yes. Something nonchalant and nonthreatening. Still, his skin feels new and uncomfortable.

"Enter, please," Reid calls to the silhouettes behind the door.

The door slides into its pocket in the wall, and there they are. Xiu, with Gustave and Selene close behind over her shoulder. His former life. His former society encapsulated in familiar faces and sensations.

"Look at you, Mr. President," Gustave says, extending his hand. "You're a tough man to get an audience with, you know that?"

Reid accepts Gustave's handshake with a nervous hand.

"It's 'Chief Executive' actually," Reid says, rising and coming out from behind the desk to meet them. "We want to distance ourselves from the political failures that made the Twentieth, and the Sociocracy, so problematic."

"Ooh," Selene says, stepping up to give him a hug. "You sound so official. Is that the Party Line, that business about problematic political failures?"

Reid smirks and nods.

"It's not always easy to turn off the language of leadership," he says.

"This is quite the office, Reid," Xiu says. "You've done well for yourself."

She doesn't offer her hand or reach out to embrace him. She merely stands there, between Gustave and Selene, a few steps away. Her hair is tinted pink and silver, wearing an expression somewhere between annoyance and acceptance.

"Thank you," Reid says. "It's coming together. You should have seen it right after the Revolution. It was just another U. S. of A. standard apartment."

"Well you certainly made it yours," Xiu replies.

And then a moment of silence falls over the four, in which the discomfort of their reunion is highlighted. Reid struggles to find the ease of communication they used to enjoy.

"Thank you guys for coming to visit me," Reid says. "I wasn't sure that you ever would."

Gustave pats him on the shoulder. Reid flinches.

"Hey, I'm not taking a swing, Reid," he says. "That's water by now."

"I'd still deserve it, I think," Reid admits.

"You might, but that's not important," Gustave says. "We would have been here months ago, but the umm... "

"Capitol Hill Free Trade Republic," Selene says quietly.

"Yes, the Capitol Hill Free Trade Republic is quite popular," Gustave continues. "It's not the easiest place to get to these days."

Reid smiles. Pride in his work is the easy refuge from nervousness.

"I've noticed a lot of new arrivals. People are really praising the FTR. I think we're doing some valuable work here, giving people the experience of purpose that they're missing out there in the..." Reid catches himself in a derogatory thought and changes direction. "In the old world.

"It's been so embraced that our Commission on Expansion and Evangelism is working on conversion plans for the Baker and Uptown Districts," Reid continues. "I've been told that it's going very well."

Gustave and Selene nod, but Xiu stands still and slack, her eyes barely focused on him or the conversation.

"So people here really work for money, and there are no robots?" Selene asks.

"That's right," Reid says. He walks to the window and waves them over.

Gustave and Selene stand close over his shoulder, Xiu tags along further behind.

"Out there on the old 13th Avenue, see all those people selling their wares, selling food, commuting from work to home, home to work, work to lunch, and on and on," Reid says. "They all have places to be, and they all have purpose. It's more beautiful that the old scene, don't you think?"

"Not just a bunch of smiling folks doing what they please anymore," Gustave says.

Selene elbows him.

"Hey, Reid knows that this is how we joke," Gustave protests.

"It's fine, Selene," Reid agrees. "Gustave is never going to embrace this new world, and that's okay."

Reid gazes out the window for a few moments, seeing himself walking with Xiu down the avenue, or running from block to block to meet Gustave and Selene for drinks, or to have sex, or to play a game, or to see a movie, or to eat an indulgent meal. He doesn't notice that they've fallen into another silence.

"So, how's the cartooning going, Reid?" Selene asks.

"Oh, it goes well. The *Origami Emu* does more than slapstick these days, and I don't draw them like I used to, but it makes me a nice supplementary income," he replies.

"I've seen," Gustave says. "It's a neat little souvenir business you've got here."

"They're artifacts of the Revolution, and historical documents," Selene says.

"I know, darling, I'm just giving Reid a hard time."

Reid turns away from the window, facing them. Xiu is still far away, for being so relatively close.

"So how long are you all here?" Reid says.

"Just for an hour," Gustave says. "Selene has a photo show this afternoon, and Xiu is touring with her new album. She's getting pretty big all over the U. S. of A."

"That's great," Reid says, looking at Xiu, but she isn't looking him.

"Can I show you all around?" Reid asks.

"No, that's alright, Reid," Selene says. "We don't want to take up too much your time."

Another silence falls over them. *Even true friends can disappear into gaps in time and space, despite what their hearts may desire.* Reid knows what he must do next. If only for himself, for his conscience.

"I owe you each an apology," he says. "I don't have a good excuse for my behavior, beyond the realization that I was so unhappy that I couldn't be anything else until I changed my life, and changed our world. I could have realized that myself, and been a lot kinder to all of you, but instead I just sort of ran away from the life that I thought was causing all my problems.

"But it was never you guys. You were the things that made my old life tolerable, and instead of treating you that way, I took my concerns out on you, and I vented all of my frustrations without realizing that I was poisoning the last days we'd spend together.

"I shouldn't have blown you and Selene off, Gustave," Reid continues. "I shouldn't have argued and been so bitter. I definitely shouldn't have hit you. It was unbecoming, and more than that, it was immature. We were brothers, Gustave, and I should have recognized that. And Selene, I was unkind and harsh and cold to you when you've only ever been a bold force of kindness and joy. I'm sorry. I really am."

Gustave grips Reid's shoulder and pulls him into a hug.

"It barely hurt, Reid," he says. "You were confused. It happens. No hard feelings."

Selene wraps her arms around Reid too.

"I already miss our art discussions," she says. "We had some good times and made some good memories. And if you ever get tired of this new world you built, you can come back and see us anytime."

"Thank you, both," Reid replies.

Xiu remains outside the hug, her arms crossed.

Gustave and Selene let Reid loose and step back. They look at Xiu. Reid looks at Xiu.

"How about we give you two a minute?" Gustave says, heading toward the office door.

"We'll be right downstairs," Selene says to Xiu.

And together, Gustave and Selene wave to Reid and say, "Goodbye. Take care of yourself."

Reid smiles to them, and feels his heart climb up into his throat. *Forgiveness is an individual's greatest power. It could almost be considered a superpower. And it's so powerful because one doesn't need to deserve it to receive it. It's a gift given with no need for a thank you note.*

Gustave and Selene's silhouettes shrink and disappear as they venture through the door and down the hallway toward the elevator and the street. Reid wonders briefly if he'll see them again. *Perhaps when the FTR expands? Or if the Sociocracy grants him an ambassadorship?* Somehow, he will, when the time is right, and when their paths are destined to cross again.

Alone, Reid looks at beautiful Xiu, just as tranquil and spectacular as the day they met. But that day is long gone, and the goodwill earned then has dissipated; worn like a stone monument in the rain and wind.

"Xiu, I probably owe you the most," Reid says. "Scratch that. I definitely owe you the most. You stood by me the longest, through all my bitter, snarky, cold, cruel, depressing bullshit. You tried so hard to make me happy and to take my side even when my side couldn't have been more diametrically opposed to yours."

"Because I loved you, stupid," Xiu says.

"And I treated you like trash."

"Only sometimes, Reid. When you weren't so obsessed with what was wrong with… everything, you were always good to me. But it just wasn't meant to be was it? I wasn't enough to ease you mind to the troubles you felt, so even I had to go. That's just the way things work."

Reid turns toward the window.

"Even after Méliès, I wanted you to be here, to see what I had done," Reid says. "I never stopped wanting you to be proud of me."

"And I never stopped being proud of you," Xiu replies. "You pushed and pushed, and then on Méliès, you were just an incredible asshole to me, and honestly, I was just exhausted. It was one thing to support you in your weird frustrations and insecurities. That was love, Reid. Love helped me do that. But when you couldn't respect my position—my feelings—when you could say those terrible things. That was the line. And what's stupid, I never stopped loving you even when I couldn't stand the sight of you. And when you never messaged me to apologize, when you didn't make an effort, I knew that was it."

Reid hangs his head.

"I'm sorry, Xiu," he says. "I never meant to lose you."

"I know, Reid," she replies. "You just fell in love with something else— with this idea, and honestly, it seems like it's actually good for you."

"It does," Reid says. And after a pause he continues, "You can stay, you know."

"No," Xiu says. "I was okay playing second fiddle to you and your cartooning, but I'm not cool with being third, behind you, and this new place you've got. I've got to be fond of me, too, Reid, and I have to do that somewhere away from you."

Reid nods, and though he wants to say something to convince her that she's wrong, he's overwhelmed with that painfully undeniable feeling that she's absolutely right.

"I'll always be fond of you, Xiu Parker," he says.

Xiu half-smiles. "Likewise, Reid Rosales."

He reaches out to her, and whether by memory or by design she falls into his arms one last time. They hold each other, and Xiu begins to cry. And then Reid begins to cry. For a moment there, before the window that looks out over Reid's grand Capitol Hill Free Trade District, they absorb each other's touch one last time. He feels her love and her forgiveness, and again, he is overwhelmed with the power of it. There is nothing greater than the connection between two individuals, the fire they tend together, and the peace they bring one another. It is tragic that all fires die some day.

"If you're ever in the area," Reid says. "We'd love to host a concert."

"I guess it depends how much you'll pay me, Mr. Capitalism," Xiu jokes.

They laugh, for a moment.

"Go on now," Xiu says. "Get back to work. I bet you have a hot date tonight you can't be late for."

Reid smiles bashfully.

Xiu nods. It's all the answer she needs.

They hug one last time, and Xiu Parker exits Reid's office, her form disappears from the window, and down the hall to the elevator and the street.

From his window, Reid watches for her to appear. There she is, on the sidewalk with Gustave and Selene. She leans into them. They hold her. She may be crying or it may be relief. Then, in a moment, she straightens up, and Gustave and Selene each place a hand on her back. Together, Reid's former friends cross 13th Avenue and walk down the blocks toward Pearl and the Tubecar station. Reid watches them until they disappear, and wipes his eyes on his suit jacket sleeve. He takes a deep breath, and then smiles, to himself, for himself. *Everything I've ever wanted, ever really wanted, is right here*, he thinks.

He sends a message to Annabelle on his wristband: "I think it went okay."

"I'm glad. I'll see you after work and we can talk about it," she replies.

Then, Reid Rosales sits down at his desk, wraps his fingers on the tabletop, and sends a message to his secretary.

"I'm ready for my next appointment, Eve."

"I'll send them right up, Chief Executive," she replies.

"Thank you, Eve."

"I'm here to serve, sir."

24

Hugo Citizens Municipality; Eastern Colorado; United Sociocracy of the Americas

September 24, 2088

12:49 PM

Xiu Parker exits the elevator on the ground floor and walks out toward 13th Avenue. She sees Gustave and Selene waiting, just a few feet into the street. Xiu wipes the thin veil of tears from her eyes, puts on a smile and strides over to join them. Gustave and Selene open their arms to her, and she slips into their embrace.

"Are you okay, darling?" Selene asks her. "Have you been crying?"

"He wasn't an asshole again was he?" Gustave says. "I knew we shouldn't have left you alone in there."

"No, no," Xiu says. "Nothing like that. He was kind enough."

She wipes her eyes again.

"It's just one of those conversations," she continues. "It's not easy to say goodbye."

"I know. It was hard for me too," Selene adds. "He's still Reid, after all. And we all shared so much."

"That's the hard part. I wish he were a dick about everything," Xiu replies. "It would make it easier."

"It's too bad this place is so good for him," Gustave jokes. "We could have gone another round."

Xiu smiles up at Gustave. She leans into Selene, and kisses her cheek.

"I'm glad you guys could come," Xiu says. "I needed you."

"Of course," Gustave says.

"We needed it, too," Selene says.

Xiu turns toward 13th Avenue, still lightly wrapped in her friends' embrace.

"It really looks good," Xiu says, watching the street vendors, commuters, lunch-buyers, and weekend warriors. "Almost like the real thing."

Xiu, Selene, and Gustave walk together down 13th Avenue. There isn't a robot in sight, just like they were promised. Each store and restaurant and theatre and bar has one or more real, bonafide human beings working behind the counters, in the kitchens, and in the projection booths. There are humans in the Doctors, with lines of individuals waiting in line to be treated for their ailments. There are even new businesses filling the old familiar places, something called a hardware store for laborers; and a bank, where people used to hide their earnings from others, fearful that they could be lost or taken, because in those days, they could be.

At the corner of Pearl and 13th, Xiu, Gustave, and Selene see a group of individuals from the Free Trade Republic holding those funny old museum devices and talking with the Citizens who have just exited the Tubecar station.

"I still kind of want to stop and test that out," Gustave says, pointing at the seated individuals with E-Meters.

"Next time, darling," Selene says. "We'll come try it together."

They descend the long stairwell into the Tubecar station that takes them below the street. After a short wait, they approach the usual location of the passenger scanners. Instead, there are just humans—Citizens—dressed in blue jumpsuits with patches on their chests that read "LoR."

"We hope you enjoyed your stay," one says. "Imprint on your wristband for reentry?"

Xiu shakes her head and pushes past. Gustave and Selene follow close behind. They walk down a corridor, passing other smiling, laughing Citizens dressed in twentieth century clothing along the way, but they never reach the platform for the Tubecars. They never see a Tubecar at all. At the end of the corridor, they queue in another line, this one leading to the exit and the entrance.

To their left, a family of four jogs by, beaming with excitement.

"I'm going to work in a record store," says the father.

"I'm going to wait tables, like my grandmother did back in the Twentieth," says the mother.

"I want a paper route," the boy says.

"No, I want the paper route," the girl argues.

"No I do," the boy protests.

They shove each other back and forth as they disappear down the corridor.

"You've got to hand it to him," Gustave says. "It's really popular."

Xiu smiles, and nods.

"Yeah," she says.

Finally, the come to the front of the line, and the pair of robots there.

"Please exchange park currency for U. S. of A. credits before leaving," it says.

"I didn't get any currency this time," Xiu says.

Gustave and Selene say the same.

Out before them is a long line of Citizens, waiting patiently, sharing their excitement about what is on the other side. The robot on the entry side of the corridor accepts credits from each citizen. Along the line, multiple robots patrol holding tablets in their hands.

"Sign up here to participate in the next quarterly uprising," one says.

"Learn more about the twentieth century and improve your experience," says another.

"Read the history of the park's creator, Reid Rosales," chimes a third.

"Schedule an extended stay here to qualify for in park housing," another says.

"Please follow all park rules during your stay," says yet another robot, pointing up to a viewscreen to the right of the entry line:

Ten Rules for this Leisure Park

1. Always maintain the illusion.

2. No outside food or beverages.

3. Please wear twentieth century attire, or be prepared to purchase some inside the park.

4. Do not discuss news or events from the Sociocracy while inside the park.

5.   Do not contact Citizens outside the park unless you are in a designated apartment or communications center.

6.   Have a twentieth century task, job, or career in mind before you enter, so you can get started playing right away.

7.   If you interact with park founder, Reid Rosales, do not discuss the park, but feel free to discuss its fictional history.

8.   Please avoid upsetting Citizen Rosales, or you will be immediately ejected from the park.

9.   If you see Citizen Rosales venturing too close to a park entrance or border wall, please distract him until a park worker arrives to help.

10.   Most importantly, have fun.

Above the rules, the titanium walls around the park rise high into the air, join with a projection dome, and close over the "Free Trade Republic." The dome features dozens of ventilators and weather machines that create the wind, rain, snow, and every detailed element that makes life believable inside. The projectors on and inside the dome replicate the sunrise, the Moon cycle, and offer reliable multi-perspective images of the Denver skyline, the Uptown District border, the Baker border, and the view eastward to Cheesman and City parks. Inside, the reproduced buildings, streets, and promenades have been carefully aged so that the copies can't be told apart from their originals. Though, no copy is perfect.

Along the outer wall, a dozen security robots stand guard to ensure that no one attempts to break in or vandalize the park wall. They also check the wristbands of several people, dressed in the blue "LoR" jumpsuits, or in carefully styled period clothes, who line up at the side entrances that spread out in a large circle around the main entrance tunnel. Atop the entrance tunnel, two poles rise up and terminate in an archway, displaying a digital readout.

Welcome to the Land of Reid

Sponsored by the Sociocracy Department of Mental Health
and Wellbeing

A new Leisure experience built by and for Citizen Reid Rosales

In the distance beyond the long line of Citizens are wide, open grassy fields decorated with solar panels and windmills. There is a sign that reads: Hugo Municipality Alternative Energy Collective. Robots wind in and out among the panels and windmills, performing maintenance and optimizing their power collection. Power from the solar and wind goes to the park, and onward to Denver. There are so many collectives covering the eastern part of Colorado, that one can look for miles north, east, or south and see shimmering fields of gold grass and glossy black and tall silent, turning blades. The sky is big and blue and high. There are layers of tall, wispy, white clouds filtering the harsh midday sun. And just a few hundred meters to the southeast, there is the Hugo Citizens Municipality, a small township, on the eastern plains of what used to be the state of Colorado, back before the Sociocracy.

"Hey," a woman's voice calls to them from just outside the entrance. "You're his friends right?"

"Yeah, that's us," Xiu answers. "Don't worry. We didn't say anything."

"I wasn't worried. He just always speaks so highly of you," the woman says.

"Does he?" Xiu asks. "And you are?"

"I'm Annabelle," she says. "You're Xiu, right?"

Xiu nods.

"You should be proud," Annabelle says. "He still talks about you. I even have a bet going that he'll be talking about you after my contract as 'love interest' is up."

"I guess you'll have to let me know," Xiu says.

"I hope there's no hard feelings," Annabelle says. "Acting is acting. And this place is really blowing up."

"None at all," Xiu says. "We were a world ago to him."

Annabelle smiles.

"Alright, my break's over," she says. "I better get back to it. This is more popular than the Sociocracy's other Personalized Leisure Parks, and the Leisure Coordinating Robot is really pushing continuity as the thing that holds these joints together."

Annabelle turns, and opens a sliding door in the outside wall of the park. The door says "Actors Entrance Only." As the door slides shut, Annabelle disappears inside.

Selene gives Xiu a squeeze, and Gustave places his arm on her shoulder.

"I'm fine," Xiu says. "Let's just get the Tubecar and go back to Denver."

Xiu, Gustave, and Selene walk the paved path back into Hugo. With nothing required of them and no limits on them, they decide to stop in a bar and order safe liquor from the robot bartender and pay with the credits they received from the morning dailies.

After their drink, they walk to the Tubecar station First Avenue and Seventh Street.

They descend the stairs and approach the passenger scanners. Xiu holds out her wristband and the scanner deducts her credits and sends her through. Gustave and Selene follow close behind. After making their way through the departure line, they climb into their Tubecar and begin the quick trip back to the Capitol Hill Citizenry District.

Instead of selecting from the in-car entertainment, Xiu Parker, and her friends Gustave Yamamoto and Selene Fitzhugh sit quietly, but sit together. Xiu gazes out the Tubecar window as they speed away from Reid's perfect new home, built with care for him. She wonders if one day, like her hair-tint pen, he'll just change the whole story all over again. But she knows it doesn't really matter because there will always be a place for him, a way to keep him and every other citizen happy. Her thoughts slip to the concert she has tonight, in the new Los Angeles Coliseum, and she mourns all the shows that Reid will never attend. A big enough wound leaves a scar, and even after it has healed, all it takes is a thought to remember everything.

"You have to admit, the Sociocracy did a nice job with it," Gustave says finally. "He got exactly what he wanted."

"We're lucky to live in a place that really takes care of its people," Selene says.

Gustave and Xiu nod.

"I'm just glad Reid's finally happy," Xiu says.

About the Author

Nate Ragolia was labeled as "weird" early in elementary school by a little blonde girl he liked, and it stuck. He's a lifelong lover of science fiction and a nerd/geek. His first book, *There You Feel Free*, was published by 1888center's Black Hill Press in 2015. A year later, he founded BONED: A Collection of Skeletal Writings. And in 2017, he co-founded Spaceboy Books LLC. Nate also creates webcomics, writes essays and articles, and pets dogs. He can usually be found in Denver, CO.

About the Publishing Team

Amanda Hardebeck has been a sci-fi & film addict since birth. When her older brother handed her a copy of *Dune* for her birthday 20 years ago, her passion for science fiction took off. She is a roller derby referee for her hometown team and is Chief Editor for Spaceboy Books LLC.

TJ Stambaugh received several commendations for his bravery as a battalion commander in the Meme Wars. After the war, TJ retired to Catonsville, MD, where he paints, enjoys movies you have to read, and is Art Director for Spaceboy Books LLC.

Learn more about Spaceboy Books at readspaceboy.com